Death Watch

Death Watch

Southern Secrets Mysteries

Carol Light

TULE
PUBLISHING

Death Watch

Tule Publishing First Printing, July 2025

The Tule Publishing, Inc.

First Publication by Tule Publishing 2025

Cover design by Croco Designs

ISBN: 978-1-966593-70-6

Dedication

To four of my all-time favorite people, and not just because they chose to marry into my family: Meg Light, RJ Roewe, Lizbeth Pence, and Jim Cloonan

Love you all!

Chapter One

TIM BIRCH HOPED there were leftovers at home, maybe some more of that beef stew Aunt Becky had cooked up two nights ago. Sure would go well with a piece of her corn bread. He'd be lucky. Audra, Becky's sister and a retired nurse who hated to cook, was staying with his six-year-old son Adam tonight. She'd practically salivated when he'd mentioned Becky's leftovers in the fridge this morning.

If he'd been home in time for supper, he might have had a chance, but there was too much work this week at the station with several officers taking a late-summer vacation before school started. As police chief, he was helping out where he could so no one else resigned. As it was, he had three patrol officer vacancies going unfilled for the third month in a row. There hadn't even been a nibble of interest. Another retirement or resignation or a flu epidemic and they'd really be hurting. He could advertise again through the state universities' job boards. The town couldn't offer the salary and benefits the larger cities offered, but Crossroads wasn't a bad place to live.

Ahead, red lights from one of the patrol units flashed at the side of Cypress. Tim slowed. The driver's door of the Kia sedan parked in front of the police vehicle was open, but both vehicles appeared to be unoccupied.

Edging forward past the civilian car, he watched for movement in the dark yard beyond. There hadn't been a radio call about a pursuit. He passed the front of the civilian car.

"Shit!" Tim whipped over to the side of the street and jumped out.

Two people lay in the grass. The young man was moaning, his head turning restlessly, but the woman, dressed in her Crossroads PD uniform, lay still, her eyes closed. A white Narcan dispenser lay just beyond her fingertips as if it had fallen out of her grasp. The carton lay open next to the male victim.

"Josie!" He reached out to check to see if she was breathing and then remembered their recent training about fentanyl and other even more dangerous drugs starting to appear around the country. If that's what this was, he wouldn't help her by going down himself due to an accidental exposure.

But seconds counted. The Narcan package she'd opened near the male victim had an unused second dose. He freed it from the package. Tilting her head back, he administered the nasal spray to his deputy, hoping he wasn't too late.

"Come on, Josie!"

There was no noticeable change. She needed another dose.

Scrambling to his feet, he hurried to his SUV and grabbed his kit. Keeping his voice as calm as he could, he called in for paramedics as he tugged on a pair of gloves.

"Dispatching an ambulance now, Chief," the operator said. "Do you have Narcan? It sounds like your officer may have been exposed to fentanyl."

"Affirmative. One dose administered."

"Is she breathing, Chief?" the dispatcher asked. "If she isn't, you'll need to do CPR. Be sure to—"

He didn't wait for her to finish.

Josie's face was as pale as the moon, her lips dark. Oh god—he couldn't lose her. "Come on, Josie," he urged, beginning chest compressions.

Her rib cage seemed so small, not at all like the overweight man he'd resuscitated two years ago. He pressed as hard as he dared, afraid to break her ribs. He counted to himself to set a steady pace and not think of the outcome he feared. "Breathe, Josie, breathe!"

The young man moaned louder, but Tim wasn't about to stop. Fortunately for both of them, the guy rolled to his side just before he vomited, probably saving his sorry ass from choking.

Josie's heart-shaped face was deathly still. Her lips had darkened into a dusky purple. Tim pumped harder, willing air into her lungs, her brain.

He wasn't sure how long it was before he heard the sound of a heavy vehicle. Flashing red lights confirmed the arrival of the paramedics. The first one to jump out was his best friend, Curt McMillan.

"Fentanyl?" Curt said snapping on gloves.

"I think so."

Curt knelt beside him and told him to stop compressions. He felt Josie's wrist for a pulse.

Tim waited, hardly daring to breathe.

Curt's lips tightened. "Was she like this when you found her?"

"Yeah. I gave her a dose of Narcan."

"Any response? Did she gasp or move?"

"No."

"We'll try shocking her." He rose.

Tim resumed compressions.

"Chief," called the other paramedic, an older guy named Mike. "How many doses has this guy had?"

"Just one, I think. I gave the second dose in the open package to Josie."

The interruption had caused him to lose his rhythm. *Please breathe, Josie. You've got to stay with us!*

Curt placed a defibrillator on the ground and opened it. Tim stopped long enough to jerk Josie's T-shirt up and expose her chest. He continued CPR as Curt applied the pads on either side of his hands.

"Stop compressions." Curt squeezed his shoulder. "You're going to need to stand back."

Tim moved out of the way. Curt tried several shocks.

There was no response.

Curt removed the pads and lowered Josie's shirt. "We've got to transport these two now."

Tim prepared to resume compressions, but Curt stopped him. "You've done all you can here. Doc needs to see them. Come on. Let's get her on a gurney."

Mike already had his patient ready to load into the ambulance. Disoriented and agitated, the guy was shouting about needing to go home. Soon both victims were inside.

"Josie?" The owner of the deep voice jostled Tim aside.

"Out of the way." Tim grabbed him and jerked him back. It was enough to allow Curt to shut the doors.

"Is she okay?" Sergeant Ed Robbins demanded. He had twenty years and about as many pounds on Tim, all muscle. He wasn't in uniform. Someone must have called him about Josie.

"They need to get her to the clinic. Looks like she's been exposed to fentanyl."

"Goddammit!" He shook off Tim's grasp as the ambulance started. "I told you she wasn't ready to go solo."

For a moment Tim was certain he was about to be punched. A struggle played out in the usually stoic sergeant's face as they stared each other down. *Go ahead*, Tim wanted to urge him. Instead, training—much of it provided by the man squared off against him—kicked in. "She needs you, Sarge," he said in a firm voice. "Go to the clinic. Let her parents know too."

Rollins glared at him a moment longer. His fists were still clenched at his side as he stalked toward the street where his motorcycle was parked. He kicked the stand up and roared off.

And then Tim was alone on the scene.

He peered into the opened door of the Kia. A baggie containing blue tablets lay on the passenger seat. Grabbing an evidence bag from his utility belt, he secured the drugs after snapping a photo of them as they'd been found. He didn't want anyone else finding them or touching them.

Fentanyl in Crossroads. They'd had the first overdoses last weekend. Four kids about to start their senior year of high school had scored some similar-looking pills laced with the powerful opioid. They'd chosen to party at a vacant house that fortunately had an observant neighbor who'd seen them go inside and called the police. By the time an officer had arrived, three of them were already unconscious. The fourth kid, who'd brought a bottle of vodka, was texting on his phone, oblivious to the life-and-death crisis his friends were in. Fortunately, the dose had been small enough and the Narcan administered quickly enough to save their lives.

Josie hadn't been so lucky. If he'd left work a little earlier or listened to Sarge about her readiness for patrol on her own, she might have had at least a fighting chance. Tim swore, furious with himself. He'd been so sure Sarge was just being overprotective. Officer Josephine Rollins was his niece.

Illegal drugs weren't new to Crossroads, but fentanyl? One of their local dealers was now selling a deadlier poison or there was a new player in town. Either way, someone had just declared war.

Chapter Two

JANA NANCE BALLED up the tissue she'd just used to dry her eyes. *No use crying over spilled milk*, Nana Sue would say. *What's done is done.*

Besides, there was too much to do. Feeling sad and sorry for herself would have to wait.

Opening the cupboard door under Nana's sink, Jana deposited the damp tissue in the yellow trash bin freshly lined with a plastic bag by her neighbor and best friend. Charlene, better known as Charly, had emptied the refrigerator and readied the house for her arrival, bless her heart. But she'd done much more than that to welcome her back to Crossroads. The sight of the hand towel with Jana's youngest daughter's small handprints and BEST NANA EVER! on it had set off the waterworks a moment ago. Where had Charly found that old towel? And before that, the Mason jar of fresh flowers on the round kitchen table had caused her to tear up.

Yes, she was going to have to toughen up and save her tears for another day that would be coming sooner than she'd like. Jana quickly put away the food she'd bought and returned outside to bring in her suitcase. She'd just opened the hatchback when Charly called a hello and crossed the yard to give her a hug.

"You made it! How was the trip?" Charly, nearing fifty as

Jana was, was looking more like her mother, Ms. Alice, as she aged, although she had the long legs and slender build of her daddy, Mr. Dex, also now a resident of Golden Pines.

"Long! I thought the drive would never end. Thank goodness for audiobooks. I finished two of them."

Charly's eyes darkened. "But you didn't drive straight through from Indianapolis, did you?"

Jana smiled. "No, I paced myself. Spent last night in Blytheville. Just had to reach the state line before I stopped."

"Well, you're braver than I am, driving this far by yourself. It's a shame one of your girls couldn't have come with you."

"Oh, they're busy with their lives, although they were pestering me with texts I had to answer every time I made a stop." Mostly Stephanie, her youngest. God love the girl, but Jana couldn't imagine spending two days in a car with her. As it was, she'd heard enough about her job and boyfriend issues to try the patience of Mother Teresa. Daniella's insecurities with her new lawyer boyfriend were almost as exhausting as her younger sister's. At least she'd had a little more experience being two years older and could laugh at herself some of the time.

"Charly, I don't know how I'm ever going to thank you for looking after Nana Sue and the house. Thank you so much for all that you've done—even putting flowers on the table. They're lovely."

"Well, I didn't want you walking into more than you already had to deal with. Are you going to see your grandmother today? I was there this morning checking on Daddy."

"Is your father okay?" She'd been too torn up over seeing

Nana in the memory care unit at Golden Pines Assisted Living to say hello to Mr. Dex.

"Oh, he's the same. Cantankerous as ever." Charly wet her lips. "Ms. Sue didn't remember me today, Jana, but that doesn't mean she won't know you when you see her."

"I did stop to see her before I came to the house. She didn't remember me at first, but then she at least remembered my mother. She asked when I was going to bring Jana to see her."

"Aww." Charly reached out for another hug, which nearly did Jana in. Fortunately, a car door slammed behind them. Charly released her to see who'd arrived at her house. She waved at the shiny blue Mustang now parked in her driveway.

The young man who emerged looked more like his mother than ever. "That's not Eli, is it?" He'd been a teenager five years ago when Jana had last been to Crossroads. Maybe a sophomore in high school? The young man walking over to say hello at his mother's urging had grown into his body. His grin was still as wide and friendly as a summer day, just as it had been when he was a baby.

"Good to see you," he said in a deeper voice than she remembered. He hugged her awkwardly. "Ma said you were coming. Sorry about your grandma."

"Thanks, Eli. That's sure a fancy Mustang you're driving. Love the color!" The boy had always been car crazy. At least that hadn't changed.

He ducked his head. "I restored it some."

"And painted it too," his mother said. "That racing stripe has every police officer in town keeping an eye on him for me."

"Ma," he protested, rolling his eyes.

Charly squeezed his arm. "Grab Jana's suitcase and put it in the house for her."

Jana protested but in the end, just thanked Eli and his mother. Soon her car was unloaded.

"I'm about to fix dinner," Charly said. "Come eat with us."

"That's very kind, but you've done more than enough already. I picked up some food in town. I'll probably just have a bite and go to bed early, if I can manage that much. It's been a long day. Maybe another time?"

"You can count on it. You call me if you need anything. Come on, son. Let's go feed you and your sister."

Eli gave Jana a shy grin and a wave. According to his mama, he was doing well as a mechanic for a car dealership. Jana felt as proud as if she'd been his mother and not just his godmother.

"Thank you again!" she called after the pair as they crossed into their yard.

"We're glad you're here!" Charly called back.

Inside, she plopped down on the sofa, found the television remote, and started watching the evening news. She was actually here in Crossroads, and she'd driven down by herself for the first time ever. That deserved a big pat on the back. She could have flown, but she needed her car here and couldn't wait for it to be transported down to Arkansas. Nana had sold hers several years ago when her eyes had started going bad, and rentals were expensive. So was having someone haul a vehicle across the country. Driving had been the only option for her limited budget.

Nana's living room had been dusted; the *Guidepost* magazines dating back several years had been neatly stacked on the coffee table. They could be recycled if there was a recycling program here. She should start a list of what she needed to check into, like trash pickup day.

A lump formed in Jana's throat. Everything was just as Nana had kept it for years, but she wouldn't be returning to her house. At this point, she might not even remember it. As Charly had said, Alzheimer's was racing to claim her and every last memory she had.

The goal had been to keep her at home as long as possible, but Della, the aide Uncle Jasp had been paying for, could no longer manage it. Nana had wandered outside at night more than once, forgot who Della was and fought her, and they all knew she needed more help.

I'll have to visit Della and take her a gift. That goes on the list too.

Later, after she'd finished her salad and rinsed out the plastic clamshell container for recycling—she could ask Charly about that—Jana turned off the television. She opened the side door that led to the carport to check that the screen door was securely fastened. For as long as she could remember, it had banged in wind gusts if not firmly latched. As she pulled the stiff handle closed, she heard men's voices from the street. The lights of a pickup truck parked in front of Charly's house shone on the dark street. The engine revved slightly every few seconds like a mechanical heartbeat. Eli was leaning on the passenger side's open window, talking to whoever was inside.

"No, I'm not doing it again," he said, pulling himself upright. "I'm finished with that."

Whatever the man inside said to him was met with an angry, "I don't care. I don't need your job anyhow." With that, he pushed away from the truck and stalked toward his house, his fists clenched at his side.

The other man shouted something, but the only word she could make out was *sorry*. Then the truck revved louder and took off. A door closed at Charly's house. Had Eli quit his job? Charly hadn't mentioned that.

That night, Jana lay in the bed where she had spent happy childhood summers and her four high school years at her grandparents' house. The window air conditioner rattled and the mattress was lumpy, but she snuggled under the sheet that smelled like her grandmother's laundry detergent.

It took her longer to find sleep than she expected. Thoughts of the blank look in Nana's eyes and her heartbreaking pleas to go home haunted her. And then her worries about the new job she'd be starting on Monday clamored for attention. She would be director of tourism for the town. It was a new position, the HR director who'd interviewed her on Zoom had said. The city council had approved the position to bring in more visitors and boost local businesses. Jana knew all about that, having worked for more than two decades at the Indiana Department of Tourism. As soon as the HR director had stopped describing the job, she'd jumped right in, sharing the ideas and experiences that had qualified her for the promotion she didn't get two months ago. He'd called back two days later to offer her the position.

Accepting meant leaving Indianapolis, but it was her dream job. And there was the added advantage of being close to Nana Sue. She'd accepted without hesitation and then had asked the fateful question: "Who will I be reporting to?"

"Oh, didn't I say?" he'd said. "You'll be reporting directly to our mayor, Deeann Donahue."

Deeann Donahue, formerly Deeann Ferris. At least she'd managed not to swear aloud. She'd never considered that her high school nemesis would still hold that office.

Better the devil you know than the one you don't, Nana Sue would have advised her, but she couldn't stay a day longer in Indiana working for a boss who hated her without further chance of promotion. So here she was in Arkansas. Her house was on the market, the contents sold, given away, or put into storage.

She had to make this job work, even if that meant having Deeann Donahue as her boss.

Chapter Three

THE NEXT MORNING'S staff meeting was somber. Tim didn't have to tell anyone what had happened to Josie; the news had traveled like lightning. He'd gone to the clinic as soon as the scene and vehicles had been secured, but Doc Bailey had already pronounced her dead. Notifying Josie's parents and two younger brothers had been the hardest duty he'd ever performed. They'd been too distraught to ask about the events leading to their daughter's death. Sarge's glare had convinced him not to stay with the family.

"I know you've all heard what happened last night," he told the officers and other staff assembled. "I've expressed our condolences to Josie's family and asked that they share service details with us." He swallowed and then cleared his throat. "Officer Rollins was a brave member of our force who showed great promise. She will be missed."

He glanced down at the floor, composing himself. Several people sniffled. When he looked up, the old guards in the back were watching him with hard eyes. If Sarge had been there, he would have been with them.

Tim summarized what had apparently happened. Josie's call in to report she was pulling over the Kia for erratic driving had been ten minutes before he'd arrived and called for the paramedics.

He then led a minute of silence, reminded them of counseling services available, and dismissed the administrative staff.

"Finn Lasher, the young man Josie stopped, is recovering," he told his officers. "I interviewed him last night at the clinic. It seems he can't remember where he scored the pills I found in his car. Maybe he'll realize how close he came to dying and help us, but I'm not holding my breath."

Nods and cynical looks greeted his last comment. "So, it's going to be up to us to find out who's supplying this poison. I'm appointing a task force, and you're all on it. Keep your eyes and ears open for any leads. What do we have on our list of possible dealers and suppliers?"

Clint Dees, his deputy chief, started the discussion. They'd been building evidence against one supplier, Robert "Pino" Bissett and his brother, Hank. So far, they didn't have enough for a search warrant, although they suspected the two were trafficking most of the marijuana into the county.

"It's possible they've expanded their product line," Clint said, "but Pino has a lot to lose if he's caught selling the hard stuff."

Pino had served eight years on assault and possession charges already and had the prison tattoos to prove it.

"There's Frank Deluca," Eamon Carey, one of his detectives, said. "Maybe he's starting a new line."

"Naw," Hal Overman said from the back of the room. "Booze is his specialty. My money's on the Bissett brothers." He folded his hands across his substantial belly. Usually on bravo shift, he'd switched with Josie last night to start her on what they'd thought would be a quiet patrol.

"I agree with Hal," Tim said. "Deluca has plenty of business selling liquor here." Chester County was dry, so residents either had to go to a neighboring county or buy the locally produced illegal hooch. Besides, Deluca wasn't so greedy that he'd push his luck by dealing hard drugs.

"Could someone be making the fentanyl locally?" Andrea asked. One of his newer recruits, she was already impressing Tim with her eagerness to learn and skills in talking to citizens. She and Josie had been close. Both had been eager to begin patrolling on their own.

"It's possible," Tim said. "The ingredients can be ordered from China and come in the mail. Doesn't take much space for a lab. It's easier to buy the pills ready-made from Mexico, but we could be looking for a local cook."

They didn't have much yet to go on, but someone in town knew something, and sooner or later, someone would talk. Tim assigned follow-up interviews with Finn Lasher's family and friends to Francine Compton, another detective. "Eamon, talk to the kid again. He's eighteen, and he's in a world of trouble with that possession charge. Cooperating could help his case. Maybe he's sobered up enough this morning to come to his senses. Let's at least find out where he was last night and who he was with. Also, check back with our previous victims. Maybe they'll be willing to tell us who gave them the drugs."

He gazed out at the team. "Meanwhile, spread the word to any known addicts that there's fentanyl in the area. Everyone should be carrying Narcan and keep dispatch aware of your location. Anything else?" There was no response.

"That's all for now. Let's find whoever's responsible for bringing this poison into Crossroads before someone else dies."

The grim faces staring back at him nodded, even the guys in the back.

JACK HUDDLESTON SNAPPED a picture of the Crossroads *Gazette* building. It might appear online in the future, but it was mostly for his personal collection. The roofless building with its soot-stained red bricks would soon be torn down, thanks to his insurance settlement due to arrive any day. Not that he'd have enough money to rebuild with the insurance money alone. He had a couple of ideas about raising the rest.

"I wouldn't think you'd want to remember what happened," Bill Parsons, the pharmacist who owned the business next to the newspaper office called as he approached Jack.

Bill held a bag from Annabelle's Café. Was it lunchtime already? He'd lost track of time this morning following up on the death of the young CPD officer last night.

"Just capturing the *before* appearance." He told Bill about the insurance money coming through. "Enjoy the peace and quiet while you can. I'm hoping to start rebuilding by October."

"I'm glad for you, Jack, but you've got to stop your subscribers from tossing Molotov cocktails through your window. Don't the police have any leads on that? It's been two months."

"The fire department hasn't issued their report yet. They

should be turning the case over to the police soon." And hopefully with some evidence that could point to the individual responsible.

"Hmm. Maybe you need that bulletproof glass or no windows at all."

"Gotta shine some light on the truth, Bill." He nodded toward the plastic bag. "What's for lunch?"

"Just a tuna melt. I have to watch my figure. I'd better get it out of this heat before it goes bad. Take care, Jack. Let me know when to expect all that noise you've promised."

Bill was tall and thin, probably because he ate healthier than most. The thought of food was appealing, but rather than heading for the café, Jack drove home, which was now also the new base of operations for the *Gazette*. His kitchen table was beginning to resemble his old office desk, with stacks of papers occupying most of the surface. Some days he carried his laptop to the library in town to write for a change of scenery and a sense of order. The library was also proving to be a good source of story leads.

He pulled a jar of crunchy peanut butter from the cabinet. It was almost empty, and he would be down to only the end slice of his white bread after he made his sandwich. Usually, he fed the heel to the birds in his backyard, so he needed to go to the store or he'd be forced to eat it. He was out of grape jelly too. He found a small jar of the mayhaw jelly his neighbor had made this summer. She'd brought it over when she'd heard about the *Gazette* fire. He unscrewed the top and tasted the red jelly. It was tarter than his usual grape, but it would be an interesting change for his PBJ fare. Even so, lunch meat was going on his grocery list. The *meow* at his feet as his cat Greeley rubbed against his legs reminded him to add cat food as well.

"You've already eaten," he reminded the tabby, "or are you just trying to tell me you missed me, hmm?"

He carried his sandwich to the one cleared area at his table. Before he could take a bite, his phone buzzed. He didn't recognize the number, but it was local.

"Jack Huddleston."

"Mr. Huddleston, this is Janelle Smith. I'm calling to tell you that my daddy, Albert Walker, passed last night. He wanted you to know. He appreciated all you've done to help us."

"Aww, Janelle, I'm so sorry for your loss. Albert was a fine man."

"Yes, sir, he was."

"I was hoping he'd see that pond cleaned up before he passed. I'm still working on making sure that's done. Are you having a service?"

"We're making the arrangements, but I'll let you know. Daddy would want you there. I hope you'll be able to come."

"I'll be there. Please give your mother and brothers my condolences. Your children too."

"I'll tell the whole family. Thank you, Mr. Huddleston."

"Please, it's Jack. Just Jack."

After he disconnected, he added Janelle's number to his contacts. Albert had described her as the one who kept them all organized and in line. She'd been the one to take Albert and his wife to their medical appointments and cancer treatments. Essie, Albert's wife, probably wasn't long for this world, but maybe now she'd consider moving away from

Crawfish Pond, which had been polluted by chemicals dumped in the past by the Southern Pines Company. A lawsuit to compel cleanup and provide compensation for the families living nearby who'd suffered an unusually high incidence of cancer had been settled almost two years ago. So far, the company had done nothing to clean up the pond. Worse, he and Albert had witnessed two men dumping liquid from barrels late at night into the murky water. Their box truck didn't have any branding, but it was identical to a model found in the company's fleet.

Jack bit into his sandwich, although he didn't feel much like eating. Albert had been a good man who'd wanted his small community of six families to have clean air and water. He'd worked for the Southern Pines Company himself until his health had forced him to quit. Jack couldn't imagine how he and Essie had coped finding out that their home where they'd raised their children had been poisoned by his own callous or at least environmentally unconscious employer.

Jack picked up his phone and found the number of the attorney in the neighboring town of Hamblen who had agreed to file a new petition to compel the company to clean up the pond. The lawsuit's original attorney, Ernie Crowell, had died not long before the *Gazette* had been firebombed. Recently, Southern Pines's board of directors had been served and predictably had filed a response asking for more time to gather information. There had to be something the attorney could do to speed things up.

The squeaky wheel gets the grease. And he was damned good at being a squeaky wheel.

Chapter Four

NANA SUE APPEARED tiny and frail in her bed at Golden Pines. Her cloud of white hair blended into the pallor of her pillow. But there was nothing weak or ethereal about her voice.

"I'm not getting up, and you can't make me."

"Nana, nobody's going to force you to do anything you don't want to do. Wouldn't you like some supper? They have fried chicken and mashed potatoes tonight. I think there's some peach cobbler for dessert."

Her scowl deepened. "You're lying."

Jana's heart broke. She'd lost her grandmother just as certainly as if she'd died. Nana in her right mind was nothing like the woman scowling at her.

"Maybe you'd like to see for yourself? It doesn't hurt to look, does it? I bet Mr. Dex is there. You remember Charly's father? He lives here too."

A look of panic crossed her grandmother's face. "Where am I? Why can't I go home?" Tears began rolling down her face, but when Jana reached out to hug her, she snapped, "Don't touch me!"

Jana sank back in her chair. Just then a nurse's aide appeared. "Are we ready for dinner, Ms. Sue? My, your hair looks beautiful today. We'll just put your housecoat and slippers on and take you to the dining room."

To Jana's surprise, Nana allowed the woman to help her sit up and perch on the edge of the bed so she could dress her.

"You must have the magic touch. She didn't want anything to do with me."

"Don't take it to heart, honey. She can't help it," replied the aide whose badge said she was GISELE. "She forgets everything right away."

Except that she wanted to go home. But from something Nana had said yesterday, she wasn't sure which home that was—her childhood house in Mississippi or the one she'd shared with Grandpa for more than fifty years and ten alone since his death. At one point she'd talked to Jana as if they were classmates at the secretarial school Nana had attended for two years in Conway. It was as if her brain had shuffled all of her memories and scattered them like a deck of cards in a game of fifty-two pickup. She was still convinced that Nana—the grandmother she knew—was somewhere in the resulting chaos of her mind.

Gisele placed Nana's walker before her, and she began to shuffle into the hall. "I think I'll go home," Jana told the nurse. She caught up to Nana, who was now making good speed down the hallway that smelled faintly of urine overlaid with a lemon-scented cleaning solution. She touched her grandmother's arm, but the old woman jerked it away and didn't stop.

"Goodbye, Nana. I'll see you tomorrow."

There was no response or reaction. It was as if she were invisible.

Dinner was served early at Golden Pines, too early for Jana this evening. There was still plenty of August sunshine when she left the nursing home just after five. Craving fresh air and a chance to stretch her legs somewhere shady, she drove to the city park, where there was a walking trail around a large pond. She wasn't dressed in athletic wear, but her khakis and rubber-soled shoes would be fine for a walk on the paved path beneath the leafy trees.

Although the heat of an Arkansas summer day had lingered, she didn't care. Indiana wasn't much different this time of year. Not that she missed her home there. Maybe a little, but she'd been rambling around in her empty house for four years since her youngest, Stephanie, had moved out for good. Truth be told, her home in Indianapolis had never been the same since Marcus had died of a brain tumor ten years ago. She'd managed to put her two children through high school and college and cope as a single mom, but now that part of her life had also ended.

The cry of a peacock startled her out of her reverie. The city had a small zoo in the park, and occasionally, a male peacock would air his gorgeous feathers, which had never failed to make her feel like Mother Nature was bestowing a gift especially for her—and anyone else who happened to see it.

"Showing off the wonders."

The jogger who'd just passed her stopped and turned around. "Excuse me?"

He was around her age, late forties or early fifties, judging by the lines around his eyes and graying hair. He was wearing shorts and a T-shirt on a body that suggested he did more than run to stay in shape.

Oh god. Did he think she was talking about him?

"I, um, I was thinking about Mother Nature." Her cheeks were hot. "She shows off her wonders, like peacocks spreading their feathers. Or rainbows," she finished lamely.

He cocked his head. "Peacocks, sure. I haven't seen a rainbow in a while. Have you?"

"No, it's been a while. It was just an example—the first that came to mind, after peacocks that is. I guess because of the beautiful colors." This was ridiculous. She stuck out her hand. "Jana Nance."

He grinned, probably accustomed to women acting like tongue-tangled idiots around him. "Clay Bailey. Nice to meet you." He released her hand. "It's a beautiful spot. Underutilized, but that's ideal for those of us who come here to exercise."

"Is it always this quiet? It's such a beautiful park. I used to come here to the zoo with my grandparents. Back then, the big attraction was a three-legged alligator, but someone told me he'd frozen to death."

Clay's mouth opened and then closed. To her surprise, he burst out laughing. "Sorry. I'm just having trouble imagining that happening here. Maybe because it's August and the heat index is in triple digits this week."

"I suppose someone could have been pulling my leg."

He laughed again. "Maybe that's what happened to the gator."

She grinned despite herself. "Come to think of it, my uncle might have told me that story. He also said the pond here was half its current size before he and his buddies started throwing beer bottles in it when they were younger." She'd also believed that story since Uncle Jasper was an alcoholic.

"He sounds like a character."

"I suspect he was then. He lives up in Jonesboro, sober for almost twenty years."

"That's good." His cell phone rang. "I have to take this call. Nice to meet you, Jana Nance. You'd better keep moving to avoid freezing to death."

"Very funny." She wasn't sure he'd heard her as he was already answering his call, but he raised his arm and waved without looking back.

She resumed her walk, increasing her pace. This park seemed underutilized. Or was it just the dinnertime hour that was responsible for the lack of visitors? Come to think of it, she hadn't noticed any picnic tables or grills. What would it take to make this place more popular?

Still considering possible enhancements to the city park, she reached the end of her loop around the pond and removed her car keys from her pocket. Nana didn't remember her, but at least she could make sure Nana was receiving the best care possible. She couldn't make up for the past five years when she hadn't visited, but she was here now. And even if her new position didn't work out, she wouldn't regret being here with Nana Sue.

Just as she'd thought, there were no picnic tables under the shady oaks close to the parking lot. That's where she would place them if she had a chance. She sighed. She desperately wanted her new job to work out. Here, she'd be in charge, able to create and promote sites that would draw visitors for miles around. Fortunately, Indiana had a policy of only confirming dates of employment for reference checks. If that HR director had spoken to her direct supervisor… It didn't bear thinking about. She needed this job and Crossroads needed her.

Whether Deeann Donahue would agree remained to be seen.

Chapter Five

THE HR DIRECTOR, as positive and jovial in person as he'd been in her interview, greeted Jana on Monday with a broad smile and a warm welcome. She was soon put even more at ease by the friendliness of her new coworkers. Jana hadn't realized she was being guided through the building with a particular destination in mind until they reached the door labeled OFFICE OF THE MAYOR. "Let's see if the boss is available," he said with a smile before introducing her to Alyssa, Deeann's assistant, who invited Jana to enter the mayor's office.

"Jana, welcome," Deeann came around her desk and offered her hand to shake. She looked just as glamorous in person as her photo online. Her blonde hair, no doubt enhanced by dye, was sculpted into a bob. She wore a fuchsia summer dress and high heels that raised her just above Jana's height. The homecoming queen had aged well. No surprise there.

"Thank you." Did Deeann even recognize her?

"And I mean that," Deeann said, surprising her by placing her other hand over their joined ones. "Welcome back to the 'hood." Humor glinted in her eyes. "Have a seat. Let's catch up. So what made you decide to come back to Crossroads?"

They settled in padded chairs in front of the desk as Jana tried to figure out how best to answer that question. The truth was always best, or at least a version of it that wouldn't send her new boss running to the HR director to have her fired.

"I was looking for a new position in tourism that would give me a chance to make a difference. When I last visited Crossroads five years ago, I could see that the town looked a little rundown. I mean, not that it looks as bad now." Her cheeks burned. Open mouth, insert foot. *Dammit!* Why did she always manage to do that?

Deeann waved a hand. "Rundown is right. You can say it. You always did speak your mind." She crossed her legs. "That's actually my mission as mayor—to revitalize this town. I convinced the city council to approve your position, and I approved hiring you because you already know this area and you've had lots of experience in tourism at the state level. Working for the city should be a piece of cake after working at the state level. Also, I know you have good ideas and a passion for what you do. Wally recorded your interview, you know."

"Oh." Most virtual meetings she'd attended were recorded, so she'd thought nothing of it. She'd never imagined Deeann Donahue would have watched it.

Deeann was nodding. "Of course some of those ideas will have to wait until we have money budgeted for them. However, I do have an important project to get you started. Your first priority will be planning our new park." She described how a property that included an *unspoiled* lake—"Willow Lake, if you remember it"—had been donated to the city by a woman named Merritt Quinn and how her staff at her suggestion had successfully applied for a federal grant to create a park for all ages to enjoy.

"Folks have been sneaking onto the property for years to swim, fish, and hunt. Anyhow, we have to submit a report to the grant program by the end of the year with our plans and progress to date."

Priority was right—it was already August. "Has there been progress?"

Deeann's chin went up. "We've been…organizing. Getting approval for your position, of course, which will be paid for this year by the grant. Also, I've formed a committee of local citizens to help you in planning this project."

That was more like the queen of their high school class that she remembered. *Bossy britches* had been one of the kinder nicknames.

"When you say my salary is being paid from the grant money, does that mean the job ends in December?" Good old Wally hadn't mentioned that in the interview.

"Not necessarily. One, there's an option to apply for a grant extension or a new grant, which we're likely to need; or two, I can find the money, especially if you prove your worth. Wally probably told you we have a ninety-day probationary period."

"I'll prove it," Jana said coolly. If Wally had mentioned a probationary period, she'd forgotten about it. "But I'm not sure I would have committed to moving down here if I'd known the job was possibly only temporary."

She stared at Deeann until the mayor gave her a tight smile. "I have no doubt you'll do well, Jana, if for no other reason than to show me that I've underestimated you. It wouldn't be the first time. So, challenge accepted?"

Jana nodded despite knowing she was being manipulated. "Challenge accepted." After all, Deeann, the know-it-all, didn't know that she was also here for Nana Sue and would have come even without the job. Besides, she did have excellent—not just *good*—ideas.

Deeann rose. "Great. Alyssa will help you set up your office and give you the details on your committee members. Check in with me at least once a week or any other time you need to run something by me." She held out her hand again. "Good luck, Jana."

Her first day at work passed quickly as she familiarized herself with her new office and read a file on the Willow Lake property sent over by Deeann. Alyssa helped her schedule a committee meeting for Wednesday morning. The clock was ticking, and she was determined to prove that she was more than capable to earn a permanent position as the tourism director, whether she decided to keep working for Deeann or not.

When she returned home after a stop to visit Nana, who again put up a fight about going to eat, she spotted her neighbor watering her flowers. Charly dropped the hose and walked over to talk to her.

"Hey, how are you settling in?"

Jana smiled. "I'm unpacked and I survived my first day of work."

"Deeann, you mean. Did you see her?"

"Oh, yeah." She told Charly about their conversation. "I think she's hoping I'll fail, although she's running out of time to meet the requirements of the grant. If I fail, she fails." Reading the actual requirements and expectations had doubled her sense of urgency.

"Sounds like the bossy bitch we remember, but you'll show her. I'm so glad you're staying, at least for a while." Charly glanced over her shoulder as a car passed by. "I was hoping that was Eli."

"He'll be home soon from work, won't he?" It was almost six, but Eli was a grown man.

"I hope so. He usually texts if he's made other plans." She glanced at the street again as another car passed. "I thought he'd be back last night from his hunting weekend. You'd think he'd want to shower and shave after being in the woods for three days, if that's where he really was. Anyhow, I'm not going to hold dinner for him. He can just make a plate when he comes home."

"It's hard when they're grown but still living at home. They're adults who come and go as they please, but they aren't always thoughtful."

Charly pulled her cell phone from her pocket and checked it. "That's it exactly. We still worry as moms, don't we?"

"Even when they're out on their own." She needed to call her two girls tonight if they didn't check in to see how her day had gone. They'd probably forgotten she was starting work today.

"We'll have to celebrate your new job—maybe pick up some dinner one night this week?"

"I'd like that." They agreed on Thursday night, and Charly returned to her house. She seemed to have forgotten the hose on the ground, which wasn't like her. Eli was going to be greeted by a relieved but frustrated mom when he showed up.

Chapter Six

On Wednesday, the mayor's assistant arranged for the new tourism committee to meet in the city council's meeting room, which seemed far too big to Jana.

"The mayor told me to set you up here. She'll stop by to welcome everyone. Of course, your meetings are open to the public and the press," Alyssa told her. Like her boss, she favored dresses and heels. "Besides, your committee's work is important to the city, and the mayor wants to communicate that."

Jana's confidence plummeted. "The press?"

"Our local press. Probably just one person—Jack Huddleston. Don't worry, we have your back."

She'd seen a copy of the brief press release the mayor's office had issued, but standing in this official meeting room with its city, state, and American flags made the work they were about to do all too real.

"The committee members were sent the agenda, but I've made extra copies for you. I'll put out some water bottles too. Let me know if there's anything else you need." Alyssa beamed at her.

"Thank you."

You can do anything you put your mind to, Nana used to tell her.

She shouldn't have worried. Her committee members, two women and three men, were friendly and down-to-earth. Marjorie Wilkie, the willowy owner of a dress shop on Main Street who loved to bake, brought oatmeal cookies with raisins. Grace Peterson, a neighbor of Deeann's who taught disabled children how to ride ponies on her ranch and had visited more than half of the national parks, welcomed her with a warm smile and a firm handshake. Dressed in jeans, cowboy boots, a white T-shirt, and a denim jacket because she knew the building would be cold, she was interested in hearing more about Indiana's state parks. Walt Grisham ran the sawmill museum Jana vaguely remembered visiting with her grandparents as a child when it had first opened. He was also a woodcarver, hunter, and fisherman.

"I know every waterhole in this part of the state," he told her. "With a little promotion, we'll get folks here in droves, not that I'm going to share my best spots." He winked at her. "More fun for them to keep coming back and discover them for themselves."

The other two men showed up minutes before ten. Cal Kinney was a member of the Southern Pines board of directors. "I haven't been here long," he told her, shaking her hand, "but this area is a hidden gem. I've spent my spare time at the parks around here. I'm also an old college friend of Merritt Quinn. I understand we're going to be talking about Willow Lake."

If he'd gone to college with Merritt Quinn, the woman was younger than Jana had pictured her. "Yes, we are. I hope I can meet her soon."

"I'll make sure of it. She's finishing up her last semester

teaching at Purdue, but I think she'll come back for the mayor's dedication ceremony for the park."

Dedication ceremony? Deeann hadn't mentioned that in their discussion. She'd have to check with Alyssa or the mayor to see if a date had been set.

The last member of the committee strode toward them.

"Doc," Cal greeted him, shaking his hand.

"Hello again," Clay Bailey said to her with a smile.

"*Doc*?" Jana asked.

"I'm the locum filling in at the clinic."

"You're just here temporarily? I didn't realize that," Cal said. "He's been here longer than I have," he told Jana, "but then most people have. What about you? Are you a newcomer too?"

"No, not exactly. I went to high school here. Anyhow," Jana said brightly, "I think it's time we started. Would everyone please take a seat?"

To her relief, no one came in to observe their meeting at first. After introductions were made, she outlined the expectations for the committee. Their first priority would be planning the new park at Willow Lake. Before they started discussing that, Deeann appeared with Alyssa to welcome the committee and express her confidence in Jana's leadership. She also mentioned Merritt Quinn's generous donation of the acreage that had belonged to her great-aunt, Mary Randall Lawton.

"My goal is to have the committee's plans finalized and approved so we can hold a dedication and groundbreaking ceremony in October."

Jana's heart skipped a beat. Two months? That meant

they would have to come up with ideas and agree on a general plan by then. In her experience, there would be research needed to price out the project and determine what could feasibly be done within their budget. Architectural plans would then have to be drawn up and approved if more than a broad idea of what was being proposed was needed for the ceremony. Did Deeann expect her to have that much done in two months? She hoped her panic didn't show on her face.

At some point, a young man with glasses had entered quietly, taken a seat in the back, and begun typing on a laptop. When the mayor finished, he approached them with a small digital camera and asked permission to snap a photo of the committee with the mayor before she left. The long-time locals teased him about capturing their best sides and asked about his building, which had apparently been destroyed by an explosion. They then took a break to enjoy Marjorie's cookies.

"Jack Huddleston," the reporter told her. "Welcome to Crossroads."

"I'm sorry to hear about your office," Jana said. "I'm glad you're rebuilding. Crossroads wouldn't be the same without the *Gazette*."

His eyes twinkled. "Does that mean you're going to subscribe?"

"Uh, yes. My grandmother used to have a subscription. I'm staying at her house."

"The paper comes out on Thursdays." He handed her a card. "I'll be happy to set it up for you. We're online too."

"Thanks. I'll do that."

She called the meeting back to order, and soon they were discussing the property the city had just acquired from Merritt Quinn.

"I haven't had a chance to see it yet," she admitted, "but I hear Willow Lake is lovely."

"The fishing's great there too," Walt said. When the two women chuckled, he added with a wink, "Or so I've heard."

"We all need to go see it," Grace said. "And it would be better together. What about now?"

"Works for me," Walt said.

"I'm clear until noon, unless there's an emergency call," Clay said. "We need to get an idea of the property and what it offers."

"Well, uh—Marjorie? Cal? What do you think?"

"As long as I don't have to drive, I'm good to go," Marjorie said.

"I'm in," Cal said. He hesitated. "It wouldn't hurt to have one of the local police go with us. The property has been abandoned for decades. There could be campers or squatters."

"I've got my rifle," Walt said. "Never heard of any trouble up there."

"All those times you weren't fishing at Willow Lake?" Grace asked with a smirk. "It should be fine. I've never heard of a problem, either, and I will admit to going there for picnics over the years. If we don't give Merritt Quinn a key to the city for her generous donation, Deeann Donahue is going to lose my vote in November!"

"Okay, it's agreed then," Jana said. "Who'd like to drive?"

In the end, they took two cars, with Cal and Dr. Bailey driving. If there was a medical emergency, the doctor warned them, he might have to leave. Cal drove a large pickup with a back seat big enough for three, so they could squeeze in together if that happened.

Willow Lake was as beautiful as advertised, with the trees responsible for the name draping tendrils of green leaves over the banks of the blue lake. The committee quickly agreed that the area near the sandy shore was an ideal spot for picnic tables and possibly a pavilion for covered eating space in case of rain.

"We'll need restroom facilities not far from here," Clay said.

"Downwind would be good," Grace said in her laconic way, which caused Walt to chuckle.

Although there was plenty of room for the picnic area they envisioned, the map of the area Jana had copied for her team showed the park land had more to offer. Most of it was pine forest, but there was a trail wide enough for a vehicle leading away from the entrance they'd used. "What's down there?" Jana asked.

"Only one way to find out," Grace said. "I'll walk."

"I'll join you," Walt said, striding off with her. True to his word, he'd brought his rifle.

"I'll take my truck," Cal said. He'd been looking around nervously while they'd been talking as if he expected someone or something to jump out of the woods. "Anyone else want to ride?"

Marjorie and Jana joined him, but the doctor followed the other two on foot. Jana would have liked to walk, but like the other woman, her shoes, although they had low heels, weren't designed for hiking. They followed the other two along the rutted path and then passed them. Cal drove slowly out of the cleared area. Around them, birds hidden in the branches of the tall trees called to each other. Pine needles dropped on the hood of the pickup and then slid off to the floor of the forest.

The improvised road seemed to go for miles, but it was probably only minutes at their slow speed before the trees parted to reveal open farm land ahead. Cal stopped.

"Looks like someone might have made this trail to cut through to that road," he said, pointing to the pavement that ended just past the driveway to a farm house.

"That's the Hardy's place," Marjorie said. "My sister-in-law is kin to Corine Hardy."

"We might want to have a second entrance to the park here," Jana said. "Something to think about anyway."

The two hikers caught up to them, and Cal rolled down the windows. "Something interesting back there you should see," Walt said. "So, have we reached the property line?"

"Close enough," Jana said, her deadline worry returning. "Another thing we might have to do is obtain a survey of the property and stake out the boundaries."

"Merritt may have one," Cal said, "or she may be willing to help with that."

"The county property appraiser should have one on file," Grace said, "but I like the idea of staking out the boundaries."

Marjorie shaded her eyes as she gazed at the farm down a slight incline from them. "Yes, and we'll need to keep the neighbors informed of what we're doing. Rich Hardy likes his privacy."

Her tone implied the farmer wouldn't be happy with more traffic in the area. Jana made a mental note to find out more about the man and create a communication plan for the project. There was so much to do. She was beginning to get a tension headache.

"Let's go check out what Walt found," Cal suggested.

He managed a three-point turn around and slowly followed the hikers back. The path they had seen was blocked by a fallen young pine, which explained why the others hadn't noticed it from the pickup. Cal parked, and the men dragged the tree out of the way. Clay rubbed his hand along the raw edge of the trunk. "It's been cut."

Jana frowned. "Deliberately to block off the road?"

"I'd say so."

Walt walked farther along the trail. "Deer stand," he called back to them. Ahead through a gap in the trees, a plywood hut with slits in the sides perched on a platform raised on four posts. He cupped his hands and yelled, "Hello! Anyone here?"

They waited together as the forest, too, seemed to be holding its breath. Even the birds were silent.

"They probably didn't want anyone to find the stand," Cal said. "This is private property. They were here illegally."

"That's why I wanted to warn them," Walt said. "We don't want a nervous hunter shooting at us."

Cal's lips tightened.

"Doesn't seem like anyone's here," Walt said. "Might as well check it out."

Jana exchanged an uncertain look with Clay, who shrugged. Then they all followed Walt.

The deer stand was in a small clearing. A wooden ladder accessed the plywood hut built on stilts. Walt called out again identifying who he was, but again there was no reply.

"It's not deer hunting season yet, is it?" Jana asked, swatting at the flies that suddenly seemed to be swarming around them. "I thought that was in the fall."

"It's November if you're using a modern gun," Walt said. "End of September for archers and October for muzzleloaders. No dogs until November, either."

"Muzzleloaders?" Cal asked, turning. He swatted at the flies. "You've got to be kidding. Is that like what Civil War reenactors use?"

"They've been around longer than that—back to the flintlock rifles. The modern ones use a ramrod and black powder but are lighter and more efficient. They're highly accurate too." He grinned. "Bows and arrows go back even further. Depends what kind of hunting experience you want."

"I suppose," Cal said.

Clay approached the ladder. "Y'all need to wait down here," he said firmly, gripping the sides and putting his foot on the lowest rung. His gaze met Jana's. "Let me check it out first."

Cal grabbed the sides of the ladder. "I've got your back, Doc."

"No," Clay said, glancing down at him. "Just give me a minute to check it out." He disappeared into the doorless opening at the top of the stairs.

Marjorie's nose twitched. "Do you smell that?"

There was an odor, a sickly sweet smell. Jana glanced around to see if the hunter had left a deer carcass or remains. The threat of a citation for shooting out of season wouldn't stop the trespassing owner of this structure from hunting.

The doctor appeared above them and began to descend. They all froze at his grim expression.

"There's a young man dead up there," he told them. "We need to call the police."

A cold chill crept up Jana's spine. Eli had gone hunting last weekend. Had he returned? She hadn't spoken to Charly since their conversation Monday evening. She also hadn't noticed Eli's Mustang in her neighbor's driveway the last two days.

"Do you know who it is, Doc?" Walt asked. Cal had stepped away to call the police.

Clay shook his head. "I didn't want to disturb the body."

"You didn't have to…check for a pulse?" Marjorie's thin face was pale.

"No, there was no need."

Jana's imagination filled in a grizzly scene. Hunter, gun, flies…whoever he was, he'd probably been dead for days.

Eli had been gone for days.

She pulled out her cell and texted Charly, *"Hi—just wondering if Eli returned?"*

No answering dots showed up, but that wasn't surprising. Charly was at work and might not see the text right away.

"They're on their way," Cal said, pocketing his phone. "I can go meet them and direct them here."

"Why don't the rest of you go back to the lake," Clay suggested. "I'll wait here."

"I'll stay with you." She felt responsible for this property and whoever the dead young man was. *Please, God don't let it be Eli.* She checked her cell. Charly hadn't replied.

"I'll stay too," Walt said, resting his rifle on his shoulder.

"No, we'll be okay, Walt," Jana said, reluctantly putting her phone in her pocket. The smell and flies seemed worse now that they knew what had caused them. "Why don't the rest of you go with Cal? I'm sorry our meeting is ending like this."

They gave her sympathetic glances before turning to follow their driver back to his truck.

"Are you okay?" she asked Clay.

He glanced at her and held up his finger as he pressed his phone to his ear. "Wilma? I might be a little later, but I'll be back as soon as I can. Is everything okay there?" He listened for a moment before giving instructions on a dosage to be administered if a patient's symptoms persisted.

After he ended the call, he said, "Not the meeting you'd planned for today, I'm guessing."

"No, this field trip wasn't on the agenda, and neither was what's up there." She gazed up at the dark opening at the top of the stairs. "Was it bad?"

"Bad enough." He grimaced. "Looks like a gunshot wound, possibly self-inflicted. The rifle was near his right hand."

"That's awful." His family was going to be devastated. *Please, God, not Eli!*

"He picked a remote place to do it, if it was suicide.

Can't rule out an accidental shooting, I suppose." He frowned.

They waited in silent thought for a few minutes. "How did he get here?" Jana wondered aloud.

"Are you speaking metaphorically?"

She wasn't sure exactly what he meant. "I mean, how did he get *here*." She emphasized the last word. "It's so remote. The road had been blocked by that tree, and there's no sign of a car." If he'd come from one of the farms on either side of the property, he could have walked. That would mean it wasn't Eli. Although she shouldn't want the dead man to be someone else's son, brother, husband, or even father.

Clay looked around. "I guess that's something for the police to look into. Good question, though."

Jana walked around the posts holding up the stand. They rested on paving stones, probably so the hut wouldn't sink into the ground if it rained. On the far side of the structure, leafy branches were haphazardly piled. She moved some aside. The bare ground beneath had tire tracks. Mustang tires? Jana suddenly felt faint.

"You should probably leave that alone. In fact, we should move away from the stand." He brushed flies away from his face, and Jana unconsciously mimicked him as she tried not to be sick. "Come on, let's go back to that turnoff where the air's fresher."

He grasped her arm, pulling her away as he steadied her. Soon the forest scent of pines filled her lungs, and she could breathe again. The fresher air did nothing to lift the heavy weight of worry from her heart.

Chapter Seven

THE DISPATCHER'S REQUEST for a unit at Willow Lake came in as Tim was on his way back to the station from a meeting with the high school administrators about the fentanyl danger. Officer Ryan Grigsby responded. Tim automatically set his cruiser in the same direction. Suicides were often messy deaths, especially hangings and shootings. A deer stand had been mentioned, so it could be either. He'd have a chance to mentor Ryan in the field.

When he arrived, the young officer was already on scene talking to two men and two women he recognized.

"Hey, Chief."

"What are y'all doing at Willow Lake?" he asked the group.

"We're on the mayor's new tourism committee," Walt Grisham replied. "Thought we'd check out the site of the new park that's going to be built here."

That made sense. Merritt Quinn had donated this property to the city after she'd been involved in a murder case earlier this summer that had shaken the town. He glanced at Cal Kinney, who had also indirectly been part of that case.

"We found a deer stand. Doc Bailey is the only one who's been in it and seen the, er, deceased," Cal told them.

"Jana Nance is with him," Marjorie Wilkie added. "She's

our new tourism director. As Walt said, our committee came out here to see what the property had to offer."

More than they'd bargained for, obviously.

"Chief?" Grigsby asked.

He should have realized the flaw in his plan to observe and mentor the young officer: His presence inhibited anyone else's independent action.

"We'll go see the death scene. Folks, if you wouldn't mind sticking around a little while longer, I'd appreciate it. Meanwhile, Cal, let me know if anyone else shows up. The coroner will be coming, although I don't know how soon."

He eyed the rifle Walt Grisham held but let it pass. The man was a licensed hunter and not a hothead.

Leaving his vehicle next to Cal's truck, he rode with his officer following the directions Cal had given. The turnoff to the deer stand was easy to locate. Doc Bailey and a pale woman who appeared to be in her forties were waiting for them where another dirt road branched off to the right. Jana Nance wore a navy dress and shoes impractical for traipsing around in the woods. Apparently, the plan to *see what the property had to offer* had been an impromptu decision. She brushed away a fly and responded with a nod to his greeting.

"He's up there, Tim," Doc said, leading them to the deer stand.

"Any idea of the cause of death?" Tim asked. The odor was faint, but he could smell the corpse as they drew closer. In this heat, it didn't take long for a body to go into decomp.

"There's a gunshot wound to the head. His rifle's by his side."

Tim kept his expression as neutral as he could. Grigsby

was watching him and waiting for direction. Unfortunately, he was about to see something that he'd likely never forget. He tilted his head toward the ladder. "Go confirm that there's only one victim and no threat up there."

Doc gave him a questioning look but kept his thoughts to himself. To his credit, Grigsby returned, paler than before but able to report, "One apparent gunshot victim deceased and clear, Chief."

Tim nodded. "Secure the scene back to the turnoff and take a statement from Ms. Nance here. Doc, I need you to come with me."

The scene was as bad as he thought it would be. Worse, maybe. They only stepped in as far as they needed to see the victim. As Doc had said, the gunshot wound to the head had resulted in massive damage and was probably the cause of death. The rifle on the floor was close enough to have been dropped when death released the man's grip on it.

"It's not easy to make that shot with a rifle," Doc said. "Could have been an accident."

Tim removed the flashlight from his utility belt. The cutout windows were narrow, and the tall pines blocked much of the midday sunlight. He clicked the light on and moved the beam around the space.

Like most deer stands, there was little furniture. The victim lay on a canvas cot. The striped lawn chair next to the cot held a bulky backpack open to reveal what appeared to be clothes. An open plastic bag on the floor nearby contained cans of food and a box of granola bars. On the other side of the space, two wooden stools sat against the wall beneath one of the slitted openings for hunters to wait for their prey. The tin roof provided shelter from rain, but there was nothing to soften the rustic hut.

"Looks like he was camping out here," Doc said, gesturing to the cans and backpack. "Wouldn't expect someone planning to shoot himself to bring clothes and food."

"No. We'll have to see what the crime scene folks and the coroner say." The flies had found them, and it was becoming impossible to ignore the smell. "Let's get out of here."

Behind the stand, Grigsby had put on gloves and was sorting through branches on the ground. Jana Nance stood nearby watching him. She hugged herself as if chilled.

"What've you got there, Grigsby?"

The officer squatted and pointed. "Looks like tire tracks, Chief. Ms. Nance here had noticed these branches piled up back here."

"We had to move a small pine blocking the turnoff when we first arrived," she told him. "There's a fire pit in the front and these branches look more like they might have been used to cover something up instead of for firewood. Maybe a car?"

Tim frowned. There wasn't a vehicle in sight, which raised the question of how their victim had arrived.

"My neighbor was worried about her son Monday night. He hadn't come home and wasn't answering his phone. She…she said he'd gone hunting. He's nineteen, if that helps."

Her last sentence came out more like a question. Tim tried to keep his expression from showing the alarm claxons sounding in his brain. "Tell her to file a missing person report if he hasn't gotten in touch. If he shows up, all she has to do is let us know to close the case. There's usually a good explanation for young adults going off the radar—lost their phone, no cell service, too busy or distracted to respond to calls or texts. No reason yet to assume this is him." But if her neighbor's son was the young man upstairs, a MP report would provide a physical description and the ability to do a DNA match.

He caught Doc's gaze and suspected his thoughts were also running along the same line.

"Thanks for your help, Ms. Nance," he said. He checked with Grigsby to see if he'd obtained her address and asked for her neighbor's name and phone number "just in case."

"Grigsby will give you a lift back to the others. He'll need to take their statements—"

The sound of a motorcycle revving shattered the quiet of the woods. Coming from the opposite side of the property from the lake, the driver swung into the clearing where they stood. He stopped and turned off the engine before removing his black helmet.

The man looked familiar to Tim in the way many residents in the county did. In his thirties with a short beard and unruly dark hair, he could have been a face from the café or the hardware store. Tim usually remembered the faces of citizens he'd stopped or arrested, although the beard might be obscuring the features he'd recognize.

"I saw the police car." The man's voice was unremarkable and didn't help Tim place him. "We try to keep an eye out on the place. What happened here?"

"Do you live around here?" Tim asked.

"Just over yonder. I'm Tucker Hardy."

Of course. Tuck was several years older than Tim and had enjoyed brief local fame as a rodeo champion until he'd ruined his knee. His skin had become worn like leather from being in the sun, aging him, and the beard hadn't been a feature back in his bronc riding days. Also, today he'd traded his familiar cowboy hat for a motorcycle helmet.

"We're investigating a crime here, Mr. Hardy. Do you know anything about this deer stand?"

"Just that it's here. It's been here as long as I can remember."

"Do you know who owns it?"

He looked amused. "This is private property, so I guess it belongs to the owner. I heard it's some woman from up north."

"That's right. Have you seen anybody around here recently?"

He shook his head. "Can't say as I have."

"Have you been up here in the last few days?"

He tapped his helmet against his thigh. "Not in the last few days. I'll confess I cut through to Jones Camp Road sometimes. Been to the lake to swim too. Lots of folks come here, but not as many recently. Not since Reverend Fletcher stopped having baptisms in it."

"Well, it's neighborly of you to look after this property, but spread the word that it's off-limits for now, okay?"

"Sure thing, Chief." He glanced up at the stand. "Stinks around here, don't it?" he said and then put on his helmet. With a quick kick, the motorcycle roared to life. Before Tim could stop him, he wheeled around, stirring up dirt and destroying any other tracks that might have been there.

Tucker Hardy always had been an asshole.

Chapter Eight

CHARLY WAS WEEDING a flowerbed in front of her house when Jana returned home after work. Her neighbor sat up on her knees and waved. From a distance she appeared to be her usually cheerful self, which might mean she'd heard from her son and all was well. Around noon she'd texted that Eli hadn't yet returned. His Mustang wasn't in the driveway.

Up close, Charly's eyes and forehead revealed her worry. "How was your committee meeting?" she asked. Charly was doing what all mothers did—trying to carry on despite her anxiety. Jana had been there too many times to count. Whoever had said girls were easier to raise than boys had never sat up waiting until curfew or an hour after for a daughter to return from a date with a boy who'd taken her out on his motorcycle, or a daughter who'd asked her about obtaining the pill as a sixteen-year-old. And those were only two times she'd been sure her hair would turn white overnight.

"That bad?" Charly asked.

She wasn't going to tell Charly about the dead young man in the deer stand. "It was … it went well. I really like the people on the committee." Deeann's choices seemed like good ones, she'd give her credit for that. She talked for a few minutes about her new team. Charly knew most of them.

"We have a lot to decide, but everyone seems really positive and committed to creating the new park. How was your day? Any word from Eli?"

Her friend rose and began to remove her gardening gloves. "No. Maddy hasn't heard from him, either. I even called Derek." She rolled her eyes. "He told me Eli was refusing to answer his calls and texts. *Refusing*, he said. He wasn't the least bit worried when I told him no one had heard from his son in days. Thank god I'm divorced from that man."

"You know, Charly, maybe you should—"

An SUV pulled into her neighbor's driveway. Tim Birch stepped out, and Charly's puzzled frown turned into raw fear.

"No," Charly whispered.

Jana reached for her neighbor's arm. Charly seemed frozen in place.

"Hi, Tim. Chief Birch, this is my neighbor, Charly—Charlene Carson."

"Ma'am," He touched his hat but didn't smile. He was still in uniform. "Ms. Carson, could I have a word with you? Maybe we could go inside." His gaze slid to her, and Jana read the sadness in his eyes. He gave a slight nod to confirm that her worst fears were true.

"Is Maddy home?" Jana asked. "We could go into my house."

Charly seemed to come out of her paralysis. "Is this about Eli?"

"Yes, ma'am."

"Let's go into your house."

Charly took the news of Eli's death much better than Jana would have in her shoes. More stunned than teary, her neighbor sat stiffly on the sofa, refusing to relax back against the cushions. Jana rubbed her back while Chief Birch explained where Eli had been found and that he'd been shot. He didn't mention suicide, and Jana was grateful for that. Accepting her son was gone was all Charly could handle at this point.

The wallet in his pocket had contained Eli's driver's license, Tim told Charly. They would do further testing to confirm identity.

"C-can I see him? I can identify him if it's Eli."

"That's not necessary, ma'am. Actually, we use DNA today mostly."

He was being kind. From what Clay Bailey had described, the fatal bullet had probably destroyed Eli's face. Charly wouldn't want to see him like that.

"If your son has any distinguishing features, such as scars or tattoos, that could help us speed up the confirmation."

"He has a tattoo of a stag on his right arm." Charly gestured automatically to her upper arm.

"He was in an accident when he was ten," Jana added. Someone needed to defend Eli. "His leg and right arm were badly broken. He was hit by a car."

Charly turned to her, her face and eyes slack with grief. "It took him months to recover. His right arm had nerve damage, and he had to learn to use his left hand." A tear rolled down her pale cheek. "He worked so hard to get his strength back. As soon as he was eighteen, he got the stag tattoo. He said it reminded him of how strong he'd had to be to survive."

The chief was frowning. "So he used his left hand for eating? Writing? Hunting?"

"Everything that required control." Charly flexed her fingers. "He could hold things in his right hand, but his fingers were stiff and didn't flex well. He still uses the rubber ball his therapist gave him." She shook her head. "It didn't stop him from being a good mechanic. He works for Newt Doncaster at his car dealership, Doncaster Motors. He's so good using his left hand now, you'd never know he was born right-handed."

Jana wasn't sure who Newt Doncaster was, but the chief nodded and made a note.

"He's really good at fixing cars, really good. You saw his Mustang," she said to Jana. "I wish you could have seen it when he bought it." She turned back to the police chief. "It's like new. You've seen it, haven't you." It wasn't a question.

Tim exchanged a look with Jana. "Ma'am, his car wasn't at the deer stand. We've put out an APB on it."

Charly frowned. "But he drove there in it. He left here…I mean, he must have driven to Willow Lake in it."

"We'll have more answers when we find it."

Charly scoffed. "It's hard to miss. It's bright blue with a wide white racing stripe that goes from the front fender over the roof to the back fender."

"That's helpful," Chief Birch said. "I understand Eli lived with you. When was the last time you saw him?"

Charly's shoulders slumped. "Friday morning. He said he was going away for the weekend, camping. He liked to do that. His father"—she sighed—"his father used to take him camping, fishing, and hunting. We divorced when Eli was twelve."

Derek Carson now lived in Lake Village. She didn't have his address.

"We'll notify him," the chief said.

"He's remarried and started a new family. Doesn't have time for his older kids."

The silence sat for a moment. "Did you know about the deer stand at Willow Lake, Ms. Carson? Was that somewhere Eli liked to go?"

"No. I knew there was a deer stand they'd built together. He and his father wouldn't tell me where it was. No wonder—Willow Lake's on private property."

"Yes, ma'am, it is. And how did Eli seem on Friday morning? Had he been sad or upset about anything?"

Charly studied him for a long moment. "Eli wouldn't kill himself." She shook her head several times. "No way. Is that what—" She shook her head again. "No way!"

"His state of mind could be helpful to us, whatever the coroner determines the cause of death to be."

Jana squeezed her friend's hand.

Charly blinked several times as she refocused. "He seemed...rushed. He said he had the day off, needed some time to himself to clear his head. He—" Her voice broke and she stopped.

"You're doing great," Jana said. "Take your time."

Charly nodded. "He was angry—at me. He said I'd been nagging him. He wanted some time away. Away from me." She put her hand to her face and sobbed.

Jana drew her into her arms.

The chief pocketed the small notebook he'd been using. "I'm really sorry for your loss, Ms. Carson." Charly didn't look up, so he handed his card to her. "Please call me if you have any questions or concerns I can help with." He explained about the need for an autopsy. "I'll also need to look at Eli's room."

Charly's head came up at that. "Why?"

"At this point, your son's death is considered suspicious until the coroner determines the cause of death. I'll also need his toothbrush or something else to match his DNA."

Charly sighed but didn't move.

"Why don't you go rinse your face in the bathroom," Jana said. "You don't want Maddy to see you like this." Even if her mother's tears weren't evident, it wouldn't take the fourteen-year-old long to sense something was terribly wrong.

"You're right. It's going to be hard enough for her." She wiped her eyes and left them.

"You haven't found the car?" Jana asked him after she heard the door to the hall bathroom close and the noisy fan connected to the light switch begin to whir and clatter.

"No."

The branches she'd noticed had been freshly cut. "He must have driven there."

"It looks like it, but he could have loaned it to a friend or had it towed away. As his mother said, it's hard to miss, so I'm hoping we'll find it soon."

Or someone had stolen it. Why had Eli gone to the deer stand and then apparently covered his car with the branches, unless he hadn't wanted to be found? But someone else had been there and possibly had taken his car.

She lowered her voice even more. “I haven’t been back to Crossroads in five years, but Charly’s right—Eli wouldn’t kill himself. I’ve known him since he was little. He was a good kid, a good person. He had his life on track, a good job. He would never hurt his mother and sister by taking his own life.”

“We won’t know the cause of death until the coroner has his say.”

Frustrated, she stared at him, trying to decipher the meaning behind his carefully worded response. Then the clatter of the fan stopped, and Charly returned.

Chapter Nine

JACK SAT IN the back of the First Street AME church in Crossroads. He'd been to funerals here before. No weddings or baptisms, no Sunday services—just funerals. Today it was Albert Walker in the satin-lined casket in front of the mostly African-American congregation. The church was almost full, a testament to Albert's large network of family, friends, and supporters in his efforts to obtain justice from Southern Pines for the toxic pollution of Crawfish Pond near his home.

"You writin' a story about Albert?" Eulie Daniels, Albert's neighbor, asked him after the service.

"Just here as a friend," Jack said, resisting the impulse to question Eulie about the pending legal action his neighborhood had filed. The attorney had stonewalled him on the phone. There was also the question about who was going to fill Albert's shoes in leading the effort to clean up the pond.

"That was a fine obituary you wrote. Albert would have liked it."

"I'm glad. And just so you know, I'm still fighting for that pond to be cleaned up."

"The company won't do nothing about that unless they have to."

"Court said they have to, Eulie. Now we just have to

hold their feet to the fire and get it done."

"Won't be any of us left to see that day." Before Jack could protest, he walked away to rejoin other mourners heading to the gravesite.

Jack sighed. Albert's family had also left. He'd already shared his condolences with them. He wasn't going to the cemetery this afternoon. He'd paid his respects. Besides, Albert wouldn't mind. He'd want him to keep working for justice. In his car, he called his connection to the Southern Pines board of directors.

Cal Kinney seemed distracted. "You want to meet? Not here."

Jack wasn't sure if he meant not at his Southern Pines office or not anywhere in Crossroads. "Then come to my place this evening." He gave Cal the address. "You can park at the library and walk. It's only a few blocks."

They agreed to meet at nine, after dark as Cal preferred. Jack rolled his eyes at the cloak-and-dagger arrangement, but if that kept his contact happy, he'd wear a disguise if necessary. But it was more than that, more than that Pulitzer Prize-winning article he'd always dreamed of writing. This was for Albert, and it was also personal. Jack had seen the sludge and sheen of the chemically poisoned water up close—too close. It was an affront to nature and to everything he valued. It had nearly been his grave. It needed to be fixed. It should have been fixed a long time ago.

That evening, Cal showed up at nine just as CNN was changing from one show to the next. The California transplant wore gym shorts, a dark T-shirt, and running shoes. He smelled of bug spray more than sweat.

"Out for your evening run?" Jack asked, inviting him in.

"Might as well work in some exercise." He accepted the offer of water, and they settled in Jack's living room.

"Nice house," Cal said looking around, clearly surprised. "The *Gazette* must be doing better than I thought."

Jack laughed. "The *Gazette* is almost breaking even. I have some family money, and the house used to belong to my grandparents. Granddad started the paper."

"Huh. So you grew up here in Crossroads?"

"Mostly in Little Rock, but I spent time here as a kid. Granddad taught me a lot. Journalism is in my blood." It was in his mother's blood, too. As far as he knew, no one here knew her biographies had won national prizes, including the Pulitzer and Nero. She'd been short-listed for a National Book Award three years ago for her biography of Orval Faubus, Arkansas's governor during the civil rights movement.

"Are you going to start rebuilding the office soon?"

"Hopefully. Soon as the permits come through. Anyhow, what I wanted to talk to you about was the truck I saw dumping waste into Crawfish Pond." With Albert late one night.

"I should have guessed," Cal said. "Nothing new there. I told you the company hasn't been dumping there for decades, and while we still use box trucks like the one you saw, they all have our name and logo on them. I checked that out myself. Did you ever figure out who the passenger was that night?"

"No, but I know I've seen him before." It was driving him crazy not being able to come up with a name for the face he'd seen when the man had briefly removed his mask. Usually he had a great memory for faces, but then again, he talked to a lot of people as the publisher, editor, and only staff reporter for his newspaper.

Cal ran a hand over his sweat-soaked brown hair. He looked more like the California surfer he'd become in his university days than the grandson of a former Southern Pines board member from Crossroads. "There is one thing I've discovered. I don't want this published, though, Jack. It might mean nothing."

A tingle ran down his spine. "Okay."

"We've been replacing the trucks every three years—whether they need replacing or not. The company advertises the inventory for sale locally, and they all sell immediately to the same place, Forest Truck Traders."

"I know it. It's out on 82."

Cal nodded. "That's it."

He didn't say any more. Jack leaned forward. "Does the pricing seem fair? Any other offers, or is Forest Truck Traders the only buyer?"

"According to what I've been able to learn, they offer a fair price, and it saves the company money not having to advertise more or keep them in inventory longer."

"Isn't Bill Grissom over transportation? Have you talked to him?"

"He's the one who assured me everything was above-board. Not that I made any accusations. I'm still playing the *new-and-trying-to-learn* card. He thinks my only concern is why we're turning over the fleet every three years. Seems like an unnecessary expenditure."

"Hmm." The company was rumored to be having some financial issues, mainly due to competition for their products in recent years from China and bigger American corporations. So far, no one had been laid off, but vacated positions weren't being filled, either. Except the board seat Cal Kinney had been offered at the beginning of the year. Rumor had it that Peter Westfield, the chair, had fought to offer the position to Cal in the hope that he'd bring new ideas to keep the company from going under. Maybe that was the reason, or maybe there had been more to it. He'd find out one of these days, but it wasn't a story he wanted to investigate tonight.

"What's the status of cleaning up Crawfish Pond?"

Cal grimaced. "Merritt asked me about that today."

Jack wasn't surprised. He'd texted Merritt Quinn about Albert's death. "SP has been served with a petition for a motion to compel the cleanup. You can't delay it forever—it's just not right."

Cal frowned at him. "Look, we have estimates. From what I understand, the EPA are the experts. They should be the ones handling the cleanup, if they'll take it on."

"That's not what the court ordered. Southern Pines caused the damage, and they have to fix it."

"Yeah, but as long as it's fixed—"

"That's not the point! Southern Pines should have to pay for what they did."

Cal frowned. "Hey, I'm not the enemy here, Jack. I had nothing to do with—"

"Yeah, yeah, you're the new guy, but you're on the board." He drew a breath and calmed himself. He needed

Cal's help and sounding like a hothead wasn't going to help. "From what I hear, you have Peter Westfield's ear. The company needs to do something, even if they have to drive their damn trucks for fifteen years like the rest of us to save money. We're talking about people's lives, families who lived in that area long before the dumping started. You know they wouldn't have poisoned that pond if white folks had lived there."

Cal flushed. "I know that, Jack. I'm pushing the others, but right now we just don't have the money. It's more complicated than you and Merritt think."

"*Complicated?* Dammit, Cal, that's just not good enough. We've already lost half the folks by that pond, including Albert Walker. Every time I write about it, I get death threats or worse. I don't want the company to go under, but it's just not right that they can trash the environment like that, kill people, and then plead that they can't afford to clean up their damn mess."

"Jack, I'm on your side. You're just going to have to give me more time to convince the others that we can afford—that we *have* to afford it. Peter's the only one willing to even consider major changes in what we're doing, and that's what it's going to take to stay in business much longer, much less find the money to do the cleanup. And that's definitely not for publication."

Jack bit back another sharp retort. Cal was on his side, even if he didn't share his sense of urgency. And why should he? The pollution had occurred more than two decades ago before Cal or any of his colleagues had been on the board. The state's department of health had reported that the toxic waste, mainly pentachlorophenol, known as PCP and used to treat wood, was an unlikely cause of the high incidence of cancer in that small community. That finding certainly hadn't helped. Even so, the residents and their former attorney, Ernie Crowell, had won a lawsuit to force SP to clean up the water. Now, a new lawsuit, if successful, could drive the company to bankruptcy, resulting in layoffs or even closure. Southern Pines was the biggest employer in Crossroads. In the entire county, for that matter. If they went under, the town wouldn't be far behind. If that happened, he'd be the last publisher of the *Crossroads Gazette*. Maybe he shouldn't rush into rebuilding his office.

"I attended Albert Walker's funeral today," he said in a low voice, his mood now as dark and murky as Crawfish Pond. "I'd hoped he'd live to see something done."

"I read his obituary. Cancer, huh? He deserved better."

"They all do. *We* all do."

Cal nodded. "I know this is personal for both you and Merritt." He held up his hand, cutting off Jack's interruption. "And important for the community. Like I told her, I'm working on it. Changing minds isn't easy."

True. Neither was changing hearts. Jack forced himself to sound calm. "I know, and I know you're doing what you can. Thanks for checking out the company trucks. I'm glad Southern Pines isn't behind the current dumping." *Not officially, anyhow.*

"I'll let you know if I hear any more," Cal said rising.

As Jack closed the door behind his visitor, he realized he did have a lead he could follow up—Forest Truck Traders. What did they do with the box trucks they bought from SP?

Presumably they sold them, but who locally owned them? Cleaning up Crawfish Pond was going to take more pressure on Southern Pines, hopefully from the court, but meanwhile the dumping had to stopped for good. If he could just place that man's face, the police could arrest those responsible for the recent activity.

Albert would be happy about that. It was at least a step in the right direction.

Chapter Ten

FRIENDLY'S FOREST INN was tucked back behind shade trees just off the highway. If Jana hadn't been looking for it, she might have missed the weathered sign with an arrow that probably lit up at night if the bulbs outlining it still worked. The drive was paved and opened into a parking lot in front of the single-story motel that she'd been told was the second largest in greater Crossroads. The Redwood Inn on Main Street had twenty rooms to Friendly's eighteen. She'd visited the manager there as her first stop this morning. The hotel was old but charming, and the central location was certainly a selling point.

She'd told Alyssa that she was leaving the office to check out the local motels and guesthouses in case Deeann was looking for her. Spending time talking to people and checking out local accommodations would be a good distraction, she hoped. She'd stayed with Charly and Maddy last night until she couldn't keep her eyes open. Not that sleep had come easily after she'd gone to bed. After Tim Birch had left, Charly had called her sister, who'd promised to come to Crossroads this morning and notify Charly's extended family. Cars had already arrived next door when Jana had left for work. She just wished there was more she could do. She hated feeling so helpless.

There were only three cars in Friendly's parking lot, which suggested either the motel wasn't as welcoming as the name suggested or business was slow. Inside the small lobby, Jana called a hello and then found a bell to ring for service. Within a minute, a stocky man appeared through the door behind the counter. His smile was broad and toothy. He wore a light-blue shirt with a grease spot in front just above his beer belly. Well, in a dry county, fried food was probably a more likely culprit for both the stain and the extra girth.

"Hello there! Welcome to Friendly's. Are you here for a room?"

Smiling, Jana extended her hand and forced herself to project more cheerfulness than she felt this morning. "Actually, I'm here to say hello. My name is Jana Nance. I'm the new tourism director for Crossroads. I'm introducing myself to all the local hotel and restaurant owners."

He clasped her palm and pumped it. "Larry Mason. Pleased to meet you, ma'am."

"Please call me Jana. Are you the owner of Friendly's? It's sure nice and cool in here."

"Yes, ma'am, er, Jana. Owner and general manager." He leaned forward as if ready to confide a secret. His breath smelled of bacon. "To tell you the truth, I do it all around here, except clean the rooms. I have a girl for that."

"You must be a jack-of-all-trades. How is business, if you don't mind me asking? My job is to increase tourism, so I'd like to know what you need."

"More tourists will do it, that's for sure. It's kinda slow, except when the rodeo's in town in June or during deer huntin' season in the fall. Other than that, I mostly check in folks visiting relatives, passing through, or staying for the night on business. 'Course most of the company's visitors—that's Southern Pines—stay at the Redbud Inn in town. It's closer for them."

Better maintained, too, if the dingy walls of this room were any indication of the rest of the place. Painting must not be a trade Larry had embraced.

Give the man a break, her conscience told her. *He's just said business hasn't been great. He may not be able to afford to hire a painter or even buy a gallon of paint.*

"Would you like a tour?" he asked. "I have some brochures here somewhere." He bent to peer under the counter and came up with a handful of glossy, folded pamphlets.

The photo of the inn on the cover appeared to have been taken sometime in the past when the exterior had been freshly painted white with dark green trim that now looked like a mottled avocado shade.

"Are these your folks?" She pointed to the older couple pictured on the back. Beneath their smiling faces was an invitation to COME JOIN US AT FRIENDLY'S, WHERE YOU'LL ALWAYS BE WELCOMED LIKE FAMILY!

"Those are my grandparents. They built the place. Their name was Friendly, if you can believe it. Sounds welcoming, don't it?"

"It sure does. And is that you playing football?" She nodded toward the two framed photos hung on the back wall. The first was an enlarged snapshot of a younger, more handsome Larry with the same wide grin suited up and crouched like he was ready to tackle anyone trying to go past him. Black face-paint slashes below his eyes added to the menacing posture. The second photo showed five young men in the team uniform grinning at the camera.

"Yes, ma'am. My glory days. You know that Bruce Springsteen song? Anyhow, happiest days of my life. Me and the guys are still close, though."

The young men in the photo looked so young. They'd probably been just a year or two younger than Eli, who would never become middle-aged like Larry and mourn the loss of his own glory days. She blinked back the tears.

The former football player leaned on the counter. "Where are you from, Jana? That's an unusual name, by the way, but it's sure pretty."

She focused again on him. "Thank you. I'm from Indiana most recently, but my grandparents lived in Crossroads, so I've spent some time here visiting them over the years."

He lowered his voice—his idea of sexy? "And are you planning on staying here now? You'd be a welcome addition."

Before she could answer, the door at the side of the lobby opened. An Asian woman emerged wearing a silky robe. She had a cascade of unnaturally red curly hair and a generous application of eye makeup for this early in the day. "Larry, hon, the coffee machine isn't working, and you know I need my caffeine before I can function in the morning." Her purring tone suggested *function* referred to more than getting her day started.

"Be right there, hon. Hey, Vivian Amber, this is Jana, uh…"

"Nance," she supplied with a smile. "Hello, Vivian." She left off her explanation of why she'd come. "Anyhow, I'll let you get back to business, Larry." She slanted a look at the woman, who gave her a sly smile as if she'd scored a point in a game Jana had no intention of playing. "Oh, do you happen to have a business card?" she asked Larry.

"Sure don't, but that number on the brochure is mine." He pointed to the back page where a sticker had been pasted on with his name, phone number, and email.

"Perfect. I'm just getting my cards printed, but you can reach me through the city switchboard. It was nice to meet you both. Thanks for your time."

"My pleasure, ma'am."

If Vivian hadn't been listening at that door, she'd wrestle an alligator. Jana smiled at the woman as she headed for the door. *He's all yours, honey.*

TIM'S MORNING BRIEFING with his officers added little to what they knew of Eli Carson or his death in the deer stand. The county coroner, Dr. Nagashi, would do the autopsy today, but he'd already agreed the gunshot wound to the head had most likely killed the young man. He wouldn't commit to saying the fatal injury appeared to be self-inflicted. He'd test for drugs, too, which should be interesting. CSI had found a baggie of blue pills that appeared similar to the ones their fentanyl victims had taken. Oddly enough, they hadn't been able to lift any prints from the baggie.

Drug user or not, Eli Carson probably hadn't died from an overdose or suicide. Dr. Nagashi had been silent on the phone when Tim had shared the information about Eli's childhood accident and him being left-handed. Tim didn't have to spell out what that meant in terms of where they'd found the rifle that presumably had delivered the fatal bullet. The coroner never said much or showed emotion, but he was thorough and weighed all the evidence, which made him good at his job. Also, Eli's mother had said her son didn't take any medications, specifically no antidepressants. No suicide note had been found on the scene or in his room, although not all victims left them. There was also the missing Mustang. At this point, it was looking like a homicide.

"What did you find on social media?" he asked Simon.

The lanky young officer turned his laptop around. "He was active on TikTok mostly, but also SnapChat and Whatsapp. Mostly what you'd expect from a teenager." He didn't glance up to see several of his older peers' lips twitch. "I did find a video about his deer hunt last fall. Looks like he bagged a ten-pointer. There's a deer stand and a couple of other guys in the video."

He turned the laptop around and clicked a few times before showing them the brief film. The white-tail deer had been strung up in a tree. Eli, dressed in camo, posed beside the carcass with his rifle in a proud hunter pose. His buddies teased him about making a lucky shot and bagging a buck so old he couldn't run if he'd wanted to.

"That's the stand where we found him," Tim confirmed.

"He also has a YouTube channel. He posted a couple of videos on rehabbing Mustangs. Looks like he was working on his own car."

"Print out a picture of the car if you can. His hunting

buddies too. So, nothing unusual?"

Simon shook his head. "Not that I found. I'll keep looking."

"Sarge, any update on the Mustang?" The BOLO had gone out last night after he'd visited Charly Carson.

"No sightings yet." Rollins had tried to avoid this briefing by claiming he needed to be on the streets supervising the new recruits, a pointed reminder about his niece's death. Tim suspected he had other reasons for wanting to be out on patrol that had more to do with catching a drug dealer than responding to citizens' calls or issuing traffic tickets. Unfortunately, no leads on the source of the fentanyl had turned up.

Tim ignored the hostility that rolled off the man like fog on a field. "Maybe having a picture will help." CSI hadn't come back yet with a report on the tire tracks they'd found at the deer stand—the ones hidden by the branches that Tuck Hardy hadn't obliterated.

"What about Eli's buddies? Did you recognize any of them from that video, Francine?"

"Yes, sir—all of them. I ran all the names Ms. Carson gave you. They're all still living in Crossroads and clean, other than a speeding ticket and a citation for driving with a broken headlight. I'll talk to them today."

"Good." He updated them on CSI's preliminary report. "They found a baggie of blue pills that looked like the ones we found the other night." His gaze met Sarge's. "They're going to compare them, but I'm guessing they came from the same source. Andrea, how are your interviews with Finn Lasher's friends going?"

"Not good, Chief. They claim to know nothing about any pills or fentanyl. They wouldn't make eye contact, so I think they know more than they're saying. I warned them that the pills could be fatal and told them their friend was incredibly lucky that Josie"—her voice cracked—"that Josie found him in time."

"And had Narcan on hand," Tim said grimly. Not that long ago, they hadn't carried it. It had saved Finn Lasher, but Josie had died with Narcan lying within reach minutes before he'd arrived. "Regardless of the cause of Eli Carson's death, given the number of pills found with him, he might have also been dealing drugs. Andrea, check back with those kids you interviewed. Did they know Eli? Ever see him hanging around the high school or hangouts teens go to during the summer? Have they heard about any new pills? Maybe they'll share something if they don't have to admit to personally using drugs. Just be careful not to suggest that we suspect Eli Carson might have been pushing them. We don't know that for sure."

"Yes, Chief."

"Simon, keep looking online into Eli's life. Check with the high school too. See what kind of student he was. Any behavioral problems there or signs of depression? You might want to talk to the school counselor assigned to him."

"Yes, sir. I can start this morning, but I'm scheduled to ride along with Sergeant Rollins this afternoon."

Tim inwardly winced. He should have realized the new recruit was still learning from the patrol officers and gaining experience responding to calls. He'd just stepped on the sergeant's toes again, drafting the kid to work on serious crimes. And not just the sergeant's toes: Some of the longer serving officers were still grumbling about being passed over for detective. Never mind that Simon already had a university degree and better computer skills than almost everyone on the force.

He glanced at Ed Rollins sitting in the back with his arms folded across his chest, his sun-aged face showing nothing. A long-time cop who'd trained Tim when he'd started on patrol, he'd never openly supported Tim's promotion to chief. Hadn't opposed it, either, although he'd worked closely and socialized with the former deputy chief who'd been presumed to be next in line for the position after their previous leader died of a sudden heart attack. His buddy had taken early retirement after he'd been passed over. What Tim had thought was a wait-and-see attitude toward the new chief had been changed by his niece's death. He wasn't sure he could repair their relationship, but he had to try.

"That training's important," Tim said, "and I'm sure you're learning a lot from Sergeant Rollins and your other trainers. Francine, tomorrow morning, you can go to the high school."

"Yes, Chief."

He received a faint nod of approval from Clint, seated in front, and ignored the disappointed look on Simon's face. He'd get his chance to prove his detective skills. In fact, maybe there should be a rotation for newbies to shadow his serious crimes team, small as it was. Sarge and the other old guard probably wouldn't approve, but that was just too bad.

"Eamon, any more information from Finn or the street

about the drugs?"

The unshaved detective in plain clothes shook his head. "Nada, although word has gotten out about the fentanyl. I did hear from an informant that some guys believed to be from a Mexican cartel were seen here about two weeks ago. He claimed he didn't know who they visited or whether they were just passing through."

"Great," Tim said. "That's all we need. All of you, check with your contacts. And Sarge, tell the patrol officers to ask around. Any whisper about drugs, I want to hear about it."

So did the mayor. As Deeann Donahue had reminded him this morning, there was an election coming up in November and her opponent was already talking about the rising incidence of crime in their town. The man was going to really love it if Eli Carson's death turned out to be a drug-related murder. Tim owed the mayor his appointment as chief. More than that, he didn't want to lose another officer or an unsuspecting teen to an accidental overdose.

He watched his team leave when he dismissed them a short time later. Sarge passed him without a glance. They had to stop the flow of drugs before someone else died. If they now had a killer to catch, they'd have to stop him too.

Chapter Eleven

JANA HAD EATEN at Annabelle's Café many times with her parents and grandparents. After her mother died when she was fifteen, her father had taken her to the café to tell her that he'd decided to accept a transfer from Little Rock to Indianapolis. She'd pleaded with him to be able to stay in Crossroads to finish high school. Starting over in a new place where she didn't know anyone without her mother had been inconceivable. She'd won that argument—too easily. A year later he'd visited and told her over another lunch here that he'd asked a woman he'd met to marry him. Fortunately, her stepmother, much younger than her dad, was nice enough, and she loved the two boys who were born while she was still attending high school in Crossroads, but Nana's house had always seemed more like home than the split-level in Indy where her father and his new family lived.

The popular breakfast and lunch spot run by the Lee siblings hadn't changed at all. The red booths and stools may have been refurbished, but the old jukebox still had an OUT OF ORDER sign. Dave, occasionally bobbing to Beach Boys songs turned low, was still flipping burgers at the grill behind the counter, and Cindy was bustling around the tables and booths, taking orders and chatting with customers. Jana could swear the man sitting at the far table spooning chili had been there the last time she'd visited five years ago.

She approached the counter. "Hi, Dave. You wouldn't remember me. I'm Jana Nance. My grandmother is—"

"Ms. Ffyfe!" Cindy finished for her. She handed her brother a ticket. "One of those burgers needs to be well done. No red at all. How is your grandma, hon? We haven't seen her here in ages. She used to come in with her card group every Tuesday."

"She's had to go into a nursing home. She's at Golden Pines now."

"Oh no! I'm sorry, hon. Alzheimer's, is it? That's what our daddy had. He passed away two years ago."

"I'm sorry to hear that."

"Well, life goes on as I always say, doesn't it, Dave? You want to sit at a table, hon, or a booth? Dave's not much company, but you're welcome to sit at the counter."

"Actually, I'm meeting Mayor Donahue, so a booth would be great. But before I sit down, I want you both to know I'm the new tourism director for the city." She gave them her two-sentence introduction spiel. "My first project is planning the new park out at Willow Lake."

"Well, I'll be," Cindy said, exchanging a look with her brother. "We'll sure welcome more trade. Wait a minute...didn't they just find a young man dead out there in a deer stand?"

"Er, yes." She didn't want to add to the gossip that seemed to be rapidly spreading. The jingle of bells on the door saved her.

"Oh, here's our mayor now," Cindy said looking over her shoulder. "Let's find y'all a nice booth."

She would need more than that to comfortably share a meal with Deeann. Her boss had texted her the invitation this morning. She probably hadn't liked her taking initiative to go out in the community. If Deeann was going to micromanage her, this wasn't going to work.

"If we're lucky, we'll be left alone for a few minutes," Deeann said, grabbing some paper napkins from the metal dispenser near the window as soon as she sat down. "Folks around here aren't shy about letting me know about their concerns. How's the community outreach going?"

"So far, so good." She told Deeann which businesses she'd visited. It had been a productive morning, although her boss might not be happy she wasn't focusing on her top priority.

They both thanked Cindy as she set their iced teas in front of them. Jana had a quick look at the menu and then gave in to the tantalizing smell of ground meat cooking and ordered a cheeseburger, medium. Deeann ordered a bowl of tomato soup. She'd informed Jana in her text that she only had a half hour for lunch. Jana had read that as a warning not to be a minute late.

They both sipped their teas for a moment, and then Deeann asked, "So what were your impressions of the places you visited this morning?"

"Tisdale's seemed okay, just dated, but Friendly's needs a good cleaning and some fresh paint. Business was really slow in all three. They were all open to developing more tourism." Larry Mason had seemed open to more than that.

"This time of year is slow, but hunters will start coming in the fall for deer season. Frankly, it's a miracle they've stayed in business these last few years." Deeann tapped a manicured pink nail against her red plastic tea glass. "If we're going to bring in more tourists, we're going to need more rooms for them." She slanted a glance at Jana. "Quality accommodations. Tisdale's and Friendly's aren't what I'd call quality, and the Redbud is showing its age."

"They're all family businesses, aren't they? I didn't meet the owners of the Redbud Inn, but Rose at the front desk told me her aunt owned it."

"Marilou is very reclusive. You may never meet her. She mostly employs her passel of nieces, nephews, and cousins to run it, but she does the books and keeps a tight rein on them from what I hear. She hasn't designated who will inherit when she passes. Probably waiting to see what cream rises to the top among them. Smart woman."

"And they have most of the Southern Pines business?"

"They do, but there hasn't been as much recently. Even salespeople are visiting less." She lowered her voice again. "It's no secret that the company has had to cut back on spending. They've been undersold by their competition, and then COVID struck. They lost a lawsuit a couple of years ago, too, and they were ordered to pay to clean up a pond where they used to dump toxic waste."

"Crawfish Pond." Jana had heard about that case.

Deeann frowned, although her forehead and brow remained smooth. Botox?

"Anyhow, if we focus on building tourism, we can help our local small businesses. I'm excited about the ideas you and your committee have already come up with for Lawton Park."

Jana had already started thinking of it as Mary's park. Tradition dictated they call it by the woman's last name, but if Lawton was her married name, it belonged more to her husband than her. Then, again, even women's maiden names belonged to their fathers if you chose to look at it from a feminist perspective. Not that she was one, but she appreciated their efforts to give women more opportunities and equal pay. As for the name, she suspected the locals would probably call it Willow Lake. She'd have to think of some way to recognize Mary at the park so folks would remember her for preserving the land for them to enjoy.

They talked about the committee's ideas for swimming and picnic area and the challenges of adding bathroom facilities until their meals arrived. Deeann seemed enthusiastic about all of them. Maybe she wasn't going to be a micromanager.

"I like the committee you chose," Jana said after they started eating. "I think they'll all be good to work with. Did you have to twist any arms?"

Deeann widened her eyes and grinned, a reaction that Jana wasn't expecting. "Me? I don't twist arms—I persuade. Actually, I didn't directly recruit Cal Kinney, although I did suggest to Peter Westfield at Southern Pines that this committee would be a great opportunity for Cal to become involved in the larger community. He's new here. I'd heard he loves the outdoors and spends his spare time at the state and national parks in the area."

"Do you mind?" Without waiting for an answer, Deeann helped herself to one of Jana's fries. "Clay Bailey is relatively new to town too." She explained about the clinic's previous long-time doctor's battle with leukemia. "He's retired officially, but we haven't been able to recruit another doctor. Clay's here as a locum, but I'm hoping he'll want to stay permanently."

"He sounds Southern."

"Oh, he's an Arkansan. He's from Fort Smith and went to the university in Fayetteville. He served in the military after graduation and worked in emergency room medicine in Little Rock most recently. Lots of experience and good references. I think he likes being a GP here in a small town. Not that there aren't emergencies here. Anyhow, folks seem to like him."

She reached for another fry. "He seems like a loner. He's renting a house from Bill Parsons, who owns the pharmacy next to the *Gazette* building—or what used to be the *Gazette* building—on Main Street. To tell you the truth, I didn't think he'd agree to being on the committee. Maybe I'm more persuasive than I think."

Too bad Deeann didn't play chess. She'd be unbeatable. No doubt she'd had more reasons for offering Jana the tourism job than she'd mentioned that first day in her office.

Deeann soon finished her soup. She glanced at her phone when it dinged with an incoming text. "I've got to scoot. Don't rush—finish your burger." After she slid out of the booth, she hesitated. "You're off to a great start, Jana."

"Uh, thank you." It felt like a pat on the head or a carrot like the ones she no doubt offered to her horses. If Deeann expected any less than a good job, she was going to be disappointed. Still, it was nice to hear those words.

When Jana later went to the counter to pay, she discovered her boss had already picked up the tab.

TIM WAS SURPRISED to find the owner of Doncaster Motors in the car dealership's showroom. Newt Doncaster had what amounted to a full-time job on the board of directors for Southern Pines Industries. Forty-something, Doncaster had inherited both the car business and his seat on the SP board from his father, who'd moved to Phoenix. Tim remembered watching his own dad, the town's popular barber, trying to chat with Doncaster Senior as he trimmed the fringe remaining around his customer's mostly bald head. His scalp was red that day. Probably sunburn from playing golf without a hat, but to Tim it looked angry like the scowl the man wore as his habitual expression.

Tim must have been about eight at the time. His legs swung below the chair seat, not long enough to touch the linoleum floor. His father had promised to take him to the rodeo that evening, but before they could go home so he could put on his new cowboy boots and hat, Dad had to finish with his last client.

The door had finally clanged shut behind Doncaster, who'd handed over cash without a thank-you.

"He's a mean son of a bitch," his dad had said, putting the money in a zipped bag in the drawer that locked. The week's earnings would have been deposited in the bank on Friday. His father, still in business today, was careful with money. He was also careful to use words Tim understood when he was a child. When he'd cut himself opening a Lego package or found the trash can tipped over and garbage scattered on the street, Dad would say, *Son of a bee!* for example. Tim knew that meant his father was really angry. He'd learned how much bee stings hurt.

He was about to ask what a *bitch* was, when his father turned to him. "And if you ever repeat that, I'll tan your hide."

"Yes, sir." He'd never wanted to make his dad carry through with that threat. "Why were you so nice to him if he's a bad man?"

His father had paused, probably deciding how best to answer that question to a child. "I choose how I want to act, son, and that means choosing how I want to react. The man may not tip well, but he gives me his business. Besides, he doesn't have much hair to cut and pays the same as a man with a full head of hair. Things even out. Does that make sense?"

Tim had nodded. It sounded like something his mother used to say before she'd died two years earlier. "You have to treat people the way you want to be treated," she'd told him when he'd snatched a toy away from a playmate. "If you're nice to others, they'll be nice to you."

That philosophy didn't always work with some of the criminals he encountered today, but like his father, he chose to be true to himself and not react with hostility. Not that it was always easy, but he chose not to take it as a personal affront when someone spit at him, cussed him out, or threatened him with a deadly weapon.

"Mr. Doncaster, may I have a word, sir?" Newt, unlike his father, had a fuller head of hair and a more pleasant disposition.

"Excuse me, Duke," Newt said to the salesman he'd been chatting with. He held out his hand for Tim to shake. "How are you doing, Chief? Come on into my office."

The glassed-in room with a view of the showroom had a clean desk. It probably wasn't used much these days other than for meetings like this one.

When they were seated, Tim said, "I'm here about Eli Carson. I understand he worked for you."

"Yes, he worked here as a mechanic." He shook his head. His thick, wavy hair was trimmed and styled by someone other than Tim's father. He probably didn't buy his fancy suits and shirts off the rack in town, either. "Such a shame. No one here had any idea he was fixing to take his own life."

"How long did he work for you?"

"Oh, you'll have to get those details from Mandy. She handles all the personnel paperwork. I can get her for you. Frankly, I'm not as much hands-on at the dealership since I joined the board at SP. In fact, you're really lucky to have caught me here."

He hadn't expected to *catch* the owner at all. "I'd appreciate that in a minute. What kind of employee was Eli—any problems you know of?"

Doncaster held both palms up. "Far as I know, he was dependable and didn't have any problems. Again, you'll have to ask Mandy. All I know was that he was good with cars. Seemed to have a real talent for fixing them. We planned to send him away for more specialized training after he'd had some more seasoning. I like to help my staff improve their skills."

"Well, I won't take up any more of your time, Mr. Doncaster. If you could just tell me where I could find Mandy, I'd appreciate it."

"Sure, Chief. By the way, you made quite a good impression solving Ernie Crowell's murder. I'm sure folks feel safer now."

Now that a killer had been caught or now that he'd proven himself? He wasn't sure how to take that comment.

"Appreciate that and for your help today."

"No problem." Doncaster's gaze was steady. "I am a little surprised you've come here in person to follow up on Eli's employment. Isn't that something that one of your officers could handle? It's not as if the boy were involved in some crime, is it?"

"I like to keep my hand in from time to time. Sets a good example and allows me to meet folks in the community."

Doncaster nodded, although he didn't appear convinced. Either that, or he'd hoped for more information on the case. Everyone in Crossroads wanted to know the latest gossip. As far as Tim had discovered, there were no exceptions.

"If you could just direct me to Mandy's office—"

"Of course. It's just around the corner. Follow me."

Doncaster introduced him to a young woman with shoulder-length blonde hair. Her blue eyes widened when he mentioned Tim was investigating Eli Carson's death.

"Oh, and if Eli has any personal items in his locker, perhaps Chief Birch here would be kind enough to give them to his family."

"Yes, sir," Mandy said.

Doncaster nodded and left them, shutting the glass door

to the office behind him.

"This is such a tragedy. We're all terribly shocked. How can I help you, Chief?"

Eli's personnel file and evaluations confirmed he'd worked for the dealership for just over a year and for two summers before he'd finished high school. He'd been rated high on his evaluations with a recommendation on the most recent one for external training in the future.

"No issues? Reprimands?"

"None at all," Mandy said. Maybe she was always somewhat wide-eyed, or maybe it was just having a police officer in her office, the top cop at that.

He leaned back in his chair and smiled at her. "Tell me about Eli. How well did you know him?"

Surprise flashed in her eyes. "I only knew him as an employee. We probably never exchanged more than a hello after he came on board."

"How did he seem recently?"

"I really don't know, Chief, but the other mechanics might be able to answer that."

"That's fine. I'll need to talk to his supervisor. Is it still whoever wrote this recent evaluation?" He couldn't read the signature.

She leaned forward to glance at the page. "Roy Holt. That's right." She sprung to her feet. "I'll take you to him now."

Holt was Tim's height and average in size. He rubbed his hands on a red rag. "There was nothing going on that was unusual. You know teenagers these days—they can burn the candle at both ends and turn up with energy to burn." His hands stilled. "Came as a shock to hear he'd shot himself. Didn't see that one coming."

"No signs of depression, talk of harming himself?"

"Hell no. He wanted to work as much as he could so he could save enough money to have his own place. Business is good, but we don't offer much overtime here."

"Did Eli have a second job?"

The rag wringing stopped. "Sure, for a while. Said he was working out at the Friendly Inn. Er, or at least he was a few months ago."

They both jumped when a wrench clanged on the concrete floor.

"Eli's annual review indicated you were pleased with his work."

"The kid was a natural. He had great instincts about motors. It ain't gonna be easy to replace him."

"I understand he asked to take Friday off."

A slight frown deepened the lines in the mechanic's forehead. "Yeah, he called in sick. Stomach issues, he said."

Tim waited.

"When I'd heard he'd been found in that deer stand, I figured he'd just wanted a day off to go hunting, even though it isn't deer season. You can never really know someone, can you? Or what's going on in their head."

"Have to agree with you there." He'd thought he'd known his ex-wife until she handed him divorce papers. "Was Eli close to anyone here?"

Holt looked around the garage. "Nah. They're older, mostly married. He got along with everybody, though. Anyhow, if that's all, I'll show you to his locker."

There wasn't much in it—a windbreaker hanging on a hook, an older pair of athletic shoes, some Snickers bars, and a striped towel wadded up and stuffed in the top part of the locker. Holt found a plastic bag for him. He placed the shoes in the bag and folded the jacket before adding it. When he pulled the towel out, something rolled out onto the shelf. Tim sighed and pulled a pair of neoprene gloves from his utility belt.

"Huh. Is that what I think it is?" Holt asked.

"Looks like marijuana." And more ounces than a single user would have.

"Well, shit!"

That was one way of putting it.

Chapter Twelve

JANA DROPPED THE bag of groceries on the kitchen table and fished her cell out of her handbag.

"Hi, Steph. How are you, sweetheart?" She began to unload the cheese slices, crackers, and grapes she'd bought.

Stephanie's long sigh was answer enough. "He still hasn't called me or texted. Not even an emoji response to my text."

"I thought you'd decided to give Noah some space." She decided to rinse off the grapes. As Stephanie started justifying why she'd changed her mind about contacting her on-again, off-again boyfriend, Jana put her on speaker and set the phone on the countertop. Where had Nana Sue kept her colander? She began opening cupboards. If she could at least find a large strainer, she'd be in business.

"...so I figured he'd at least reply to tell me he'd bring my hair straightener over."

Aha! A plastic colander.

"Mom? What are you doing?"

Jana squatted to shift the other food prep equipment nestled inside the colander.

"I'm listening. It sounds as if he's more upset than you realized."

"Do you really think so?"

Knowing the question was rhetorical, Jana didn't answer.

Sure enough, her younger daughter continued without really wanting her opinion, which she seldom seemed to accept anyway. Muting her phone, Jana ran cold water over the grapes.

"What if he's serious this time about leaving?" The tears were about to start.

She turned the water off and unmuted the phone. "If he doesn't appreciate you, he doesn't deserve you. It's time to move on."

"You always say that, but what am I going to do? I love him!"

Rolling her eyes, Jana tore open the plastic covering the tray of cheddar slices. If she cut them into fourths, they'd be perfect for the crackers and ready in the unlikely event she had any visitors. "He's not the first man you've loved, and he won't be the last. Trust me. You're a beautiful, talented woman. Now dry up your tears and go out for a walk."

"It's too hot, and I just don't feel like it." More crying and a sniffle followed.

She stacked the slices on Nana's wooden cutting board and reached for a knife from the butcher's block. "Go to the gym then. Even if you only stay fifteen minutes on the treadmill, you'll feel better, Steph. Do not wallow—keep busy. Either he'll come to his senses or he won't. You can't make him love you."

Silence. She waited, her knife poised. Was Stephanie really listening to her this time?

The slam of a car door drew her closer to the kitchen window. Deeann emerged from her SUV in Charly's driveway with a foil-covered dish. Of course Deeann had known

Charly in high school, probably earlier than that. It was still a surprise to see her paying her respects with a home visit. Jana returned to her chopping board and began cutting the cheese into smaller squares.

At last Steph sighed again. "If it's so easy to find another man, why didn't you remarry after Dad died?"

The knife came down on her thumb.

"Ouch!" She grabbed a paper towel and pressed it to the cut. Blood soon soaked through.

"Mom, are you okay? What happened?"

"I just cut my thumb—no big deal." Who knew Nana Sue's knives were so sharp? "Steph, I'm sorry, but I need to go. Promise me you'll go out somewhere for a little exercise?"

Her thumb was still bleeding. She threw away the first paper towel and replaced it with a fresh one. In seconds, it was soaked with blood.

"You sure you're okay?"

"Yep, I'm sure Nana Sue has a Band-Aid around here somewhere. Call me tomorrow, okay?" She really didn't need to ask; they talked every day at least once. "Love you."

"Love you, too, Mom."

Jana disconnected. The bleeding didn't seem to be stopping. She replaced the paper towel again, reluctantly peering at the injury. She must have nicked a blood vessel, a major one. She wrapped her thumb up and sat at the table with her hand elevated above her head.

A sharp knock came at the side door. "Jana?"

"Come in—it's unlocked."

Charly's eyes widened. "What on earth…" She set a Tupperware container on the table and examined the wrapped thumb.

"I cut myself. The bleeding doesn't seem to be stopping."

"You're probably going to need stitches. Come on. I'll drive you to the clinic."

THE CROSSROADS CLINIC was a rambling, single-story white building with a concrete ramp leading up to the entrance.

"You're in luck—Doc's still here," the gray-haired woman behind the desk told them after asking Jana's name and the nature of her emergency. "Have a seat. I'll let him know."

Jana couldn't believe she'd been so careless. "You don't have to stay," she told Charly. "I can get a ride home or even walk."

Her friend squeezed her arm. Despite all the casseroles dropped off at her house the last few days, Charly's face was pinched and her shirt hung loosely on her already thin frame. "I'm not leaving you. I'll let my sister know where I've gone. I told her I needed to get out of the house for a while. She's there with Maddy to answer the door if anyone else comes." She lowered her voice. "Deeann Donahue stopped by. I couldn't believe it!"

"I saw her pull up. What did she bring?"

"Mac and cheese. Looks homemade too."

"Wonder who cooks in her family?"

"Not Her Honor, I'm sure."

They both giggled. Then Charly abruptly stopped and sighed. A hunted look appeared in her eyes. "I didn't think

I'd ever laugh again."

Jana nudged her with her shoulder. "You'd better let your sister know you're here with me before she worries."

Charly had just started texting when Clay Bailey emerged. He glanced at Jana's bandaged thumb. Blood had already seeped through the layers of paper towel. "Let's get you back to the exam room so I can have a look at that. Your friend is welcome to come too."

She introduced Charly, who said, "I'll just stay right here, unless you'd like me to come."

"No, I'm fine," Jana said rising. "Hopefully this won't take long." It was embarrassing enough to have Clay take her elbow. She wasn't feeling faint, just annoyed with herself.

In the exam room, he had her sit on the side of the raised bed and sat on a stool next to her. Pulling a rolling tray closer, he unwrapped her makeshift bandage.

"So what happened?"

His eyes were more gray than blue, and his touch was gentle as he unwrapped and then cleaned the wound.

"It's so silly. I was talking on the phone to my daughter and unpacking cheese slices. I decided to cut them into smaller pieces to fit on crackers, and the knife slipped. Or maybe my thumb got in the way. I don't know, except suddenly I was bleeding, and I couldn't get it to stop."

"It's a deep cut. It's going to need two or three stitches. I'm going to inject something to numb it before I stitch it. Are you okay with injections?"

"Yes, I get my flu shot every year and whatever else I need. Besides, I have a high pain tolerance. I gave birth to two daughters and survived their teen years."

He chuckled before placing her hand on a towel-covered tray on her lap and giving her the injection. "That might explain why women generally do better than men as patients."

"I'm just so annoyed with myself. All this trouble when all I was doing was cutting cheese."

His lips twitched, and she realized what she'd said. A giggle burst out of her. "Did I just say that?" She couldn't help it now and burst into laughter.

His face eased into a broad smile. Soon he was chuckling too.

"You have a great laugh," he said, still smiling. "Okay, let's get serious and get you home. I'm going to start stitching here, so I need a steady hand unless you want to end up with a crazy quilt pattern on your thumb."

She giggled again, receiving a mock frown from him in reply. "Okay, okay," she said. "No more laughing."

She watched the procedure, curious to see what he was doing. "You don't have to watch," he said.

"I don't mind. I don't feel anything. I like to sew, and I've caught my finger a few times with the machine needle." She stifled a giggle, taking care to stay still. Good grief, he was going to think she was some kind of masochist.

It took three stitches before he was satisfied. The bleeding had stopped. He opened a package of gauze. "Your neighbor seems to be…coping. I heard it was her son we found."

Poor Eli. She wondered again what he'd seen up in that deer stand. "She's doing about as well as you'd expect. Luckily, she has family here and a clumsy neighbor to distract her."

"Mmm. Grief can hit folks in a lot of different ways. She'll have good days and bad days for a while."

He knew what he was talking about. Who had he lost? "Did it look like suicide to you? Charly didn't believe he'd kill himself."

He hesitated. "That's not uncommon. Families tend to see what they expect and miss signals. Boys that age can be impulsive, too. Sometimes it's a sudden decision."

But Eli hadn't seemed the least bit depressed, and Charly knew her son better than anyone.

"BUT YOU MUST have a professional opinion about how he died. You didn't really answer my question."

His hands stilled and he met her gaze. She read his answer in his gray eyes. "It could have been an accident," he said.

"Eli was skilled with guns. He's been hunting since he was a boy."

He nodded slowly before breaking eye contact and resuming his bandaging. "Anyhow," he continued, "the coroner, Dr. Nagashi, will determine the cause when he does the autopsy." He finished wrapping her thumb and looped the gauze around her palm. "Was that his deer stand?"

"I guess so. Charly knew Eli and his father had built one, but she didn't know where. I doubt his father's hunted much there since the divorce, but after Eli was hit by a car, his dad encouraged him to learn to shoot left-handed. That must have been when he built it—after the accident." Derek hadn't been a total loss as a father, especially back then.

Clay's head came up. "Eli couldn't use his right hand?"

"He could use it, he just didn't have fine motor skills with those fingers any more. The limited functionality made writing with that hand difficult. He became skilled enough with his left hand to become a mechanic. He was really good with cars." The shiny blue Mustang he'd so lovingly restored was proof of his skills. She wondered if the police had found it.

Clay shook his head. "It's a damned shame."

"It is. Eli had a future and he wouldn't give up on life. Do you really need that much bandaging?" He'd wrapped enough gauze around her thumb to make it twice its normal size.

He chuckled. "We're trying to use up a surplus." Then he crisscrossed the gauze around her palm before tying it off. "There. It'll heal faster if the stitches are held in place. Keep it on for a week, and then come back to have the stitches removed. Have you had a tetanus shot recently?"

"Not in a while. It's probably been at least eight years." Or longer.

"I'm going to give you one, and then you'll be free to go. How are you feeling?"

"Better," she said, surprised. Her thumb didn't hurt at all and somehow their conversation or his patient bedside manner had calmed her and quelled that internal voice telling her she was an idiot.

When he escorted her to the lobby, Charly said, "I heard lots of laughter back there. I'm not sure who kept who in stitches, but I was beginning to regret not joining the party."

"I'll tell you later," Jana said, meeting the doctor's amused gaze. "Let's go home."

Chapter Thirteen

THE OFFICERS NOT on the task team had been dismissed, leaving Tim with the small group working on the fentanyl and Eli Carson cases. He'd hoped to be proven wrong and close the latter case this morning, but now that he had the coroner's preliminary report, they were going to have to investigate further. It wasn't a good start to the new week.

"According to the coroner, while there's no question a bullet from the rifle found at the scene killed Eli Carson, it's unlikely he fired the fatal shot. There's evidence of bruising on the jaw that happened before death. Also, the rifle was found beside the victim's right hand. Turns out he was left-handed."

"No chance he dropped the weapon on his right side after the shot?" Clint Dees asked.

"He died instantly. His hand would most likely fall straight down."

"Could he have used his right hand for some reason instead of his left?" Eamon asked. "If he'd been in a fight—"

"No," Tim said. He explained about Eli's childhood accident.

"Also, the school counselor said he'd never been in any trouble," Francine said. "No signs of aggression. He was an average student—mostly Cs. Seemed to get along well enough and had friends."

"Anything back yet from forensics?" Clint asked.

"Plenty of prints in the deer stand. The rifle had only the victim's prints—from his right hand."

Even Rollins, again seated in the back with his arms folded across his chest, sat up a little straighter at that one.

Tim rose. "Simon, lend me your arm for a moment. Hold it out—it's close enough to the length of a hunting rifle. Agree?"

"Yes, sir. Close enough to a twenty-four-inch barrel." The young officer held his arm out stiffly with his index finger pointed at Tim.

"Now if I'm Eli intent on killing myself by eating a bullet from this rifle, I'm going to probably need to do two things: hold the weapon into position and somehow get a finger around the trigger, which is about where Simon's armpit is." He grinned at his officer. "You're not ticklish, are you?"

After some chuckles and a shrug from Simon that was as good as an admission, Tim said, "Just kidding. I don't need an assault charge today." He clasped Simon's arm with his left hand and then mimicked pulling a trigger finger near his armpit.

"You can see the problem with using a rifle to kill yourself. From this end of the gun, the most logical digit to use is your thumb. The partial print on the trigger matched Eli's trigger finger, not his thumb, as if he'd shot the rifle the normal way." He moved behind Simon and mimicked pressing a trigger below his outstretched arm. "And given Eli's limitations using his right hand, the shot would have been even more challenging. He would have used his left hand."

He clapped Simon on the back. "At ease. Thanks for helping with my demonstration."

Grinning, the officer returned to his seat amid applause and a few cat calls.

Tim rested his hip again on the table at the front of the group. "There's another problem: The forestock and gun barrel had been wiped clean. Maybe he didn't hold it there, even to get it in position, but that seems odd to me. We need to consider that someone else may have been with him."

Clint asked, "Anything on the tire tracks, Chief?"

"The only tracks found near the stand could match the victim's Mustang, given the size and type. That road that cuts through had tracks probably matching Tucker Hardy's motorcycle. It's mostly pine needles in the clearing where the deer stand is, so CSI didn't come up with much. They're still trying to match the fingerprints they pulled from the stand, but most of them aren't in the system."

"Could be his friends," Clint said. "The ones in the video."

"I asked them when they'd last been out there," Francine replied. "All four admitting going there to hunt last year. Said they'd been looking forward to going with Eli again this fall. They didn't seem to realize they weren't supposed to be hunting on that property."

"But none of them had been out there recently?" Tim asked.

"No, sir. They all denied that they'd returned since last fall. One's attending college at Monticello, and the other two are working at the paper mill. They've seen Eli occasionally, but they say he's been busy working and saving money. Seems he had a girlfriend, too. He told them he was saving for a place of his own."

"His mother didn't mention a girlfriend," Tim said. "Do we know who she is?"

"Not yet. None of his friends knew her full name, only Jenny. They think she went to Hamblin High."

"Francine, follow up with that, would you?" Tim asked. "Also, when you find her, do some background. CSI confirmed the pills found in the deer stand match the ones in Finn Lasher's car. Interestingly enough, Eli's baggie had no prints on it. Also, when I visited Doncaster Motors, I found a stash of marijuana in Eli's locker. It's being analyzed at the lab now but also had no prints on the package."

His gaze met Sarge's. Would he regret keeping him on this task force? "Our two cases are related because of the drugs. Either Eli was selling or was set up to look like he was. Either way, there's a dealer who might know something about his death and the fentanyl. We know he was trying to save enough money to have his own place, so he might have been tempted to sell. Besides the car dealership, he was working at the Friendly Inn doing odd jobs."

"Seems odd that Larry Mason had money to hire him," Ed Rollins said. Heads turned to the back. The others had probably forgotten he was there.

"Why's that, Sarge?" Tim asked.

"The motel doesn't have a lot of business, especially this time of year."

"I stopped by there," Tim said. "He claims he hasn't employed Eli since May or June. He agreed with your assessment of his financial status." Eli had done the jobs assigned—some landscaping and helping his boss haul away junk. Mason had promised to provide the dates and hours Eli had worked there as soon as he could check his records, but Tim wasn't holding his breath. The payments had no doubt been cash off the books. The information probably wouldn't be needed anyhow.

"Okay, to sum up, we need to find the girlfriend and interview her." Tim nodded toward Francine. "He might have confided in her. Eli had planned to stay a few days in that deer stand, judging from the food he'd brought, and it wasn't like him to lie to his employer about needing a sick day. Was he lying low in the woods for some reason? I'll talk to his mother again. Now what about tracking the pills? Andrea, you were going to follow up with Finn's friends. Did any of them know Eli Carson or see him hanging around the school or other places?"

"No, sir. They knew who Eli was from when he was in school, but none of them hung out with him, and all claim they haven't seen him since he graduated. I did get a name of the possible supplier of Finn Lasher's pills—Wilson Webb. The party that night was at his house."

"Webb… Is that Anson Webb's son? The banker?" The head of First Crossroads Savings was a long-time customer of his father's.

"Yes, sir. They live in South Crossroads, near Franklin Estate. The boy who told me had overheard part of my conversation with one of Finn's friends. He hadn't been invited to the party and had heard about the drugs and the overdose incident. He's Baptist and doesn't approve of drugs or alcohol."

"Or parties. Probably why he wasn't invited," Eamon said.

"Hmm. Still, it's a place to start. Andrea, go back to the school and talk to young Mr. Webb. I'm betting his folks didn't know about his little bash. See what he's willing to tell you about where he does his shopping for party supplies. Eamon, you go with her. Sarge, you and Simon go have a word with our local bootlegger. I doubt that he'll tell you much, but we need to start getting word out that we're on the hunt for whoever's bringing fentanyl into Crossroads."

Rollins scowled. "Deluca doesn't do hard drugs. The Bissetts are either behind this or know who is."

"We'll get to them soon. Let's see what we can get from Wilson Webb. If he points the finger at the Bissetts, we'll go in with a warrant and search the place."

Sarge's lips curled, his disgust obvious.

Tim gazed around the room. "Anything else? Fine. Keep digging. We'll turn up something. And let's find that Mustang!"

WORKING AT HIS customary table at the library, Jack finished typing up the brief article about the discovery of Eli Carson's body. From what little he'd learned from the city's public relations contact, the nineteen-year-old had been found in a deer stand built on the property Merritt Quinn had donated to the town. For decades, the property had been owned by her great-aunt, who had lived in Washington, DC, and done nothing with the land. Locals had picnicked at Willow Lake, even though it was private property. They'd also fished in the lake and probably camped there too. Jacob Fletcher, minister of the glass-walled Cathedral on the adjoining property, had used the lake for baptisms in recent years. He'd tried to buy it to expand his empire, but Merritt's aunt had refused to sell, which, as it turned out, had been a fateful decision for both Merritt and the town.

Obviously, Eli had hunted there, although the police hadn't released information about the owner of the stand. Were there other deer stands on the grounds? He opened another file that contained his article on the new tourism committee. According to the police, the body had been discovered by its members while they were checking out the property. Walt Grisham, the only one of the committee who'd returned his call so far, had said it was actually Doc Bailey who'd climbed up to look inside the structure where Eli had died.

"Doc had smelled death and wouldn't let the rest of us go near," he'd said.

Jack leaned back in his chair. The official police statement said that cause of death was still being determined, pending an autopsy. He'd been stonewalled when he'd asked if the death had been accidental or not. They wouldn't even provide an estimated time of death. For now, he was going to leave his article as it was—a brief report on a body found. He still had another two days before he had to put his weekly newspaper to bed and send it to the company that did his printing in Pine Bluff. Maybe he'd have more details tomorrow.

Meanwhile, he could add Eli's obituary. He checked his business email, but the only obituary submission was for an elderly woman who'd passed at eighty-seven. The photo they'd attached subtracted about twenty years, but it probably represented how the family wanted to remember their beloved grandmother and great-grandmother. Eli Carson would look too young to die, even if his family used a recent photo. Most likely, they would use his senior picture if they submitted a photo at all.

Curious, Jack secured his laptop screen and crossed to the reference section where the library's collection of Crossroads High School yearbooks was kept. This year's edition wasn't there, so he browsed through last year's edition. He found Eli's name beneath his photo in the senior section.

Jack peered closer. The face looked familiar. He closed his eyes, and his mind immediately replayed the night he and Albert Walker had watched two men empty the contents of half a dozen barrels into Crawfish Pond. When they'd finished, one man, the passenger in the box truck, had briefly removed his mask and spit.

The face he'd seen had been Eli Carson's. He was sure of it.

Chapter Fourteen

JACK RISKED A stalking charge the next morning by waiting in the parking lot at the police station for Tim Birch to arrive. Marva Hawkins, the receptionist inside, had made it her life's mission to keep him away from the chief ever since Jack had failed to mention her niece's third-place win in calf roping at the rodeo last year. Never mind that he'd only had enough space to name the first and second place winners; Marva was determined to place herself like a boulder between him and her officers, especially the chief. Today he was in no mood to try to sweet-talk the woman, and he doubted she'd believe he had important information to share pertaining to an investigation.

"Chief!"

Tim Birch glanced up, the determined set of his jaw easing as he approached. "You ambushing me in the parking lot now?" He sounded more amused than angry. He'd probably guessed why the subterfuge was necessary.

"Yeah. Just thought I'd catch you before you got busy. I have some information about Eli Carson." He explained about searching for a photo of the boy for his article. "Eli is one of the two men I saw dumping liquid from barrels into Crawfish Pond in May."

"I remember your article. Didn't know you'd seen their

faces."

"Just his. The driver of the truck never removed his hood or mask, but Eli did for a moment. I couldn't figure out where I'd seen him before. Still can't."

"He worked at Doncaster Motors as a mechanic. Ever have your car serviced there?"

Jack snapped his fingers. "That's it. We had quite a talk about how he'd figured out the noise I was hearing. The kid seemed to love what he did."

"I need you to do a statement, Jack. Come on inside. Marva's off today, by the way."

"Good to know," he muttered. "By the way, any confirmation on cause of death?"

Tim swiped his card and opened the back door. "The coroner confirmed he died from a gunshot wound."

"Looks like suicide, though, right?"

"He was shot in the head, apparently by his own rifle, but that's all I can confirm now. I know you'll respect how hard this is for his family."

"Of course." He followed the chief into an interview room.

"Have a seat. Someone will be in to take your statement."

"Chief, that truck I saw. It didn't have any markings, and Southern Pines states it wasn't one of theirs. Do you have an open investigation about the dumping?"

The chief frowned. "I'll have to check. Thanks for coming in today. Next time, use the lobby like everyone else, okay?"

"Sure, Chief."

The interview room was cold and gray, and the metal chair was hard. Any investigation of the dumping probably had gone nowhere. He'd reported it in the *Gazette* back in May in the same edition he'd reported the murder of the town's beloved attorney, Ernie Crowell. The Crossroads police had been busy with that investigation and subsequent events related to that case. Now they had another murder and the fentanyl death of Officer Rollins. Still, he wasn't going to let them push the illegal dumping aside, a dusty case forgotten on a back shelf.

The firebombing of the *Gazette* office had also occurred after that same issue of the paper had been published, and it was still unsolved. The fire department had yet to turn their evidence over to the police to pursue charges—that is, if they had found enough evidence to point to a perpetrator. Come to think of it, the fire chief owed him a return call on the status of their arson investigation.

He squirmed, trying to position himself more comfortably on the hard chair. Maybe Tim Birch and his team would now look more closely at the dumping since Eli Carson had been involved. Meanwhile, he'd continue asking questions, however many it took. The two men hadn't been yahoos getting rid of a broken appliance at the side of a road. They'd worn protective clothing and looked professional or at least prepared to work near the toxic water. Whatever they'd dumped was something they—or someone—had wanted to dispose of quietly.

They hadn't counted on Albert Walker seeing them one night or him joining Albert to witness their visit the second night. How many other nights had there been and what had they added to the pond's dark waters?

The memory of his own struggle to avoid being forced into the pond returned as it did too frequently these days, although mostly at night. A chemical stench filled his nostrils. Hands grabbed at him as he fought to move away. Grunts as they struggled. Twigs and dirt stinging his face as it was forced into the earth. Another blow to his aching head. Pain and stars disorienting him, obscuring his vision. His fingernails clawing into the earth. The dark, murky water only inches away waiting to claim him—

The door opened as an officer came in to take his statement.

JANA MENTALLY PATTED herself on the back as she stowed her purse in her desk drawer. She'd learned all of the names of everyone she passed entering each day, and others, such as the cleaning staff and the city attorney, who didn't keep the same hours. The HR director had introduced her to most of them last week when she'd started, but the names and faces had been jumbled in her mind that first day. Now her bandaged thumb ensured everyone recognized and remembered her. "Thumbs-up!" had become a silly way to elicit some smiles.

She'd be glad to take the bandage off on Friday when the stitches were removed. The cut didn't hurt, but the oversized digit kept getting in her way. It also confused Nana Sue. Each evening when she visited, Jana had to explain again what had happened, sometimes more than once. Last night, her grandmother had looked concerned and called her by name.

"You need to be more careful, Jana, honey."

She'd barely had time to process what she'd heard before Nana Sue's eyes had emptied of all remembrance. The haunted, confused look that tore Jana's heart in two returned. A minute later, her grandmother had again asked who Jana was. Tucking her bandaged hand beneath her good one to avoid another explanation of her injury, Jana had assured Nana that she loved her.

She had to remember to buy a box of tissues for the car. Tears always followed her visits.

But today was going to be a thumbs-up day. Her committee was meeting again this morning. There was no time to waste before the grant expired. They'd agreed on an earlier time and would be here soon.

Walt and Grace were the first to arrive. They were exclaiming over her injury when Marjorie entered the meeting room toting a plastic carrier that smelled of chocolate.

"Just some muffins," she said. She produced paper plates, polka-dot napkins, and plastic forks from a grocery bag.

Cal and Dr. Bailey soon joined them, and they all settled around the table with their muffins.

"We're going to need more hiking trails if we're going to be eating Marj's baked goods every week," Walt joked. "Not that I'm complaining. Well, hello, Larry."

Jana followed his gaze. Larry Mason, the motel owner, smiled at them near the front of the section of chairs set up for visitors. The door opened admitting Jack Hutchinson, who took a seat behind and to the side of Mason.

"Has anyone heard what happened to that young man we found?" Marjorie asked. "I heard he was identified." They all turned to look at the doctor.

"It was Eli Carson," Jana answered. "He was my neighbor's son."

"Suicide, was it?" Walt asked after they'd commiserated with her.

"The police are still investigating. I don't know if they've confirmed the cause of death," Jana said. Clay Bailey nodded in agreement.

"Okay, I'm calling the meeting to order. I'm sorry our tour ended so abruptly on such a tragic note, but I think we know now that some folks have been using the property for different purposes, like hunting and cutting through from Jones Camp Road to Bluegill Lane." She pointed to the map of the property she'd asked Alyssa to enlarge. Printed on posterboard, it rested on an easel. "We might want to consider adding an entrance to the park from that direction."

"Connecting to Bluegill?" Grace said. "Don't know if the Hardys would be thrilled about that. Their farm is closest to the new park."

"If we don't, we'll have to block off that trail so folks don't cut through," Walt said.

"Just a suggestion for now," Jana said, "but you're right, Walt. We'll probably need to decide what to do with that trail. Let's talk about next steps now that we've seen the property."

"Only part of it. We need to survey the entire property," Cal Kinney said. He hadn't shaved, but the look suited him. "We also have to make sure it's safe, even for us to visit."

"Of course," Marjorie said, "but how are we going to do that? Do we need to pay for a survey? Do we have any money for that?"

"I'll have to check," Jana said, "but I'm guessing the city council or at least the mayor would have to approve it."

Cal leaned forward. "I think hiring a surveyor who uses a drone would be the best way to check out the entire property. It's more than four hundred acres, and I'd estimate at least half is forest and the lake."

"Don't know if a drone could see through those trees," Walt said, "and that's where any deer stands would be."

"The stand we found was in a little clearing," Cal said. "I think we'd see those. It's safer using a drone than risking surveying on foot. Look, I took Merritt Quinn to the lake when she was here in May. Someone shot at us. And now we have someone dead by gunshot."

"Oh my," Marjorie said.

"Do you know who it was?" Jana asked. Why hadn't he told them about this when he'd suggested a police escort? No wonder Cal had seemed nervous the day they visited.

"We didn't see them. We left. I reported it to the police."

"It could have been your neighbor," Grace said to Jana. "Maybe he didn't want his deer stand discovered."

Local residents had visited the lake to picnic or fish for years. Had there been other incidents of shootings? She glanced nervously at the two people in the audience. "I wish you'd said something, Cal. We shouldn't have gone if it was dangerous."

"No one shot at us," Walt said. "And none of the rest of us have heard of any trouble out there." Marjorie and Grace nodded. "Besides, I had my rifle."

The reporter was scribbling a note. The last thing she needed was a story about the future park being dangerous or poking fun at her armed and clueless committee. Jana managed a smile. "We appreciated you being prepared, Walt, and, fortunately, there wasn't any shooting during our visit. Even so, I'll talk to Chief Birch about the incident involving Cal and any other reports they've had. Maybe the police did a search of the property at that time."

They all nodded and she breathed a sigh of relief.

"I like Cal's suggestion," Clay said, speaking for the first time. "A survey's a good place to start, so we know what we have to work with. I think a lot of surveyors use drones now. Even if it wouldn't show much through the trees, we'll have some aerial pictures of the property."

They all agreed to pursue a survey as a next step, with Jana taking the lead on researching that action item. She assigned them each to talk to friends and family and come up with a list of features they'd like to have in the new park. The city also had a social media presence where they could post requests for suggestions. She would check with Alyssa about that. And just before they ended their discussion, Grace reminded her that it would be a good idea to talk to the neighbors and keep them in the loop as their plans progressed. Jana added that to her growing to-do list.

The property was vast, with lakes, forest, and open land cleared for farming decades ago. Part of that section had been retained by Merritt Quinn and leased to Bryson McMillan, who lived across Jones Camp Road from the prospective park. Even so, there was plenty of room to incorporate many features, although maybe not all at once. She still needed to have a better idea of the current budget and how far it would stretch. For now, though, all options were on the table, and how exciting was that?

"Thank you all again for volunteering to serve on this committee. And thanks, Marjorie, for the muffins. I think we're all in chocolate bliss!"

"We're going to build a wonderful park together," Grace said, sounding determined to make it happen.

"That's the truth," Walt agreed. He winked at her. "We have a good leader and a good team."

Jana touched her palm to her heart in reply. Her team had bonded.

"If it's okay with you," Cal said to her as the group broke up, "I'll go with you to talk to Tim Birch."

The others were still chatting with each other and the two men in the audience. Marjorie had offered Larry and Jack muffins. "Oh, do you mean now? That's fine with me. We can at least see if he's available."

She wasn't sure what to make of Cal. He seemed charming most of the time, but why hadn't he mentioned being shot at? It hadn't been an oversight—more of either a lack of good judgment or ego. Because he hadn't hunted down the shooter? He'd had Merritt Quinn with him, so driving away in that moment made sense.

He seemed young to be on the board of Southern Pines. He didn't look much older than her daughters, maybe thirty. From what Deeann had said, he'd probably been encouraged to join her committee by his boss to represent Southern Pines, either to gain more knowledge of the community or because he was new and nobody else on the board wanted to do it. She needed to learn more about Cal and *the company*, as people referred to the sprawling industry across the highway from the end of Main Street.

"You sounded like you've had experience with drone surveys," she said as they walked to her office.

"The condo complex where I lived in LA had a roofing issue, and the contractor who came out to give us a quote used a drone to check the roof. The building was two stories. It took him about five minutes, and he didn't even have to bring a ladder." He flashed her a smile. "Seems like the best way to go, especially with a big property. That is, if there are surveyors around here who use drones."

"Oh, I bet we can find one." Arkansas wasn't as backward as he seemed to think. People here had computers and cell phones; the stores had scanners too.

"We'll see. Hope you're right."

Fortunately, Chief Birch was available and invited them to his office.

Chapter Fifteen

CAL GREETED TIM with a broad smile and handshake. Tim hadn't spoken to him since June, when there had been a send-off party for Merritt Quinn.

"I understand this has to do with the new park at Willow Lake?" That's all the information Jana had given him on the phone.

"Yes, or more specifically about security there." She explained about her committee and their decision to look into surveying the property. "After we came across the deer stand, we wondered if there were others and maybe hunters who wouldn't like their territory invaded. Cal mentioned he'd been shot at in May when he'd visited the lake with Ms. Quinn. We were wondering what your officers found and whether they searched the area at that time."

Shooting? He'd read the incident reports, but he didn't recall that one. Gunshots being fired were reported periodically, and sometimes they were called about possible hunters operating out of season. He didn't recall any incidents at the Willow Lake property. "I'll have to look it up. The report was filed in May?"

"Late May or maybe early June. I had to report it for my insurance claim for the bullet hole in the rear of my truck."

Jana winced, but Tim didn't think it was a close call. A

skilled shooter would have hit his target. It sounded as if someone had been warning Cal and Merritt off the property, rather than trying to shoot them. Could have been Eli Carson or another hunter, but he could think of another reason for someone not welcoming visitors.

"We checked the area around the deer stand last week, but not the entire property. As for your shooter in May, since some time had passed between the incident and the day you reported it and no one had been hurt, an extensive search wouldn't have been warranted. The shooter would probably have been long gone."

Cal started to argue, but realizing how accusatory he'd sounded, Tim raised his hand to stop him. "There could be other deer stands or campsites. A survey makes sense. We could have an officer accompany whoever does it." It was a generous offer, considering his staff shortage.

"Do you use drones?" Cal asked.

Tim's long stare was probably answer enough. If it were up to him and the city gave him a generous budget, he'd have drones and a helicopter, but this wasn't LA. He managed a simple *no*.

"It would be wonderful to have one of your officers there," Jana said, her gaze darting between the two men. "We don't want anybody hurt. Do you know of any property surveyors we could contact?"

"There's a company in Hamblin called Boundary Markers, and there are others in surrounding towns, like Bastrop or possibly Monticello. I don't have any personal experience with any of them, but I haven't heard anything negative, either."

"That's okay. I'll check online," Jana said with a smile. She hoisted her handbag over her shoulder and started to rise.

Cal didn't take her cue. "Chief, we've had two shootings on this property. I think we need the forested area searched. I'm not sure surveyors or even a drone can handle that. We may need people on the ground."

"If you're asking for my officers to do it, I'm going to have to say no. I can provide an officer or two on scene in case of trouble, but with no one's life in immediate danger—"

"Our lives were in danger," Cal said, "and hunters have been using the property illegally. Why was that deer stand still allowed to be used? Maybe if it had been removed—" He glanced at Jana and didn't finish his thought. "Why didn't your investigating officer discover it, assuming my complaint was followed up on?"

Anger surged up from Tim's chest, but he kept his voice calm. "I need to look into it, Cal, and talk to the responding officer. If you want to give me your phone number, I'll give you a full report."

"We'd appreciate that, Chief," Jana said, shooting a concerned look at her companion. "Thank you for your time. I'll keep you informed about any surveying we schedule. Cal?"

The golden boy from California reluctantly stuck out his hand but didn't smile. "I'll look forward to hearing from you, Chief."

"Glad to help," Tim replied, not feeling the least inclined to go out of his way for Cal Kinney. Jana Nance, the new tourism board, and the mayor they reported to were another story. And despite what Cal thought, public safety was important to him and should be his officers' first priority.

The complaint for criminal mischief of a motor vehicle was easy to find searching with Cal's name. The incident had happened just after six P.M. on a week night. While the sun would still have been up, it was late for hunters to be out, unless they were night hunting. How keen of a hunter had Eli been? Many local hunters enjoyed shooting deer in season but didn't bother with possum, raccoons, or feral hogs during the off-season. If the deer stand was Eli Carson's bolt-hole, he could have been there after work just hanging out. Charly Carson might be able to shed some more light on Eli's hobbies at their appointment today during her lunch hour.

He flipped the report over and groaned. The officer who'd followed up had been Hal Overman. His brief note stated that nothing and no one had been found. Tim would bet his bottom dollar that Hal hadn't looked very far, if he'd gone out to the property at all.

Clint Dees's lips curled in disgust when Tim summarized the incident and Cal Kinney's anger over his report not being taken seriously.

"Follow up with Hal. What did he actually do to check out this incident? He needs to provide more details. If we ever get body cams—" He couldn't be bothered finishing his statement.

Clint chuckled. "I predict a sudden increase of suspicious activities at the Dairy Queen needing investigation on the night shift when we start wearing those."

"And that's another thing. Why did *he* handle this complaint?" Hal usually worked nights, although recently he'd been scheduled for some day shifts to cover for vacationing teammates.

"I'll check on that too."

"CSI found evidence of a possible campsite about fifty yards from the crime scene. Looks like there might have been a four-pole tent or something rigged up on poles. The ground beneath had been cleared and showed recent shoe prints of multiple individuals. They also found traces of ecstasy on a rag that had been left behind."

"Sounds like someone cleared out in a hurry. You think they were partying or making the stuff?"

"Whichever it was, they were there recently and could have something to do with Eli Carson's death."

"Maybe he saw something he shouldn't have."

He'd told Clint and the team this morning about Jack Huddleston's revelation about witnessing Eli dumping waste in Crawfish Pond. "Or he did something that his associates didn't like. We need to find out what was dumped in that pond and who the other man was with him."

They also needed to know who'd been using the Willow Lake property. The survey the tourism committee had proposed would be a start. "Let's map out CSI's crime scene perimeter and see how far Hal searched. I want to know if he noticed that deer stand. If he did, that should have been in his report." He shook his head, but he was just as angry at himself as he was at Hal. There were some broken links in his chain of command. He was going to have to find them and fix them fast.

TO HER SURPRISE, after she returned from the police station, Jana received an invitation from Deeann to bring her lunch and join her in her office. The mayor had already opened a Tupperware container filled with a green salad when Jana arrived. Her large desk had been cleared of everything but a vase of flowers and a lamp with a sculpture of a horse as its base. Behind the desk were the US and Arkansas flags. Deeann had already pulled up a chair across the desk from her and invited Jana to sit.

"It's impressive," Jana admitted. "Seeing you here in your office with those flags behind you—"

"And don't forget my ego wall."

"Okay, that too." The framed pictures showed Deeann posing with dignitaries. Apart from the current governor of the state and a senator who enjoyed appearing on television, Jana didn't recognize them.

"Thank you. How's your thumb?"

"Annoying. I'll be glad to have the stitches out and the bandage removed."

"And your grandmother? I understand she's at Golden Pines."

Jana unwrapped the ham and cheese sandwich she'd packed as she fought her annoyance at Deeann knowing her personal business. Still, where Nana lived wasn't exactly a secret, especially not in this small town.

"She has good days and bad. I think she knew who I was the other day, but then she disappeared back into that mental black hole. She has Alzheimer's."

"I'm so sorry. My grandmother had that. It's just heartbreaking—that blank look in their eyes when they don't know who they are anymore."

"Mmm," Jana agreed, chewing. Her sandwich tasted like cardboard.

Deeann was smart enough to realize that she didn't want to talk about Nana Sue. "So, how did the committee meeting go this morning?"

She had copied her boss on the agenda, so she started with the survey proposal. "We agreed that we need to make sure there aren't any other trespassers on the property. Cal suggested hiring a surveyor who uses drones, although we don't think they'll be able to see much through the tree canopy. Do we have money for that?"

Deeann thought for a moment. "The grant money that partially funds your position should be used for activities more closely related to promoting tourism. If it's a safety issue... Have you talked to Tim Birch?"

"Yes, Cal and I met with him after the meeting. He offered to have an officer there while we had the property surveyed. He's checking, but the area they searched after they found Eli Carson didn't go far beyond the deer stand where he was found, or at least that was my impression." She wasn't going to mention the earlier shooting incident unless she needed reason to persuade Deeann.

"Hmm. Well, send me three quotes, and we'll find the money somewhere. Maybe Merritt Quinn will pay for it if the council won't. We need to know what's there. I'm assuming you'll want to tear down that deer stand when the police are finished with it."

"Yes." She should have asked Tim about that and when

the coroner would release Eli's body so Charly could have his funeral.

As if reading her thoughts, Deeann said, "I'm so sorry for Charly. If I lost one of my sons—" She shook her head. "He didn't kill himself, if that's any consolation. The coroner determined it was murder staged to look like a suicide. That's between us for now."

"Oh my god. Does Charly know?"

"If she doesn't, she will soon. Tim's going to talk to her today."

Deeann switched their discussion back to the committee meeting and jotted down points she could share with the city council. Then she put her pen down.

"So, you're settling in okay at your grandmother's house?"

Still uncertain of the sincerity of the mayor's interest, she faked her own friendliness. "The house needs some work, but that will keep me busy on the weekends."

Nodding, Deeann said, "I suppose so. Let me know if you need me to form a committee to help you."

It took a second to realize her boss was joking. "Actually, it could be worse. Charly has been looking after it the last six months or so since Nana went into Golden Pines."

"Ah, well, it's good to have friends." She sounded wistful, although that was hard to believe. Everyone knew the mayor, and she'd been voted in with a clear majority from what Charly had told her.

Maybe it was lonely at the top, but that was where Deeann had always chosen to be. Besides, she still had her husband and at least one son living at home. Jana refused to feel sorry for her.

Chapter Sixteen

JACK WAS RELIEVED to have the mystery solved: Eli Carson had worked at Doncaster Motors as a mechanic. No wonder he'd looked familiar: He'd repaired Jack's ancient Honda about four months ago when the brake pads had needed replacing. He'd seemed shy, but he knew cars and had clearly explained exactly what he'd done to fix the brakes. He'd also admired the engine's condition. Considering the Civic was fifteen years old with high mileage, Jack had welcomed the mechanic's praise. Like a good doctor checking a patient, Eli had also looked beyond the reported complaint to make sure no other problem was looming.

But what had the young mechanic been doing unloading barrels of some unknown liquid into Crawfish Pond at midnight?

His assumption had been that Southern Pines was once again dumping toxic waste. The box truck appeared identical to those in the company's fleet, although the branding had been painted over. According to Cal Kinney and the company's official response to his inquiry, dumping in that pond had ceased more than two decades ago. So was Doncaster Motors involved? Their mechanics drained oil, brake and transmission fluids, and gasoline when they serviced vehicles. Were they cutting corners by illegally disposing their waste?

Jack parked in the back of Doncaster's car dealership outside the service department. A curly-haired woman with glasses smiled at him through the plexiglass at the customer window.

"Hello, do you have an appointment?" The question in her voice indicated she knew he didn't.

"No. Is Roy Holt available? I'm Jack Huddleston with the *Crossroads Gazette*."

"I'll check. Let me page him for you."

Holt didn't look familiar. Average build and probably nearing fifty, he wore blue coveralls with the company name on the front. Judging from their stained appearance, the supervisor was still keeping his hand in at the repair business.

Jack introduced himself again. "I'm following up on Eli Carson's death. Thought I might get some quotes from folks who knew him."

Holt glanced back into the shop where several cars raised on lifts were being serviced. The noise of a radio playing country music and mechanics at work would obscure anything he said, but, for whatever reason, the man seemed uncomfortable.

"Uh, I can't speak for the company. Maybe you want to talk to someone inside."

"Sure, but Eli was a mechanic, right? He worked here in the garage and you were his supervisor?"

"Yeah, but Mr. Doncaster likes all the press to be handled by him."

"Okay, so off the record, was Eli a good employee? Someone who'll be missed?"

His brow furrowed. "Oh, sure. He was a good kid. Good

mechanic too. Or at least that's what I thought before."

"Before?"

"Before he died." His gaze shifted away. "You know how it is when someone passes. No one wants to think or say anything bad about them. But Eli, he was a good mechanic, and I never had any problem with him."

Jack nodded, not sure what the man had learned recently that had changed his opinion of the young mechanic. "Eli fixed my Honda earlier this year. He was very good, the way he explained what was wrong with my brakes. Did he just work on cars or trucks too?"

"Anything on wheels. He loved motors. Fixed up a Mustang he bought from a customer ready to sell it for scrap metal. He was sure proud of that car."

"You don't say. That probably took some money for parts and stuff. I heard Eli had a side gig helping someone who drove a white box truck. Do you know who that was? I might try to get a quote from them."

"No idea." His puzzled look seemed genuine. "They might know inside, but he never mentioned anything to me."

Jack was about to thank him and walk away. "Hey, one more question. Does anyone bring white box trucks here for repair?"

He thought a minute. "Haven't seen one in a while. Southern Pines has some of those, but they have their own mechanics. You might try Forest Truck Traders. They sell new and used trucks and have a repair shop. They're about two miles north of here on the highway."

Jack snapped his fingers. "Hadn't thought of them.

Thanks for your help. I'll go inside and see if I can get a quote from your bosses."

The woman in HR made a phone call and then told him that he could say that the team at Doncaster Motors was deeply saddened over the death of Eli Carson, and their thoughts and prayers went out to his family. No surprise there—it was a standard PR release for the tragic loss of an employee.

"Mr. Doncaster sent his mother a condolence card and flowers," she told him, as if that, too, wasn't expected.

All nice and professional, he thought as he jotted down the quote. Just what he'd expect from Newt Doncaster. After all, everyone knew he planned on becoming the next chairman of the board of Southern Pines when Peter Westfield retired. He had his staff here well trained. Ms. HR wouldn't divulge any other information about Eli, other than to say she was sorry to hear of his death.

Forest Truck Traders was busy. Jack wandered around their showroom to the lot behind the office building. Fenced in, it was mostly out of sight from the highway. They had an impressive assortment of trucks of all sizes, including several semitrailer cabs, flatbed trucks, trailers, and box trucks of various sizes. One side of the lot featured used vehicles. He'd just spotted three white box trucks when a muscular man in chinos and a navy polo shirt approached.

"See anything you like?"

His voice was as deep as his neck was wide. Heavy black eyebrows made up for the lack of hair on his shaved head. His smile didn't reach his dark eyes.

"Just looking around. I've never been out here. You have

a big inventory."

The man's eyes narrowed. "You look familiar."

"Jack Huddleston, *Crossroads Gazette.*"

"Tom Fielding. Are you planning to write a story about us?" His frown didn't communicate any eagerness for that to happen.

"Thought you might be interested in advertising with the paper." He smiled apologetically. "I was having a look around to see what your business was all about. Your sign says you lease as well as sell."

"That's right." The man's dark gaze never wavered. "Sometimes folks just need a truck for a move or a brief job. Not worth buying a truck in those cases."

"Makes sense. Guess that puts you in competition with U-Haul and Ryder. Your boss might want to consider an ad in the paper. You could also notify our subscribers when you have a sale." He handed him a business card.

Fielding looked amused. "I'll mention that to the boss."

Jack looked around. "I understand you do repairs as well."

"We service the vehicles we sell and rehab the used ones that are traded in. The garage is over there."

"Ah, so it is." He'd painted himself in a corner with his excuse of coming to sell advertising. He couldn't think of a reason for wanting to talk to the head mechanic. "Tell your boss to call me about placing an ad. I'll give him a discount on the first one."

"I'll be sure to do that." He still looked amused. "Have a good day."

Jack glanced back once as he crossed the lot. Fielding had

moved to the rear door of the building but was watching him head to the open gate at the side where he'd entered. The wire fence enclosure had warning signs posted about camera surveillance. Thieves and nosy reporters weren't welcome here.

He'd check further on Forest Truck Traders and who might have purchased the truck he'd seen at Crawfish Pond. One of Eli's friends might also know about his night job. He had to identify the driver to uncover who was behind that dumping. Only then could he make sure it never occurred again.

"I KNEW HE hadn't killed himself," Charly told Jana that evening. The sun was setting, but there was a faint breeze stirring the humid air on her neighbor's front porch. Inside the house, canned laughter erupted from a television show Maddy was watching.

"I'm so sorry," Jana said. Regardless of the cause, the young man was dead long before he should have been. "It must have been a shock to hear how he died."

"I thought anything would be better than him killing himself. I've been driving myself crazy trying to think of what signs of depression I might have missed. But murder..."

The silence lengthened. Remembering how unhelpful platitudes had been from friends when her husband had died, Jana didn't offer any. As much as her heart ached for Charly, she was furious at whoever had snuffed out Eli's young life. "Does Chief Birch have any idea who might have killed Eli?"

"No. He asked me again about his friends, coworkers, even who he talked with online. I told him what I know, but apart from his closest friends, I couldn't think of anyone. Oh, apparently he was dating a girl and saving money to move out." She sniffed. "That's the first I'd heard of that."

"You know how it is at that age. They're anxious to be independent." And stupid enough to get themselves into trouble.

"I thought Eli was happy here. I mean, I knew he'd move out one day." The swing creaked as Charly pushed it with her foot. Somewhere out in the yard a frog responded with its own call. "I even threatened to kick him out once. Eli had been using marijuana. I saw some in his room and told him that I didn't want that in my house. I made him throw it out."

The silence following that revelation lengthened. Sure, her girls had smoked some weed—maybe they still did. She'd done it herself at that age. But Eli? She just hadn't accepted that he'd grown up in the last five years since she'd been away. She shouldn't be surprised Charly had discovered a stash. As for not kicking him out, she would have done and said exactly the same thing.

"Was that recently?"

"About six months ago. I admit I've looked in his room to see if there was any more, but I've never found any again. I told the chief that. He said they found marijuana in Eli's locker at work and pills in the deer stand." Her lip quivered again.

"Oh, Charly."

She wiped a tear from her cheek. "They think his death might be related to those drugs, that maybe he was selling to make some quick money. I told him Eli wouldn't have done that. He's heard all his life about how dangerous drugs are. He would never, never hurt anyone. Selling drugs...it's just evil!"

Chief Birch must have been as blunt with poor Charly as he had been with Cal this morning, not that Cal hadn't deserved a little pushback. Jana tried to think of something comforting to say, but she drew a blank. She couldn't imagine the pain her neighbor was feeling. Eli had kept multiple secrets, including an apparent involvement with hard drugs. She couldn't help it. Now her anger was directed at Eli.

"He knew that. You're right—kids today know all about the evils of drugs, alcohol, cigarettes. At nineteen, they still don't have great sense and they feel invincible. Maybe the chance to make a lot of money quickly was more temptation than he could resist."

The swing jerked to a stop. "I don't believe you just said that."

"Charly, there were things Eli didn't tell you, and they found all those drugs... I-I just think you need to be prepared in case—"

"You need to leave." She rose, towering over Jana. "Now."

"I'm sorry—really." But Charly was already through her front door. She closed it firmly behind her.

Inside Nana's kitchen, Jana plopped into one of the

kitchen chairs and rested her elbows on the table. She buried her face in her hands. How could she have been so thoughtless to suggest that Eli had been selling drugs, even if that appeared to be true? Charly was grieving the loss of her son. She needed a supportive friend, a listener—not someone daring to point out that her son may have been committing crimes. She'd just said a moment before that she didn't believe he'd been involved in illegal activities, despite what Tim Birch had told her about finding drugs in his possession.

Stupid, stupid, stupid!

And Eli was her godson! What was wrong with her? She should have been defending him. He might have been desperate or tempted or even forced by someone to do something bad, but he was a good person. If he'd had the chance, he would have matured into a fine man.

She remembered his sweet smile when she'd arrived and helped unload her car. Then that same night she'd seen him arguing with someone. Could that have been about the drugs? Had he been refusing to be involved? The next day he'd left, apparently to go to that deer stand where they'd found him. The argument might have something to do with his death.

Tomorrow she'd mention it to Chief Birch. Meanwhile, how was she ever going to make things right with Charly?

The call from the nursing home came before she had a chance to think any more about it.

Chapter Seventeen

"WE HAD TO sedate her," the director of Golden Pines, a competent-looking middle-aged woman said. "It's a mild sedative. We're very careful, and the dosage was approved by our physician."

Her grandmother was asleep in her bed, her face relaxed and peaceful. She looked nothing like the crazed woman the director had described on the phone.

"You said she attacked one of your staff?"

"Yes, in the dining room. She suddenly started shouting that we were trying to poison her. She threw her food on the floor and then lashed out at Etienne, who was trying to calm her. He's okay, but your grandmother wouldn't stop fighting us. We had to restrain her."

Nana Sue's arms lay beneath the sheet and light blanket that covered her. Jana lifted the bed covers, but there were no straps holding her in place.

"They were removed as soon as she was sedated. I'm sorry, but we really didn't have a choice. The other residents sitting at the table with her were in danger."

"It's just hard to imagine her doing that." Nana had always been patient and kind. Jana had never seen her lash out at anyone, even verbally.

"It's the disease, and it's becoming more advanced. Paranoia often develops as their world becomes more confusing to them. Tomorrow she probably won't even remember what happened."

"Did the doctor come check her out?" Nana had always complained about bruising easily. In that agitated state, she might not have even realized if she'd hurt herself.

"We have a nurse on duty, an RN. She examined her after the incident."

"But you said you cleared the dosage with a doctor—"

"By phone. He'll be here tomorrow. That's his day to visit our facility."

Jana brushed her fingers across Nana Sue's white hair. "She seems okay for now." But what was she going to be like when she awakened? And what if she had hurt herself?

"Yes, and we'll check on her throughout the night. Unfortunately, if this kind of violent behavior keeps recurring, we may have to ask you to make other arrangements. Hopefully, that won't be the case."

Jana stared at her. "Make other arrangements?"

"She might be happier somewhere else."

And you certainly would be. But that wasn't fair. Their staff didn't deserve to be attacked or the other residents upset or possibly injured. What if Nana had thrown a dish at one of them? She still couldn't image her grandmother in a rage like that, but it had to be true. What if it happened again? They couldn't keep restraining her, whatever that had entailed, and what kind of quality of life would Nana have if she had to be sedated regularly?

"Again, we hope it doesn't come to that, Ms. Nance. I'm sorry you had to come out tonight."

"I had to make sure she was okay. Thanks for calling me right away, and please let me know if anything else happens, no matter what time. I'll stop by tomorrow morning and follow up with you about the doctor's visit."

She hadn't yet bought tissues for her car. When she returned home, she threw a box from the bathroom into the front seat. At this rate, it wouldn't last long.

THE SUN WAS already flexing its solar muscles at seven. For the second day in a row, Adam didn't want to go to school. Not for the first time, Tim sympathized with kids having to be in classes in late August instead of after Labor Day, but school start times had changed.

"But Dad," Adam whined. "Can't I just stay here with Aunt Becky?"

"She isn't coming over until this afternoon when school lets out."

His son pushed his cereal bowl away, crossed his skinny arms over his chest, and poked his lower lip out as he huffed his frustration.

"Is there something about school that you don't like?" His aunt Audra, a nurse and his other babysitter, had suggested he question the boy about his new teacher and classmates. Adam had started first grade two weeks ago. Something had to account for this change in behavior that seemed to be related to school.

"Everything." The lip remained poked out. "Why can't I go to work with you?"

Tim smiled. "Because only people who finish twelfth grade can work at the police department. You have a few years to go yet."

A tear as fat as a gumdrop rolled down Adam's cheek.

"Do you like your teacher, Mrs. Crumb?"

"She's old and bossy."

Tim's lips twitched. The woman had seemed old and bossy when she'd taught him, too, but she'd also known what first graders liked and how to handle them. "She's a good teacher. She knows a lot, and she's been teaching a long time. She taught me in first grade."

"I know. She told me. She told everyone."

He was beginning to guess the problem. "What did she say?"

"That she taught you and now you're the police chief. She said it's an important job, and she's proud of you."

She'd said that to him at the open house before school had started. Adam hadn't seemed to mind her saying it then. "And what did the other kids think of what she said?"

"They said I'm teacher's pet, and they have to be nice to me or you'll put them in jail. I told them that was a bunch of horse pucky."

Thanks to his great-aunts and his grandfather, Adam had a variety of expressive word choices to use other than the adult four-letter ones. "You know what, son? They're just jealous. They wish Mrs. Crumb would say something nice about their fathers."

"They won't play with me. They told me to play with the girls."

"Well, there are some nice girls at that school, but I'm

guessing not all the boys in your class are mean. Sometimes they're afraid to speak up. They might be afraid of being teased if they do. Do you think there are one or two you might play with? Maybe we could put a few extra chocolate chip cookies in your lunch box that you could share with them."

His gaze shifted to the ceramic cookie jar on the counter. "Maybe."

"Would you try it for me today? If that plan doesn't work, we'll come up with another one. We'll figure this out. Usually, folks treat you the way you treat them, so be friendly to everyone. Just laugh if they tease you. They'll be so surprised that you're not mad, they'll probably walk away."

Adam picked up his spoon and scooped a bite of Cheerios. "We have music today."

"You don't want to miss that." Crisis averted for now. Who knew there could be so much drama in the first grade? Unfortunately, dealing with people wouldn't get much easier for Adam in the years ahead, but hopefully he'd develop a thicker skin and more skills to handle them.

The team was beginning to put together a picture of Eli Carson's life, although they still hadn't come up with his girlfriend's name. It seemed Eli kept his private life to himself. That made sense if he was involved in selling drugs or illegal activities.

Tim was reviewing the previous night's incident reports at his desk when Marva called him.

"Derek Carson is here to see you," his receptionist said. "He's Eli Carson's father. He's insisting on speaking to the chief. I put him in the interview room."

"Be right there."

Carson, red-faced and overweight, wasn't coping well with the August heat or his anger. The underarms of his light-blue polo shirt were sweat-stained, and his face glistened with perspiration. "I told that woman I want to speak to Bob Bowen, the chief," he said angrily after Tim introduced himself.

"I'm chief of police now. Bob passed away last December. Can I get you some water, Mr. Carson?" The man looked about ready to have a coronary.

"No. Thanks," he added grudgingly. "Hadn't heard about a new chief." He still looked skeptical. It was the *you're too young to be chief* look Tim had come to expect.

"I'm sorry for your loss. I asked the Lake Village police to contact you." It had taken several visits to catch up to Eli's father, from what he'd been told.

"I want to know what happened. His mother said he was shot with his own rifle out at Willow Lake."

"That's right. He was found in a deer stand I believe you built?"

His flush deepened again. "I want to know who shot him. I want his killer caught. If you won't do it, I will."

"When did you last see Eli, Mr. Carson?"

"What the hell's that got to do with anything? I loved my boy."

"I was hoping you could give us some information about your son's life and who he might have known recently that could have done this. When did you last see him—or talk to him?"

"Haven't seen him in a few months. He's over eighteen. Couldn't make him come visit if he didn't want to."

His ex had guessed Eli hadn't seen his father in almost a year. "We've confirmed he was working at Doncaster Motors as a mechanic and picking up some side jobs. Did he tell you anything about those?"

"I knew he wanted to move out of his mother's house. I told him I couldn't help him with that. I have two more kids at home in Lake Village. My wife doesn't work, but that's none of your damned business."

No, but it explained why the nineteen-year-old may have felt unwelcome at his dad's new home. He would have been another mouth to feed and a reminder of the man's first marriage and the child support he didn't pay until the state came after him for it. Eli's mother had said he owed her more than twenty thousand in back support for Eli and his sister.

"So you have talked to your son recently." Tim waited until the man became uncomfortable with the silence.

"I called him that Thursday. I keep in touch with my kids."

"What time was that?"

"What the—I don't know. Around noon."

"How did he seem then?"

"He told me he was working and couldn't talk."

They could check Eli's phone records. If the call had been around noon, he'd probably been at Doncaster's garage.

"So you didn't talk long."

"I just told you. Didn't want to get the boy fired, did I?"

"Did Eli have any problems with anyone you know

about?"

"You're saying you don't have any suspects?" He slapped his hand on the table. "Hell, how long is this going to take? If Bob Bowen were still in charge, he'd have someone in jail by now. What's this town coming to?"

Okay, screw the grieving father status. "As soon as we find out why Eli was hiding in that deer stand you built on private property, I'll notify you. Meanwhile, if I hear you're taking matters into your own hands, you'll have more to worry about than the trespassing charge I'm considering. Is that clear?"

Carson glared at him.

"Now is there anything else you can tell me about your son that may help us find his killer, or are we finished here?"

Carson rose. "You damn well better call me soon or I'll be talking to the state police, maybe the FBI. Hick town," he muttered as Tim escorted him back into the lobby.

Marva's eyes narrowed to mean slits. Fortunately, their visitor didn't notice and headed straight out the front door Jana Nance had just opened. She stepped back to let him pass.

"Was that Eli's father?" she asked when they were seated in his office. Tim hadn't wanted to use the interview room he'd just come from.

"Do you know him?"

"It's been years since I've seen him. The last time was probably not long before they split up. He's put on some weight since then." She pulled out her cell. "Maybe I should warn Charly that he's in town."

Carson probably would look up his ex. He needed someone to blame. He wasn't facing up to his own obviously poor relationship with his son in recent years.

"Has he ever been violent?"

She glanced up. "They used to fight when he'd been drinking. I know she'd appreciate not being surprised in case he tries to see her or Maddy."

"So, how can I help you?" Tim asked after she finished texting. "Is this about the tourism committee and your survey?"

"No, it's more to do with Eli's murder. Charly told me that you've determined he was murdered. The first night I arrived—the Thursday before Eli left—I heard an argument outside between Eli and another man." She described what she'd seen, which unfortunately didn't include a look at the driver's face or a license plate number.

"I only heard the last part of the conversation. Eli had started walking away, so his voice was raised a little. He said, *I'm not doing it again* and that he was finished with it. The man in the truck said something back that made Eli mad. He then said he didn't need the man's job anyhow."

Not doing it again sounded like a one-off. Whatever it was, Eli had been paid, but it wasn't worth the money to do it again. And the last part about not needing the man's job. Was that just bravado, or had he found another source of income?

"Is there anything more you can tell me about the truck? Anything that stood out to you?"

Her brow wrinkled. "I can't even be sure about the color, except it wasn't white. It was just too dark. And it was an average-sized pickup." Her eyes widened. "It was an older one, I think. The paint finish seemed dull—" Her eyes brightened. "The engine revved. It could have been the driver doing it, but it was more like the timing was off or something, not that I'm a mechanic."

Tim made a note. That detail might be helpful, but it wasn't much to go on. Still, what she'd overheard could be another piece of the puzzle they were putting together. An argument meant someone hadn't been happy with their victim.

"I'm afraid that's all I remember. I know it's not much."

"Well, I'm glad you came in. We're trying to learn more about Eli to figure out who might have killed him. Every bit helps."

She looked away, her eyes sad. "I told Charly that kids that age, probably boys especially, don't tell their mothers everything. They want to be independent."

"That's true." It was unlikely Eli had confided in his father, either. Jana looked so unhappy, he changed the subject. "So, how are the plans going for surveying the new park grounds?"

"I have the go-ahead from Mayor Donahue to provide her with some quotes from three companies, which I'm trying to finish up today. I'm hoping the city council will approve an expenditure tomorrow when they meet. Do you go to those meetings, Chief?"

"Not usually, unless they ask me to come or there's a budget item to support."

To his relief, she didn't jump on the opening he'd just given her. "With the mayor behind our request and the grant money we have, I think it will pass. I'll let you know and take you up on your offer to send an officer when we do the survey. I, um, I'm sorry Cal was so upset at you the other day."

"Not your fault. He's right to complain about not receiving a response. I'm still reviewing the incident, but I'll get back to him personally today."

"Thanks for your time. You have a lot on your plate."

"You do too. Let me know if you remember anything else about that truck or the conversation you overheard."

After he escorted Jana out, he checked his email for any new responses from neighboring police chiefs or the state and federal drug enforcement agencies. Nothing he'd received so far indicated that their fentanyl problem was elsewhere in the area. Then he opened the email with Josie's name in the subject line. Her funeral was scheduled for Saturday.

Chapter Eighteen

JACK HAD HIS newspaper ready to submit early, and it worried him. Either he was missing something he should have included or a story was about to break just before his deadline. He was seldom finished before the drop-dead hour. Or maybe he was just working faster these days, his experience and increased efficiency at last making his job easier.

Nah. Wishful thinking. Then again, he had been writing and editing more stories throughout the week to post more frequently online. With sleep hard to come by, he often wrote in the middle of the night. Anything to keep his mind busy and the nightmares about the *Gazette* fire and his near-death experience at Crawfish Pond at bay. Some of his online feature stories would appear in the print edition with no changes. All he had to do now was bring his news stories up-to-date. Eli Carson's death, for example, which had been ruled a homicide. He'd try the police department for a last-minute update just before press time.

But before he could click into his contacts, his phone rang. Tim Birch's name popped up.

"Hey, Jack. I'm calling to let you know that we have an open case on the dumping at Crawfish Pond you reported. I've updated it with your identification of Eli Carson as one of the men involved. We'll try to find out who he was working for as part of his murder investigation."

"But nothing's turned up yet?"

"Not yet. Have you heard about any more dumping at Crawfish Pond in the last week or two?"

"No, nobody's called me. Didn't hear anything at Albert's funeral, either. Why? Have you had a tip?"

"No, just something that came up today that might have nothing at all to do with the dumping."

"Something related to Eli Carson's case? Before I go to press, I'd appreciate any updates."

There was a pause. No surprise there: The chief was no doubt considering what to release. "No update. The coroner ruled it a homicide, so we're investigating who the victim knew and his movements in his final days."

That could be promising if it led to the driver's identity. "No persons of interest in the homicide?"

"We're looking into everyone who knew him, but no one in particular stands out at the moment."

"Nothing from forensics that was helpful?"

Another pause. "At this point, we don't know how helpful the information we received from CSI might be. Fingerprints and DNA don't help unless they're matched up, and not everyone is in CODIS."

Tim was becoming good at PR speak, but Jack didn't hold it against him. Some details had to be kept under wraps so they could confirm whether informants or suspects knew about the actual crime or just what they'd heard or read about it.

"And what about the drugs?"

"We're still tracking down the pills we found with the

body in the deer stand."

Whoa. No one had mentioned Eli Carson had been found with drugs. His question had been meant as a follow-up on the fentanyl pills and tragic death of Officer Josephine Rollins, not about the Carson murder.

"If you hear anything more about the dumping or the man working with Eli Carson, let me know," Tim said.

"I will, Chief, but there's something else related to the illegal dumping." He told Tim about the white SP box trucks being sold to Forest Truck Traders when the company replaced them without revealing his source. "If you could get a list of who they were then sold to, I could follow up. I think I'd recognize the one I saw."

"I'll have someone talk to them, but I can't promise we can get a list of their customers without a warrant."

Well then get one! He wanted to say but didn't.

"Forest Truck has mechanics. It could be that Eli Carson worked on the side for them. Those automotive places have a lot of oil and other fluids to dispose of."

"I thought you didn't know what they were dumping."

"I don't, but it had to be hazardous waste of some kind or they would have poured it down a sink."

There was a pause. "I'll have someone check with Forest Truck," Tim repeated. "You have a good day."

"Thanks," he said, not meaning it. Everyone wanted him to *have a good day*, but no one was willing to help him. He stared at his computer and the article about Eli Carson's murder. Maybe Tim would follow up with Forest Truck's sales records, but he was clearly just going to send one of his officers to do it. Jack removed his glasses and rubbed his eyes. Short of breaking into Forest Truck, he couldn't see any way to get his hands on those records. He'd have to give Tim a chance to check into it. All he could right now was check back with Cal Kinney and keep the pressure on the board to start the cleanup of the pond. But first, he had a sentence to add to his headline story about the Eli Carson murder investigation. He put his glasses back on and began to type.

CHARLY MUST HAVE been watching for her to come home after work. She knocked on Nana Sue's door only two minutes after Jana returned. She'd only had time to put her purse down and slip off her shoes.

"Thank you for the warning," Charly said stiffly, ignoring her invitation to come in and not returning her smile. "Derek was waiting in the parking lot when I got off work." Her cheeks were flushed and her eyes hot. "He blamed me for not knowing what Eli was doing and for telling the police that he'd built that deer stand. I could tell he'd been drinking too."

"Did he come to the house to see Maddy?"

"Oh no. After we argued, he hightailed it back to Lake Village to his wife and *his* kids."

Jana's heart ached for the girl. Her daughters had been about the same age when they'd lost their father, who'd been a wonderful dad. Marcus would have given anything to have lived longer and spend more time with them.

"He doesn't care about Madison, except when the state

pressures him to pay support. Then it's all about *his* rights and how I'm keeping him from seeing *his* kids. I remind him that he's the one who stayed away from home and *our* children when he started seeing Rayellen. I can't tell you how glad I am to be divorced from that man."

That last sentence sounded like the friend Jana had feared she'd lost. "Charly, please come in."

Her face tightened. "No, I'm not ready to forgive you yet." She turned to leave.

"I went to see Chief Birch today," Jana said. "I told him I'd heard Eli arguing with a man the first night I arrived in Crossroads."

Charly turned back around. "What man?"

She told Charly about the conversation she'd witnessed between Eli and the driver of the pickup truck. "I realized last night that the argument they had might have something to do with what happened to Eli. Maybe if they can find the driver of that truck, they can find his—whoever did that to him."

Charly frowned. "I didn't realize he'd gone outside. Maddy and I were watching TV. Most of the evening he was texting, sitting in Derek's old recliner with his legs draped over the side—" Her voice hitched, and she stopped.

"I wish I'd paid more attention to the pickup truck," she said, giving Charly a moment to compose herself. She wished they weren't standing on opposite sides of the screen door. "I couldn't even tell what color it was, but I told the chief that my impression was that it was old."

"Derek has an older pickup." Anger replaced the sadness in Charly's eyes. "He told me that he'd talked to Eli that

Thursday. He claimed Eli wanted to borrow money from him because I wouldn't help my son. Eli never asked me! Not that I would have said yes. After all, he had a job, two according to the police. He had to learn to support himself." She looked to Jana as if for confirmation, and she nodded.

There had been a girlfriend, too, to spend money on—something else he hadn't told his mother about. Making money had been a big concern, but he wouldn't have asked his father for a loan if he was making money selling drugs. If only Charly knew how much she hoped Eli hadn't been involved in that. At least her friend didn't seem ready to end their conversation.

"I think maybe it was Thursday night when Eli's phone kept dinging with texts. I asked him what was going on. He said it was Derek and he wasn't going to answer. I didn't ask why or what his dad wanted." She sighed. "I guess I didn't blame him for not wanting to talk to his father. Maybe I was even happy about it. How petty is that?"

Jana stepped outside but stayed on the carport step several feet from Charly. "Do you think that might have been Derek outside that night? Maybe he came to talk to Eli in person." He wouldn't have wanted to knock on the door and have to explain why he was there after dark to see his son.

Charly looked troubled. "I don't know. Derek had gotten to where he didn't like driving at night. Said there were too many cops out. The truth is he'd usually had too much to drink by then."

"The argument I heard concerned some kind of job Eli had been doing. Did Derek ever pay Eli to do work? Or maybe he'd arranged some part-time job for him?"

"Pay Eli? You have to be joking." Charly rolled her eyes. "He wasn't that involved with Eli recently, at least not that I knew about. I don't know what he was texting him about, but Eli was ignoring him. Derek would have been pissed off about that, but I can't see him driving his butt over here after dark." Her lips twisted. "He never liked missing a meal, either. He's probably being fed by his new wife in Lake Village right now." Her eyes widened. "I need to go see about Maddy's dinner."

Jana's heart ached as she watched her friend cross the lawn. At least they'd talked, and Charly had said she wasn't ready to forgive her *yet*. Jana was placing all her hope that their friendship could be healed on that one little word.

Later, after Jana listened to her girls complain about their lives, she wished she had someone to hold her, someone to step in and assure her that she didn't have to cope alone. Charly was a hugger. They'd first met when they were about seven. Charly's grandparents had then owned the house next door. As girls, they'd both looked forward to Jana's visits several times a year and exchanged letters and later calls the rest of the year. They'd been in each other's weddings, Charly making her first trip to Indianapolis to be her bridesmaid. What a whirlwind visit that had been with last-minute wedding preparations, but they'd found half a day to explore the city. So many good times.

Charly had been in the last month of pregnancy with Maddy when Marcus had died and couldn't travel, but she'd called Jana every day for weeks until her baby had arrived. Nana Sue had come to Indianapolis, leaving Grandpa here. She'd stayed for two weeks, cooking for her and the girls, who'd been teenagers then.

Jana sighed. This morning Nana Sue hadn't recognized her but lit up when a cheerful aide arrived to take her to have her hair done. At least she'd shown no signs of trauma from her meltdown last night. The administrator at Golden Pines had called later to tell her the doctor had checked Nana Sue and found nothing new or unexpected. Unfortunately, paranoia was common in Alzheimer's patients, and sometimes they had to be restrained and sedated for their own safety as well as that of others around them. Jana still couldn't wrap her brain around Nana Sue needing that kind of intervention.

She hadn't stopped by after work and still felt guilty about that. Although her grandmother was in her nineties, her heart was strong and she was still mobile. She could live several more years, although her brain would continue to be destroyed by a disease that had already robbed her of her memories, judgment, and intellect. The woman who looked like her grandmother but didn't recognize her most of the time seemed more and more like a stranger.

Even so, Jana didn't want to lose her. Nana Sue had always been her touchstone, especially after her mother, a brittle diabetic, had died when she was fifteen. Her mother's health had always been fragile, and as a child, Jana had felt like disaster was poised to strike any minute. Only during her summers in Crossroads could she feel free to play, knowing that Nana Sue was watching out for her mother. Her father would come down on weekends to stay with them, and he, too, had seemed more relaxed with someone else to help share the burden.

She reached for a tissue. She was losing Nana Sue and she may have lost Charly, despite that reassuring *yet*. Oddly, Deeann's comment about it being nice to have friends popped into her head. Not that they were friends or ever would be.

At least her job was giving her purpose here. It was something positive in her life. Tomorrow she should have those three surveyor quotes ready. Soon they would have a plan for a park, something everyone in town could enjoy for generations. A legacy?

Suddenly, she knew what feature she wanted to incorporate into their plans—a memorial to Eli. Whatever the reason he'd been killed, he hadn't deserved to die. A memorial would be a visible reminder of him and a place Charly and Maddy could visit. And Derek. After all, he was Eli's father. She hoped Charly was right about him not being the man she'd seen arguing with Eli that night. He'd been abusive when he drank during the marriage, although it had taken a long time for Charly to confide in her about him striking her. It hadn't happened often, or so Charly had said, but what if Derek had reacted with violence toward his son? Could Derek be Eli's killer?

She brushed her tears away. Here she'd been feeling sorry for herself when Charly and Maddy were the ones who might need a whole army of hugs. Somehow, she was going to have to patch up their relationship and soon.

Chapter Nineteen

THE TIP CAME in the next morning. Wilson Webb, afraid of his parents finding out that he'd had more than a couple of friends over while they were gone, had texted Andrea that his drug dealer, known to him only as Bags, was in his spot near campus. The end of the week was apparently prime selling time, and now they had a chance to catch him in the act. Bags wasn't an early riser, but he'd arrived early enough to be available for lunchtime customers. Tim had dispatched Andrea and Eamon to make the arrest.

Meanwhile, Hal had shown up as ordered to meet with him. His green CPD polo shirt stretched over his belly into the brown belt below it. His khaki pants looked clean and freshly pressed.

"Have a seat, Officer Overman," Tim said. Clint Dees took the other guest chair in his office.

"Chief Deputy Dees here tells me your follow-up on Callum Kinney's complaint about someone shooting at his truck was substandard."

Hal glared at Clint. "Chief, like I told him, I went out there, had a look around, and didn't see anything. There was no one there. He didn't file the report for a couple of days. How am I expected to find a shooter who's long gone?"

"When you *had a look*, did you find any evidence of trespassers?"

He shifted in his seat. "What do you mean? I didn't see anyone. It was dead quiet."

"Any campsites? Trash? Shell casings?"

He folded his arms. "I didn't see anything by the lake. That's where he said he was shot at."

"Shot at by a rifle, most likely," Clint added, apparently knowing where Tim was going, "according to the report."

"Which means the shooter could have been two hundred yards away or more," Tim said. "But you only looked at where Kinney was parked by the lake. Have I got that right?"

"Chief, it's forest!"

"You've sworn to protect citizens—and their property. Merritt Quinn was with Kinney, and it was her property. And I happen to know there are trails through that forest, not to mention a deer stand where the shooter could have been hiding. But you didn't see that, did you?"

"I—"

Tim waved the complaint at him. "Officer Overman, your response to this complaint is unacceptable. If that deer stand had been reported, something could have been done about it before Eli Carson died there. And if you'd searched an adequate perimeter for a rifle shot, you would have come across it. Even given the area you claim you investigated, your report is unacceptable." He read the brief sentences aloud. "You give no specifics about where you searched or what you could be expected to find."

Hal frowned in obvious confusion.

"No shell casings found, no obvious signs of hunters or campers…" Tim suggested.

Hal's brow smoothed. "Yeah, I didn't see any of that, Tim, er, Chief. Hey, I'm sorry I didn't write more. Just trying to keep it brief. We're stretched pretty thin around here. I've been switching shifts, filling in wherever I'm needed. Guess I rushed through it."

Tim studied the man. Hal was an average cop at his best. Always had been, always would be until he collected his pension in another ten years or so. He was right, too, about the delay between the incident and reporting it. Yet, none of that excused sloppy work.

"I'm giving you a warning, Officer Overman. I'll be checking up on your reports. You're going to need to regain my trust in your ability to do your job with the care and concern we need to provide to our citizens. I don't expect a long report, but I'd better be able to read some specific details on who, what, when, and where you investigated. Is that clear?"

"Uh, yeah, Chief. I'll do better."

"You're dismissed."

"Hope he recognizes you're not just talk," Clint said when they were alone. "He'd be making a mistake."

"Hard to tell. Hal's been coasting for a long time." He suspected his predecessor had put up with the officer for the same reason he had—chronic staff shortages and not enough time to really mentor and monitor officers.

"Do you want more follow-up on the shooting report?"

"Let's see what the tourism committee wants to do. They should get approval today to hire a surveyor. If they've found one with a drone, they'll start with some aerial surveillance. Not sure how much they'll be able to see through the trees, but it could show any other camps or deer stands."

"Lotta ground to cover if we have to do it on foot."

A knock at the door was followed by Andrea and Eamon reporting.

"He's being processed," Eamon said. "He tried to run but didn't get very far before Andrea cuffed him." He smiled at the trainee detective.

"So who is Bags?"

"Ray Bagoli, age twenty-six. His DL address is in El Dorado. He has a few priors, including possession with intent to sell, petty theft, and loitering near a school. Only served eighteen months in prison," Andrea said.

"What was he selling today?"

"Marijuana, ecstasy. None of those blue pills, Chief," Eamon said.

"Not today anyway," Tim said. Yesterday's paper had an article about the fentanyl incident. Maybe the dealers were waiting until the news died down. "I want to talk to him after he's processed."

Not surprisingly, Bagnoli wasn't willing to give up his source for the drugs he was pushing. He claimed he didn't know anything about the fentanyl-laced pills and denied recognizing Eli Carson when shown a photo. Tim didn't believe him. At least one dealer was off the street for now, but he had no doubt another one would soon take his place unless they could arrest whoever was supplying the Bags of their community.

JANA WASTED NO time in arranging for the survey after the city council approved the expenditure. She invited the committee to come to Willow Lake on Tuesday at nine, and they were all able to make it. As promised, Chief Birch sent an officer, a young woman named Francine Compton, who was waiting for them when they arrived. Tall and lithe, the sergeant had a face that could have appeared on the cover of any fashion magazine. Her minimal use of makeup—lip gloss only—and chestnut hair twisted up off her long neck emphasized her large brown eyes and full lips.

"I checked the immediate area, ma'am, and it's clear," she told Jana, who'd introduced herself.

"Thank you." She'd convinced Walt not to bring his rifle. He and the two women seemed to know the sergeant and had asked about her family. Cal was glancing around as if looking for a rifle barrel poking out between the trees. Dr. Bailey stood apart from the others, talking on his phone. He'd driven his own vehicle in case he was called out on an emergency.

The surveyor arrived a few minutes later in a white van. Aaron Reese, not much taller than Jana and stocky, nodded to the committee and unloaded his drone. It was bigger than the ones Jana had seen in stores.

"Yes, ma'am," he told her. "This beauty has a camera here and can fly up to forty minutes. It even has a defog mode and night vision, not that we need that today."

"Sure don't," Walt said. "Perfect day for it."

"Do you think forty minutes will be enough time?" Jana asked, anxious to get started. "This is a large property."

"I've done my research, ma'am, and we'll be just fine.

Like we discussed, you should even be able to see through these pines enough to tell if there's a structure below." Mostly talking to the men, he wasted more time pointing out more of the drone's features. At last, he said, "Now if everyone could stand back, I'll get this bird in the air."

He started over Willow Lake, monitoring the drone's flight on his cell phone attached to the control device that reminded her of video game controllers. She wanted to watch over his shoulder but resisted the urge. They would have the video soon enough. But why was he spending so much time over the water? She'd told him the forested area was what they were most interested in surveying.

"No one on the lake today," he chuckled, glancing at Walt. "Guess the fish aren't biting."

"It's not open to the public yet," Grace told him.

"Right. Heading around to the northeast corner now." He stepped away from them.

"Everything okay?" Jana asked Clay, who'd pocketed his phone and joined her. The others had moved closer to the lake's edge.

"Just giving instructions for an eight-year-old with a fever. Sounds like strep throat, but Wilma can take care of it for now. Didn't see you at the park this morning."

They'd met up a few mornings to walk together. Jana had begun to look forward to both the exercise and the company. They'd also had time to chat on Friday when she'd gone to the clinic to have her stitches removed.

"I wanted to make sure I had everything ready for today, and my younger daughter called. She's still not listening to my advice to move on from her boyfriend."

He smiled. "At least she's not making plans to marry him."

"Not yet, thank goodness. Not ever, I hope."

"How's your grandmother?"

"No more calls from the administrator so far." She'd told him about the paranoia and threat of having to move Nana Sue to another facility. "I feel like the axe is about to fall any day, though."

"You need those morning walks. Caregiving is stressful, even if you aren't the one providing the full-time care."

Did that mean he enjoyed their walks? The possibility made her smile. "I'll consider that a prescription and be a good patient."

He grinned. "That's what I like to hear."

Ten minutes later, as Jana and her committee were blocking out where a children's playground could be, a shot rang out.

"No!" Aaron Reese cried staring down at the drone controls. "No, no, no!"

"Take cover!" Cal cried at that same time. Jana and several of the others had ducked.

Sergeant Compton's hand was on her gun. "Everyone, move over there." She pointed to the vehicles they'd arrived in.

"Sounded farther away to me," Walt said, apparently unconcerned. He pointed east. "Somewhere over that way."

After making sure they were out of danger, Sergeant Compton hurried to the surveyor's side. He hadn't moved. She looked over his shoulder at the screen he'd been watching. Her right hand still gripped the butt of her gun.

"He shot down my drone!"

Her gun hand relaxed, lowering to her side. "Can you play it back?"

"Yeah."

Jana cautiously moved out in the open to join them. There hadn't been another shot, but if the drone had been the target, they weren't in immediate danger. Also, a single bullet seemed to have done the trick. The replay showed the landscape the drone had been filming and then suddenly the screen went black.

"Looks like your drone may have been over a farm property," the sergeant said. She turned to Jana. "I'd suggest y'all go back to town. I'll go talk to the farm owner."

"I'm going with you," Aaron said. His florid face was beaded with sweat. "That drone cost me over four hundred dollars!"

"No, sir. You need to let me handle it. I'll make sure we retrieve it for you." Before he could argue, she pulled out her radio and requested another unit.

"Someone's going to pay for this," Aaron Reese mumbled. His angry gaze fastened on Jana. "This is your fault."

"What? I wasn't directing the drone! Why were you flying over that farm? I sent you a map." Dammit, she hadn't followed up on talking to the neighbors as Grace had suggested, but this idiot wasn't going to pin his mistake on her.

"My bird was circling around to start a pass on that side of your property. It's normal operating procedure." Taking a step closer to her, he practically spit out the last three words.

Still rattled by the gunshot so close to where Eli had

died, Jana couldn't help herself. "You were out of bounds! We never directed you to fly over that farm. You should have controlled your *bird* better."

He moved closer, glaring at her. Another step and they'd be chest to chest. "Look, lady—"

"Okay, folks." Sergeant Compton stepped between them. "I think we're finished here today. Sir, give me your contact information. Ms. Nance, I'd appreciate it if your group left now."

Jana took two steps backward and shook her finger at him. "We're not paying for it." It was childish to want the last word, but he needed to be clear about who was responsible, and it wasn't her.

"We'll see about that," he replied.

Chapter Twenty

TO TIM'S FRUSTRATION, Bags had been released on bond at his first appearance and allowed to return to El Dorado, where he supposedly had a sick mother waiting for him. In the judge's defense, the bail amount had been high enough that he probably hadn't expected the scruffy-looking drug pusher to afford it, but someone had come through with the bail bondsman.

"Any hint of this guy reappearing in Chester County for anything other than his next court hearing, I want to know about it," Tim told his officers at Monday's briefing.

"Chief, there was another OD last night," Clint said. "It was out at Friendly's. The victim was a prostitute who claimed not to know what she took other than it was a blue pill. Lucky for her, the owner of the motel, who lives on the premises, found her and gave her Narcan. The paramedics reported it."

"Did someone take a statement from her?"

"Officer Overman reported to the clinic, but she'd left. Dr. Bailey said she refused further treatment."

"Let's see if we can track her down. Sergeant Rollins, I'm assigning that to you. Bring her in for an interview if you can. Sounds like our fentanyl pills again. Any other drug-related incidents this weekend?"

Clint looked around the room before answering. "Seems like a quiet one."

That had suited Tim. After Josie's funeral Saturday, he'd given his aunts a break and spent time with his son. He'd taken Adam to the Chennault Aviation and Military Museum that afternoon and fishing with Curt on Sunday. Adam had been so tired last night, he'd gone to bed at eight without complaint. They'd both had a great time, and his sorrow over his officer's death had been somewhat soothed by the happier moments with his son and his best friend.

"Francine, any update on the drone shooting?"

Chuckles rolled around the room. His sergeant had definitely taken some teasing about the incident. Some of the jokes he'd overheard were about enforcing drone hunting season and her running afoul of farmers protecting their livestock from Chinese spy planes.

"No, sir. I updated Ms. Nance and the drone owner about my conversation with Richard Hardy. As I said in my report, Mr. Hardy didn't appreciate being spied on."

Tim nodded. Her report had been thorough, quite a contrast in detail to Hal Overman's typical product. "There was no crime, so they'll have to settle any disagreements in civil court." Both men had already threatened to sue the other for damages, including pain and suffering.

"Did the drone camera pick up on anything out of place on the park property?"

"I haven't seen the video, but Mr. Reese, the drone owner, has it recorded on his phone. He started over the lake and then turned north. He hadn't reached the southern part before the incident."

So, they still hadn't checked out the entire property, including the forested area where they'd found the deer stand. Cal Kinney hadn't seemed satisfied when Tim had called him Friday afternoon to let him know that the May shooting incident had been checked out and nothing found. Cal had pointed out that if the committee hadn't discovered the deer stand and Eli Carson's body, not even that area would have been searched. He was right too. Most likely the shooter had been hiding closer to the road on the east side of the property. Neither Hal nor CSI had checked that area.

"Good work on that assignment," he told Francine. The property still needed to be checked for trespassers, and because of Hal's sloppy work, he felt responsible for ensuring that happened. He'd contact Ms. Nance later about that.

"Let's talk about Eli Carson. Andrea, what did you find out about his father?"

The young woman sat up taller. Determined to be the team's first Black female detective, she'd been excited when Tim had included her on his drug investigation team, which was now also involved in the young man's homicide. "Derek Carson lives at the address he provided in Lake Village with his second wife, Rayellen, and two mutual children under eight. She wasn't very cooperative, Chief. She confirmed she's a stay-at-home mom and claims her husband was with her at home Thursday night."

"She would, though, wouldn't she?" Eamon said, echoing what Tim was thinking.

"What about the hardware store where he works?"

"The owner confirmed he worked there *for now.* And he'd called in sick that Friday, Chief. That didn't go over well with his boss. He said Mr. Carson was lucky his son had died or he'd probably fire him."

"Compassionate guy," Tim said. If Derek was an alcoholic as his ex had claimed, he'd probably taken a few too many sick days. A winning personality might have appeased his boss, but he seemed to be lacking in that department. "So, it's possible he could have come to see Eli Thursday night or Friday when he'd called in sick. Did you ask his wife about that?"

"Not yet, Chief. I visited her before I talked to his employer." She hesitated. "Their house was a wreck." She wrinkled her nose. Andrea took care with her appearance and maintained a tidy workspace, but she wasn't known to be judgmental.

"That's okay. We'll leave it for now." If Derek Carson wasn't involved, he and his family were victims of the killer, too, and deserved compassion. "Francine, any leads on Eli's girlfriend?"

"No, sir. I've checked every Jenny, Jen, Jennifer, and Ginny with a G who attended Hamblin High in the last five years. None of them had even heard of Eli Carson."

"What about Virginia?" Clint asked.

"I tried that too. No joy."

"Try the other high schools in the county," Tim said. "Or pull driver's licenses with those names for women between seventeen and twenty-two."

"Yes, sir."

Unfortunately, the only prints found in the deer stand they'd been able to match so far belonged to Eli, his three deer hunting pals, his father, and another local man who'd once been arrested for a DUI. Presumably, he was a buddy of Derek's who'd hunted with him at some point. The only prints on the gun had been the victim's. The killer must have worn gloves. The absence of prints on the baggie with the pills also supported that theory and suggested they might not have belonged to Eli.

Tim scratched his cheek. "Eamon, follow up with Larry Mason out at Friendly's to see if he's found his records of Eli's employment. Had he been trying to rehire Eli? See what he drives. That conversation Ms. Nance overheard had been about a job, so maybe he'd been the one in the pickup that night trying to rehire Eli. Let's ask him. Also, ask about our most recent OD victim—how long she'd been staying there, any visitors, et cetera. I thought Friendly's was a family motel. What's a hooker doing there? And who else was there last night? Maybe somebody saw something if she entertained a visitor or had a delivery."

"Yes, sir."

"Okay, anything else?"

"We had a chat with Frank Deluca," Rollins said from the back of the room. As usual, he had his arms crossed over his chest and a bored expression on his face. "He claims he doesn't touch drugs. Not the kind we're asking about anyhow."

"Not expanding his product line then?" Tim asked.

"No, but he did say something interesting." He paused, probably to ensure he had everyone's full attention. "He said only fools and the Bissetts mess with those Mexican cartel types who come through here every Thursday night."

Tim's heart beat faster. This could be the break he'd

been hoping for. "Seems like our Mexican visitors haven't been officially welcomed yet. I'll coordinate with the state police. Maybe we can put the Bissetts out of business and stop that fentanyl trade before our supply of Narcan runs out. Good work, Sarge."

Rollins just shrugged. It was going to take a lot more than a compliment for doing his job to win over his former trainer.

JACK TIMED HIS departure from the pharmacy to catch Marjorie Wilkie as she unlocked her dress shop on Main Street. As he'd hoped, she carried a large plastic food container.

"Here, let me help you with that," he said, putting his Coke down. He couldn't tell if he smelled chocolate, cinnamon, or a combination of both.

"Thanks, Jack." She inserted her key in the lock. "Looks like a beautiful day, doesn't it?"

"Looks like you've been baking again. Something sure smells good."

"Well, bring that in here, and I'll see if I have a spare treat or two. Any news on your office?"

"I've lined up a contractor. Still finalizing the plans." The fire bombing of the newspaper office had done enough damage to need the remaining structure to be demolished. The architect he'd hired in Hamblin had shown him the initial plans Friday, and he was still trying to wrap his brain around the more modern design that would include second-story office space he could rent out.

"Oh, I'd love to see them."

"I'll bring them 'round soon." His mouth began to water as he watched her place two chocolate chip cookies and a cinnamon-sprinkled sugar cookie inside a baggie. "How are the new park plans coming? Are you enjoying being on the committee?"

She grinned. "I haven't had so much excitement in a long time." She told him about the surveyor's drone being shot down. "There we were crouching next to Doc's car only to find out no one was shooting at us. Rich Hardy took that drone down with a single shot. Can you imagine? Seems he thought he was being spied on. Poor Jana felt terrible that she hadn't warned him ahead of time. I hope Mr. Reese was insured."

Jack shook his head. "Umm. First y'all discover a body and now this. Maybe Hardy was extra nervous after hearing about Eli Carson's murder so close to home."

Marjorie's expression turned serious. "Oh, that poor boy, and here I'm talking about my own foolishness hiding from a gunshot a mile away. Have you heard if the police have arrested anyone?"

"'Fraid not. Thanks for the cookies, Marjorie!"

"The chocolate chip ones have cherries in them. Just so you know."

Outside, he picked up his Coke can. It was too warm to drink, so he threw it into the trash bin in front of the hardware store. Luckily, he'd already finished most of it while talking to Bill at the pharmacy.

Damn, his timing was perfect this morning. The young

man emerging from the hardware store carrying a plastic bag with something that rattled as he came down the steps was a familiar face on the local rodeo scene. Jack had interviewed him on several occasions.

"Hey, Tuck. You're out early this morning."

Tucker Hardy laughed. Mid-thirties, he had the rugged looks that women seemed to love and a swagger to match. "We get up early on the farm. It's almost midday. Bet you're on your way to breakfast—or is that what you're carrying?"

He ignored the sneering look the other man was giving him. "Just a gift from a friend. I heard there's been a lot happening out your way. Is it true your dad shot a drone down yesterday?"

The sneer turned into a hard stare. "Damn right. Some surveyor was filming over our ranch without permission."

"I understand he was meant to be surveying Merritt Quinn's property—the part that's going to be the new city park."

He clicked open the door to his black pickup. "They had no business on Hardy land. Reckon they've got the message now." Tossing his bag in, he slid into the driver's seat and slammed the door.

"Guess they do," Jack said to himself as the truck started with a roar. He headed back to his car parked in front of the ruin that had been his newspaper office. His neck was tingling now about this drone shooting news. Hadn't it taken just one shot—*the shot heard 'round the world*—to start the American Revolution? He needed to find out the city's reaction to Hardy's action. Clearly, not everyone was happy about the new park.

Chapter Twenty-One

JANA FOLLOWED ALYSSA to the conference room. Deeann's assistant had told her that only her presence was needed in a meeting with the city attorney. A summons by the boss to meet with a lawyer? She held her head up higher. If they were going to terminate her over that stupid drone incident, she was going to give them an earful before she left.

When she entered the room, her boss and the attorney, an older, bald man in suit and tie, broke off their conversation and glanced up. Deeann didn't offer a smile.

"Jana, this is Conner Douglas, the city attorney. Conner, Jana Nance." As usual, Deeann's blonde bob had every hair in place as if she'd just styled and sprayed it. Jana wished she'd had time to run a comb through her hair and touch up the lipstick that she'd probably chewed off.

"Nice to meet you." *Don't let them see you sweat.* She folded her hands on top of the table. Deeann had directed her to a chair across the table from the two of them. She was in the hot seat. It wasn't the first time.

"Unfortunately, we may be facing a lawsuit from Mr. Hardy," Deeann said. "Conner?"

"He's filed for a cease and desist order," he told her. "He's claiming trespassing, invasion of privacy—his attorney is probably testing the waters for a civil suit in an attempt to squeeze money out of the city."

Jana's heart beat faster. She'd expected the surveyor to be the one suing.

"It's ridiculous, of course," Deeann said. "There was no intent to film his property."

"That's right," Jana said. She had to say something here. "My instructions to the surveyor, Mr. Reese, were to survey the park property."

"Did you notify him in writing of that?" Connor asked.

"Yes, I sent him an email with a map. I'd highlighted the boundaries for him."

"Hmm. If anything, this seems to be Mr. Reese's fault, not that it hasn't already cost him losing his drone," Deeann said. She'd heard the whole story as soon as Jana had returned to the office from the park.

The attorney cleared his throat. "Mr. Reese was working for the city, so we could be found culpable. Also, I had a call from an attorney in Hamblin asking about the incident. Apparently, Mr. Reese is also looking to claim compensation for his loss. I'll need that email and any other correspondence you have with him."

He gave her his card. "Don't talk to either party, and let me know if they try to contact you. You can refer them to my office."

"Okay."

"And feel free to call me if you have any questions." His smile was kind. "A lot of this is just posturing to see what we'll offer to make this go away."

"Thanks, Connor," Deeann said.

He nodded and rose. "Pleased to meet you, Jana. Welcome aboard."

"Deeann—" Jana started to say when the door closed behind him.

"Let me say something first. Mr. Reese's attorney told Connor that you were rude to him and accused him of causing the incident."

"He did cause it. If he hadn't flown beyond the property line, Mr. Hardy wouldn't have had any cause to shoot down his drone."

"That may be, but it might help calm the waters if you apologize to the man."

"Apologize?" Maybe she should quit right now. If anything, Reese should be apologizing to her and the committee. They'd probably have to pay him, if he had any video to share, but he didn't deserve an apology.

"Yes. You may not like the man, but you're working for the city. Your actions reflect on all of us here. Just take the high road, Jana, and forget about blame. If this does go to court, everything you've just said about him flying the drone beyond the area you told him to survey will come out. If we can avoid court, though, that would be even better."

"Your attorney said not to talk to him. Not to talk to either of them."

Deeann sighed. "He's a lawyer, but I'm a politician. Trust me, it's that personal connection that matters. Just don't start arguing with him again or say anything we'll all regret. Can you do that?"

Jana bit her lip. She wanted to say *no* so badly she had to physically struggle to keep the word from shooting out of her mouth. She wasn't going to be hasty this time. She still had her job, and she didn't want to lose it, dammit. But Deeann was asking her to lie to that jerk, to stroke his little ego. She wasn't sure she could even look at the man again without saying something that would get her into even more trouble. If Deeann had known what she'd said when her supervisor in Indy had informed her she'd been passed over for the promotion she'd worked so hard for, she'd know the answer to her question had to be—

"Yes, I'll do it."

Deeann's perfect eyebrows rose. "I thought you were going to say *no* for a moment there. Is he really that bad?"

Now she was really pushing it, trying to be friendly. Or was she laughing at her?

Don't be hasty. You need this job, even if it costs you a little of your pride. "I suppose we were both upset. I'll go see him."

Later, Chief Birch stopped by. He'd removed his green ball cap and hadn't bothered to smooth his brown hair, leaving it with a spiky appearance. Clean-shaven today, he looked even younger than she'd guessed, although his eyes were those of someone older who had seen more tragedy than she could imagine.

"Ms. Nance—"

"Chief, please call me Jana. I hate to say it, but the way things have been going, I may need to move my office next to yours. We seem to be seeing a lot of each other."

His slow smile softened his guarded expression. "There does seem to be something about that property that attracts trouble. And my friends call me Tim."

"Are you here about the drone incident? I've already had a meeting with the mayor and the city attorney this morning.

I understand Mr. Hardy is still upset." He couldn't be here to arrest her, could he? She hadn't trespassed. "By the way, your sergeant was wonderful. She made sure we were all safe when we heard the gunshot."

"Actually, I'm here to offer our services. Before your committee starts building a park out at Willow Lake, we need to make sure no one's camping or hunting out there. I'd like to organize some volunteers to search the property on foot, if that's okay with you and the mayor, of course. I'll check with her if you're okay with it."

"Okay? It's wonderful! I'd be willing to volunteer, and maybe some of the other city employees would help." She could put up a sign-up sheet in their breakroom. "How soon do you think we can do it?"

"I'll aim for Saturday morning. A couple of hours should do it."

Her eyebrows shot up. The chief wasn't wasting any time.

"I appreciate your interest in volunteering, but given the shooting incident in May and the murder, it might be better to have trained first responders do it. I understand the drone filmed the lake area, so it's mostly the forest south of the road that needs to be checked out. Beyond that is open field, which won't take long."

"You seem to know the property."

"I know the McMillans who live on the other side of Jones Camp Road. Used to play there when I was growing up. 'Fraid I might be responsible for some dirt bike trails here and there."

"Ah, so obeying laws was something you picked up later

in life."

He grinned. "Part of the job description, or so they tell me. Anyhow, thanks for your time."

"I'm serious about being there, Tim. This is my responsibility. Besides, I've been there twice with my committee, and no one has shot at us."

After a moment he nodded. "I'll be in touch."

Jana smiled as she typed an email to her committee about the chief's—Tim's—offer. Now they could really focus on their plans and know visitors would be safe. The sooner they could move forward on the park, the better.

After she hit Send, her excitement turned to annoyance. She'd promised to apologize to the surveyor. She found his card in her desk, but she hesitated. As Deeann had said, it would be best to apologize in person, but she didn't want to drive to Hamblin only to discover he wasn't there. She fingered his card. He might refuse to talk to her. If that happened, she could tell Deeann she had at least tried.

The call went to voicemail. She disconnected without leaving a message.

EARLY FRIDAY MORNING Tim and four officers were spread out around the Bissett brothers' property as a SWAT team from the state police and a federal DEA agent shouted "Police!" and ordered everyone to come out with their hands up. The brothers, caught buying from two Hispanic men who'd arrived in a van marked WINTER CHILL AIR-CONDITIONING, were already cuffed. Four handguns had been confiscated. Hardly the usual accessory for an AC repair.

Still holding his rifle, Tim watched as the vehicle was searched. To the casual observer, the van and its cargo looked like it belonged to the advertised business. Two air-conditioning units, still in the manufacturer's boxes, sat in the center. A carrier filled with well-used tools sat conveniently near the door, and hoses and other legitimate parts on racks lined the side walls of the van. The marijuana the men were examining when police burst on the scene had to be just a sample.

"Tear it apart," the state police lieutenant named Anderson told two of his men.

A woman's angry voice distracted Tim. Two women, still in nightgowns, had been routed from the house. The one loudly protesting carried a toddler whose cries competed with his mother's shouts. An older boy, maybe four years old, clutched the other woman's hem and tried to hide behind her. Two additional men had been rousted from the barn where they'd been sleeping, judging by their tousled hair and bleary eyes. Dressed in worn jeans and white T-shirts, they blinked in the early morning sun but kept quiet. Tim hadn't seen them around town. They also looked Hispanic and seemed more disappointed than angry at being captured.

"All clear," one of the agents called, emerging from the barn.

Per their planning session in Hamblin yesterday, Tim called his officers on his walkie-talkie. "All clear. Begin your search."

Several clicks answered him. Five minutes later, Eamon Carey broadcasted a find: a shed hidden in the trees containing drug packaging materials and traces of weed on the floor. Francine soon added her own discovery: an extensive marijuana grow shed covered with a camouflage net.

"I noticed the electric wire in the trees," she pointed out when he joined her. "It started about twenty yards back that way." As it turned out, the wire coming from the house had been buried up to the tree line. No doubt they'd discover the brothers paid more than a normal household for their power each month.

"Any evidence of the pills?" Tim asked.

"Not yet," she said.

"Keep searching, but be careful."

Eamon wasn't far away. Tim asked him the same question.

"There's some powder residue in the shed, but not much," Eamon replied.

"We'll see what CSI says," Tim said. "I'll see if they're cleared to come in. Stay out here and make sure no one tries to access." When his other two officers reported in without any further discoveries, he assigned each of them to one of the two drug locations.

Back in front of the house, a stash of pills, white powder, and hash had been found in one of the boxed air-conditioning units.

"Looks like mostly heroin and ecstasy pills, but we'll check it out," the DEA agent said as a state police officer photographed the back of the van and the contents of the AC unit.

"What about fentanyl?"

"Wouldn't be surprised if there isn't some in there, but we'll have to run tests."

None of the pills that Tim could see were blue, but the buildings and property still had to be searched more thoroughly. The important thing was that no one had been hurt. This raid had been textbook.

Chapter Twenty-Two

"I HOPE THOSE are old shoes," Walt said Saturday morning, frowning at Jana's athletic shoes. "We're going to be walking through a lot of brush."

She looked at his feet. "I don't have any boots like yours. I'll be fine." He'd insisted on joining the search, at least until he had to go to the sawmill museum to open it to visitors at ten. Clay Bailey had also volunteered. He, too, wore sturdy hiking boots. At least she'd worn jeans and a long-sleeved shirt, knowing that mosquitos would probably be biting. She'd also found an old, floppy sun hat of Nana's that should protect her hair from branches and insects.

"You need any sunscreen?" the doctor asked her.

She smiled at him. "Already applied."

They joined the group assembling around Tim Birch. Dressed casually in jeans, an olive-green jersey, and a ball cap, he'd assembled about ten men and two women, in addition to her threesome. She recognized Sergeant Compton, whose long ponytail was pulled through the back of her ball cap. She pulled on work gloves more appropriate for trekking through a forest than the light, floral-print gardening gloves Jana had brought.

"Good morning," the chief said, raising his voice over the friendly banter of a group of fit-looking men. "First, thanks for coming this morning. It isn't often the police and the fire department spend a Saturday in the park, or future park." Laughter and whoops greeted his comment. "Unfortunately, we're not here for a picnic—"

"What? You promised, Tim," a blond fireman interjected, grinning.

The chief pulled a granola bar out of his knapsack and tossed it to him. "That's because I knew food was the only way to get you out of bed this early, Curt."

When the laughter died down, Tim introduced the three members of the tourism team. "Ms. Nance is the new tourism director for Crossroads," he said as everyone stared at her.

"It's Jana," she yelled back. "And thank you all for being here!"

"I think y'all know Doc Bailey and Walt Grisham. They're members of Jana's committee planning this new park. But first, we need to make sure this property is cleared of anything or anyone that doesn't belong here. Unfortunately, we had a shooting incident a few months ago and more recently a homicide in a deer stand just through the trees over yonder."

Smiles disappeared as the volunteers considered the seriousness of the recent crime that had happened so close to where they now stood.

"We're going to walk from here to the south edge of this forested area to make sure there are no vagrants or other illegal structures on the property. My officers will spread out so they're mixed in with the rest of you in case there's trouble. If you come across a campsite, deer stand, or any other evidence of people being here, call out. My officers and I have whistles in case we're too far away to hear you or if anyone needs assistance."

With a few more instructions to organize the volunteers and warn them of natural dangers, like poison ivy and snakes, they spread out and began the search. By unspoken agreement, Walt and Clay fanned out on either side of Jana. Sergeant Compton was within sight just beyond the doctor.

The undergrowth beneath the pines wasn't as bad as Jana had feared. Sunlight became mere dapples of light as they trekked through the forest. Afraid of stepping on a snake or tripping over something, Jana watched her feet. She didn't want to end up as a casualty and cause Tim to regret letting her participate.

"Don't forget to look up. Sometimes deer stands are built in trees." Clay Bailey smiled at her. He'd found a large stick that he used to push low-hanging branches aside.

"Do you think we'll find any more?"

"I wouldn't be surprised."

"Pretty remote out here," Walt said. "Good place for all kinds of illegal activities."

"Like what?" she asked. They hadn't come across any paths or roads cut through the forest. Wouldn't criminals need some way to access whatever enterprise they were running?

"Drugs," Clay said, glancing up. "Not sure there's enough light to grow marijuana, unless they've cleared a spot we haven't found."

"Timber could be worth stealing," Walt said. "Used to be farmers would sell their trees to the company. Someone could've been harvesting these. Doesn't look like it so far."

This forest could have been stripped in the years it had been unoccupied and possibly no one would have noticed. "I understand that Merritt Quinn inherited this property and it's been vacant for years."

"That's right." As she'd hoped, Walt, their local historian, launched into a history of the property. "The McMillan family settled this part of the county when they came here from North Carolina sometime in the 1850s. Doug and Bry still farm their properties on the other side of Jones Camp Road. Curt—that's the paramedic with the granola bar—is Doug's son. Doug's brother, Bryson"—he chuckled—"well, that's a long story for another time. Anyhow, their uncle, Angus McMillan, had inherited this parcel of land and chose not to farm it. He lived in town where he practiced law and later became a judge."

"And he left it to Merritt's aunt?"

"Great-aunt, but yep, that's what happened."

A squirrel scampered up a tree and out of Jana's way. "So these trees could be very old."

"Now you've done it," Clay said with a grin. "I take it you haven't been to the sawmill museum?"

"No, not yet. Sorry, Walt. I'm going to visit you there soon. I promise."

"That's okay. You've had a lot on your plate since you've arrived. Anyhow, the short answer to your question is that pines can live between one hundred and one thousand years. There's one in California that's 4,600 years old. It's a Great Basin bristlecone."

"That's amazing!" She gazed at the rough trunks on either side with new respect.

"Yep. We don't have bristlecones around here. These are shortleaf pines, also sometimes known as yellow or southern pines. They're plenty hardy. 'Course, climate can affect how long they live. They like cooler weather than our summers. Fire, disease, and bugs can get them too. This forest has done well."

"I think you spoke too soon," Clay said.

Ahead, a fallen tree blocked their path. About five feet in diameter, there was no room to go under it. Jana was considering whether they could boost each other over it when Clay called, "Come this way."

They followed him to where Sergeant Compton waited. The stump and the end of the broken pine were both jagged. No person had cut down this tree.

"See that?" Walt pointed to a blackened edge of the pine. "Lightning strike. That's probably what took her down."

Jana couldn't see the top of the tree from here. Maybe it had stood taller than the ones around it until a lightning bolt had struck it.

"Do you think it made a sound when it fell?" Clay teased her as they regrouped on the other side of the pine to resume their search.

She grinned. "I'd like to think the other trees heard it, but there's no sign of humans around here, is there?"

"That's what we want, isn't it—not to find anything or anyone to have to clear out?"

"Yes." Her feet crunched on the pine needle floor as they moved forward once again. "I think we should consider preserving this forest as much as we can."

"We might not have enough room for all those suggestions folks are coming up with if we don't clear some of the trees," Walt said from her other side. "Not that I'm objecting to your idea."

When they reached the edge of the forest, they emerged onto a grassy plain. The tall apex of the glass cathedral about a quarter mile south of them sparkled in the morning sun. Shading her eyes, Jana saw that other volunteers had already emerged. Her group joined the them as they waited for Chief Birch. He arrived looking serious, which Jana had learned was his usual expression.

Curt McMillan separated from him. "Didn't hear any whistles. Is everyone okay?" Like a few of the others, probably fellow paramedics, he had a first aid kit attached to a utility belt.

"Just waiting on you, McMillan," one of the other men answered. "Did you stop for lunch or get lost? We were just planning a rescue mission."

"Aww, thanks, guys. Tim here just likes to be thorough."

"Anyone see anything? Any sign at all of campers or hunters?" Tim asked, removing his ball cap and running his fingers through his hair before putting it back on. The day had heated up since they'd started their search. Jana was looking forward to removing her gloves and hat.

"Nothing but squirrels," another fireman answered. "Just a walk in the woods."

Tim thanked them again. "You can cut over that way and follow the road back up if you want more exercise. Eamon is coming back in a minute in his truck." His gaze fell on her team. "He can drive anyone who's tired of walking back to their cars."

Walt raised his hand. "That's me. Gotta head to work."

"CPD team, over here with me. Jana, you too."

"I need to get back too," Clay told her. "If you're interested, I could take you to the sawmill museum sometime."

"I'd like that. Maybe next Saturday? I'm going to Eli's funeral this afternoon." She guessed the museum was closed on Sundays.

"Sounds like a plan."

He headed in Walt's wake toward the road to wait for a ride back. Jana joined Tim and his team of three.

"Jana, I came across an area used for drug production. It's been cleared out, but it looks like it was recently in use."

"Oh no! You didn't blow your whistle."

"No. No need to stop everyone to see it, not that there's much to see. Besides, I'd rather word didn't get out on what we've found for now." He glanced at his officers, who nodded.

"Okay. I won't tell the committee."

"I'll call the mayor and update her," he added as if he'd read her thought. "I'm going to call CSI. There's really not much left, so you can proceed with the park plans. CSI should be able to finish today. I'll make sure all traces of the operation are removed. It'll just look like a former camp site."

"Do you think they'll come back?" The whole idea of today's outing had been to ensure the area was safe.

"I doubt it. If they hadn't already closed it down, news of the murder would have scared them off. They'd know police would be out here looking around. The latest *Gazette* had an article about your committee beginning work on the park, so they'll want to find a quieter place to hide what they're doing."

Her heart sank.

"Do you think Eli knew what was going on? Maybe he came out here to stop whoever was involved." But she realized how naïve she sounded. Eli could have removed the evidence to hide what he'd been doing or what he'd decided to stop doing. Either way, wouldn't he have known about the drug activity in the woods?

Several feet shifted as the officers looked at their chief. "That's something we're investigating. Until we have more facts, rumors and speculation don't help us."

"Or Eli and his family. His funeral is this afternoon. Don't worry; I won't say anything." Charly wouldn't believe her anyway. She didn't need to drive the wedge between them in deeper.

"I appreciate that. Eamon is coming back in a minute. He can give you a ride back to your car."

Driving back to town, Jana tried to lift her mood by thinking about Clay's invitation. Or was it a date? If so, it would be her first in a long time. At her daughters' urging, she'd gone on a few just before the COVID epidemic struck, but they'd been awkward for both her and the men who had asked her out. She couldn't help but compare them to Marcus, and none had come close to stirring any romantic feelings in her heart. No, this wasn't a date. Clay was a friend and colleague on her committee. So was Walt, whose sawmill museum was a tourist attraction she needed to visit so she'd know how to promote it.

Tim Birch didn't know her well if he thought she was going to broadcast news of a drug operation at the new park grounds. Eli's murder had already cast a dark shadow on the beautiful property. And then there had been the drone incident. She'd tried calling Aaron Reese again yesterday without success. If Deeann hadn't been out of the office all day, she probably would have asked her if she'd apologized.

No, she didn't need any more trouble associated with her or the park. But why had Eli been killed? Hopefully, he hadn't been involved in whatever had been going on at the camp site the chief had discovered.

Chapter Twenty-Three

A MODEST-SIZED CROWD of mourners attended Eli's funeral that afternoon, mostly younger people and Charly's friends, coworkers, and family. A lifelong resident of Crossroads, she had two brothers who lived in the area and a number of cousins, aunts, and uncles. Her sister had returned as well. She and Charly's parents sat next to her and Maddy, hunched over with their heads bowed during the service. Derek and his wife, Rayellen, sat in the front row on the other side of the aisle—the groom's side, if it were a wedding. Some of the older people in the rows behind him bore some familial resemblance. Jana slid into a pew several rows behind Charly.

The Methodist service wasn't long or drawn out. The minister didn't talk as if he'd known Eli. His words were what Charly must have shared about her son. Sadly, Marcus's eulogy had been similar. They'd stopped attending church regularly several years earlier, even before he'd become ill. The girls had complained about being forced to attend Sunday school and had never shown much interest in church activities. It had been easier to choose not to fight that battle each week, especially after the minister she and Marcus had both liked was reassigned and replaced with a less inspiring preacher. He'd been kind, though, in talking to

Jana about her husband, and those who had attended had praised the service.

It was hard to believe Marcus had been gone fourteen years. What would he think of her quitting her job and moving to Crossroads? She seemed to keep bouncing back here: Little Rock to Crossroads to Indianapolis to Crossroads again. What did it all mean?

A young woman moved to the front and began to sing "Amazing Grace." The hymn always moved Jana to tears. In front of her, Charly's head drooped and her shoulders shook. Maddy's arm encircled her mother's back and they leaned into each other. Jana's heart ached for them. She fumbled in her handbag for a tissue and wished Nana were here to pat her knee.

When the service ended, Jana followed the others to the church hall, where food and drinks had been set up. A linen-covered table held photos of Eli at various ages. Some of his contemporaries were pointing at them and talking about him. One young woman stood apart. Clutching a cloth handbag, she looked more forlorn than anyone Jana had ever seen.

"Were you a friend of Eli's?"

She glanced at Jana, startled out of her reverie. "I—Yes. A friend."

"I'm Jana, his godmother."

"Ginny. Ginny Matthews."

"Did you go to school with him, Ginny?" The girl didn't seem to know the half dozen grouped around his photos.

"No, we met last year. I live in Bastrop." She sniffed. "He came into The Last Rodeo. That's the bar where I work.

The first time he was with some friends, but the next time he came alone. We talked, and he asked me out." Her smile was sad. "I just sensed he was a nice guy, you know?"

So this was the mysterious girlfriend. "You have good instincts. He was a nice boy. His family lives next door to my grandmother's house, so I've seen him grow up." Although she hadn't been there the last five years, had she?

"We talked about moving in together." A tear rolled down her cheek. "We were saving our money…"

"Oh, honey." Years of comforting her daughters made gathering Ginny into her arms seem natural. The girl didn't stiffen; she sank into Jana's embrace and moaned softly.

"Why?" she whispered before straightening and using her finger to brush away her tears. "Who would hurt him? Eli wouldn't hurt anybody."

"Have the police talked to you?" She was surprised when the girl shook her head.

"Ginny, you might be able to help. If Eli confided in you—"

She backed up a step, shook her head again. "He wasn't in any trouble. I-I know he smoked a little weed, but he promised he was giving that up."

"No, but he may have told you some things about his work or people he knew that might help them. Chief Birch is a good man. I know you want the police to find whoever did this, don't you?"

She looked scared and skeptical. "I—"

"Would you like me to go with you?" Jana offered impulsively. Clearly Ginny was here on her own. She'd probably never walked into a police station before, or, if she had, it might not have been a pleasant experience. "We could go right now."

Ginny took another step backward. "No! I have to get back. I need to be at work by noon."

"Okay, I understand. Please, let me give you my phone number. Maybe we can go on Monday. Does that work for you?" She wished she had a business card to give her. "Do you have your phone with you? Even if you don't think you know anything that would help, I know Chief Birch would really appreciate you trying. I think Eli would too."

The girl reluctantly pulled her phone from a small shoulder bag hanging beneath her arm. To Jana's relief, she let her type in her name and cell number but shook her head when Jana asked for hers. A call on Monday might be as likely as snow in August in Crossroads.

JACK DIDN'T MIND a healthy meal or even driving to Hamblin to enjoy it, especially when Cal Kinney was paying. However, if Cal thought meeting in the closest town to Crossroads was going to be an escape from prying eyes, he was deluding himself.

"How'd you discover this place?" he asked when they were settled in a booth at the Hamblin Harvest Table. Cal had opted for the illusion of privacy the booth offered instead of choosing seats at the long communal table in the center of the room.

"I brought Merritt here. She wasn't happy with the quality of salads in Crossroads."

"Shoot, I didn't know folks ate salads in Crossroads," Jack joked, "other than potato, bean, or macaroni."

"The café offers green salads, but apparently they aren't good."

"I don't see Dave Lee tossing lettuce, but he sure can't be beat for hamburgers."

"That's the truth."

They each studied the one-page menu for a few moments. The dishes listed actually sounded good, even if they were healthier choices than he usually encountered. Jack decided on a Mexican bean bowl with black beans, sweet potatoes, a homemade mango salsa, avocado, and corn. He told the server no cilantro. That was one green he could live without. Cal opted for the three-bean chili with corn bread.

"I've found out—" they said simultaneously and then stopped.

"Go ahead," Jack said.

"I've been looking at past purchase and sales orders." Cal had lowered his voice. "I've made a point of getting to know more of the SP staff, including one of our accountants. She's relatively new, on the job only two years, and tired of being treated like an assistant to the others in the finance department. The woman moved here from Atlanta and is a CPA. She's also Black, which she suspects is another reason her talents are discounted. Personally, I think it's more chauvinism than anything from what I know of the guys she works with. She seemed very interested in helping me look at the books. She's pulling together some information she thinks I'll be interested in seeing."

"Did you tell her what you suspect?"

Cal sipped his Coke. The server, a thin dude with a soul patch, had looked disappointed when he'd ordered it. "No, at least not yet. I told her I'm trying to catch up on what's been going on in purchasing as we get ready to discuss the budget for next year, which happens to be true. She'd heard I was suggesting changes, trying to cut costs. I'm more the corporate type she's used to."

"And not one of the good ole boys."

"Right. Anyhow, she's been helpful already in providing me with purchase and sales information on the big ticket items, including the box trucks—"

"Which are being sold to Forest Truck Traders every three years." He told Cal about his visit. "I didn't see the dented box truck that was at the pond that night, but they had several similar ones on their lot. Unfortunately, that truck could have been sold to someone else who's doing the dumping."

"So you're not really any closer to finding out who's doing it."

"Maybe. I recognized one of the two men. It was Eli Carson."

"Eli—The guy we found in the deer stand on Merritt's property?"

"Technically, it's now the town's property, but yeah, that's who it was. Eli worked for Doncaster Motors, which is owned by—"

"Newt Doncaster. I know."

"They referred me to Forest Truck Traders when I asked the head mechanic about who services box trucks. Eli did extra jobs to earn money, so I thought he might have picked up some work at Forest Truck. They didn't seem very happy about me poking around, so I tried to sell them advertising in the *Gazette* and didn't mention Eli."

Cal grinned. "Worth a try while you were out there."

"No sale yet. I just wish I could find the driver of that truck. That would lead us to whoever's behind this. Any progress on the cleanup?"

"We've contacted the EPA. That's not for publication yet, Jack."

So they were trying to pass the buck. He should have seen that one coming. "They'll take forever to do anything. Is this another stall tactic by the company?"

Cal frowned. "Not if I can help it. I want that pond cleaned up as much as you do, and I'm not going to let it drop. The EPA are the experts, and they'll continue to monitor the water and surrounding soil after they remediate it. Contacting them is progress, Jack."

"Has the EPA committed to do the cleanup?"

"Well, not yet. They're testing the water and soil this week. They'll then do a plan to clean it up, depending on what they find."

Jack pursed his lips. "I can wait on publishing the story, but I want to know what they learn and have an exclusive when you can release it."

"I'll do what I can, but no one can know I'm working with you on this. There's more at stake here than a polluted pond."

"A toxic pond you mean. And there *is* more at stake—people's lives."

Cal stared at him. "Hey, I get that you're upset, but I'm

not the bad guy here."

"Yeah, sorry."

The server arrived with their lunches. The young man glanced at each of them before placing their bowls before them. He must have sensed the tension.

"You doing okay?" Cal was still watching him. "You look tired."

"Sure. Doing fine." Jack unrolled his cutlery. "Have you talked to Merritt recently?"

"Yeah. She's planning to come during fall break in October. Said she's looking forward to enjoying Crossroads when it's cooler."

"That's about when the mayor's planning a dedication ceremony for the park, isn't it?"

Cal nodded and chewed for a moment. "Assuming nothing else stops us between now and then."

"You worried about something specific?"

"No, just that things keep happening. Actually, we should be in good shape now that the area's finally been searched. Tim wouldn't admit it, but I don't think they looked very hard back in June when I reported that Merritt and I had been shot at when we were at the lake."

"I thought the drone was shot down before the survey was finished."

"It was. Tim organized a group to do a walk-through this morning."

"You included?" Jack patted his shirt for the small pad he usually carried for notes, but he hadn't brought it.

"No, I decided to leave it to the professionals. Anyhow, Jana emailed that it went well. No other structures were found, and we're clear to go ahead." He spooned a bite of his chili. "We're going to put up NO TRESPASSING signs and a chain across the road to the lake. Tim thought that would help."

Cal sounded as if he didn't believe it. An area that large had many access points. Meanwhile, there was still a murderer to catch, but Eli Carson's killing probably had more to do with the victim than the place where he'd met his fate.

The black bean bowl was delicious—the best meal he'd had in a while. He waited until Cal had also enjoyed most of his entrée before asking, "So what do you really think is going on at SP? Is someone cooking the books?"

Cal's alarmed look was quickly replaced by a casual shrug. "Probably just some you-scratch-my-back-and-I'll-scratch-yours kind of deals. Still, I'd like to know why some of the other board members are so resistant to my suggestions to make the company more profitable. At least Peter is encouraging me to develop a proposal on a sustainable packaging line."

Jack only half listened to Cal's explanation of what cellulose fibers were and how they could be used. If and when the board at Southern Pines voted to move forward in that direction, he'd dig into it. But what if there was corruption and the dumping at Crawfish Pond was somehow connected to the company's used box truck sales? Maybe kickbacks were involved. Eli Carson had worked for Newt Doncaster, one of Cal's colleagues on the board. Maybe he'd been offered the job to dispose of whatever had been in those barrels at his workplace or by someone who'd known him from there. Just because SP wasn't officially still using the pond for waste disposal didn't mean there couldn't be a side hustle going on, like illegally dumping and then billing the company for what it would have cost to properly dispose of it.

And now Eli was dead. "You know, Cal," he said when the other man stopped his discourse and returned to eating. "You need to be careful. Something's going on that's turned deadly."

Cal pushed his empty chili bowl away. "You think that guy's death in the deer stand had something to do with whatever may be going on at SP? I don't see it. Seems more like a drug deal gone wrong."

"Maybe. Even so, watch your back." He'd have to watch his too.

Chapter Twenty-Four

MARVA MAY HAVE been annoyed to have Jack Huddleston waiting in the lobby until the Monday morning staff briefing was finished, but Tim didn't mind seeing the reporter today. After all, the raid on Friday had been a complete success. The state police officer in charge had issued a statement in time for the evening news, with a representative from the DEA standing next to him. Although they failed to specifically mention the Crossroads police in the comments about the *joint effort* and *cooperation from local police*, Tim had given his team full credit at this morning's meeting. He hadn't seen their mood so positive since he'd become chief. Even Sarge had given him a nod.

Jack had his pen and notebook out almost as soon as his backside hit the chair in Tim's office. "Congratulations, Chief. I saw the news about the raid on television. I understand the Bissett brothers have their first appearance this morning after spending the weekend in your jail."

Tim glanced at his watch. "Ten o'clock, I think."

"Do you think they'll get bail?"

"Depends on Judge Wooten's mood this morning, but we did confiscate a truckload of marijuana and other drugs. With luck, they'll be out of business for a long stretch." Technically, the state police had done the confiscating, but it had been *a joint effort.*

He confirmed other details on how the raid had come about, glad to have a chance to brag on his team.

"I understand three teens were treated Saturday night for fentanyl overdoses at a party. Did the drugs come from the Bissetts?"

Tim stared at him, his expansive mood evaporating. He hadn't yet reviewed the weekend's reports, but no one had notified him or mentioned the incident at this morning's briefing. Then again, the officers working the night shift hadn't been there.

"We're still investigating that possibility," he managed, sounding like every other clueless politician or law enforcement spokesperson blindsided by a new revelation.

Jack's gaze sharpened. "I suppose they could have purchased the stuff before your raid. I hear one of the kids is critical—the one they airlifted to Little Rock. The other two are still hospitalized but expected to recover."

Shit. "We're doing all we can to keep fentanyl out of Crossroads, Jack. My officers are on the front lines, you know, and I've already lost one of them."

His angry words hung in the air between them for a moment.

"Hey, I know," Jack said. "I think Friday was the biggest drug raid we've ever had in the county. I'll have to research that. In any case, I don't recall anything like it in recent years."

"Not since I've been on the force," Tim agreed, regretting taking his anger at himself over Josie's death out on the reporter. "Fentanyl's everywhere these days, even here."

Or maybe drug dealers who had avoided Chief Bowen's territory now thought they could get away with it under his watch. Tim's jaw tightened. If so, they'd misjudged how determined he was to keep his people safe and catch whoever had caused Josie's death.

"So, any update on Eli Carson's murder? Was he working for the Bissetts?"

Tim frowned. "What makes you think that?"

"You told me last week you'd found drugs—pills—in that deer stand. If the Bissetts were the source and Eli had more than enough for personal use, he had to be pushing them."

"We haven't found any link yet or confirmed his death was drug-related." There was also the small amount of evidence CSI had bagged up on Saturday at the abandoned site on the park grounds he'd discovered. It would probably be processed today. A single broken blue pill, apparently trampled on, had been uncovered by an observant tech. But even if it matched the pills found with Eli's body, it didn't prove he'd been manufacturing or selling them. They needed to nail the Bissetts by linking them and their Mexican visitors to the fentanyl. So far, the brothers were denying any connection to Eli Carson or involvement with his death.

"No suspects yet for the murder?"

Tim shook his head, noting the dark smudges beneath Jack's eyes. His face seemed thinner, too, as if he'd lost weight. "Anything else I can help you with?"

"Did Forest Truck turn over their sales records?"

He stared blankly at the reporter a moment too long before recalling the box truck connection. "Not yet."

Jack's face tightened. "You haven't even checked it out."

"We've been a little busy around here." He hated making excuses, however true. "I'll get someone on it today."

"Yeah, right." He rose abruptly, the chair screeching as it was pushed backward. "I'll check in on Wednesday for updates unless something breaks before then."

Yeah, let's hope so, Tim thought, but it wasn't the weekly newspaper's print deadline that concerned him. At least his team had been able to celebrate a win, but if fentanyl wasn't found in the drugs confiscated in the raid, they still had a serious threat to the community to stop. And if Eli Carson's murder was connected to the deadly drugs, the perpetrators had already claimed a second victim. Or maybe more. As soon as Jack left, he began reading the weekend's incident reports.

JANA FOUND HERSELF checking her phone every ten minutes or so at her desk Monday morning. She had no idea when Ginny Matthews woke up or what her schedule was. Ginny was young and worked nights, so she probably slept in. Then again, was the bar open on Sundays? Had she worked last night? For all Jana knew, the girl could have left town after their conversation at the funeral.

A sharp knock on her open door jerked her back into the present.

"Good morning," Deeann said. "Tim updated me about the search on Saturday. He said you were there."

"I thought I should be." Had she done something

wrong? "Besides, it was a nice morning to be outdoors."

The mayor hadn't sat down. "Tim said that we can go ahead with our planning." She paused, her gaze direct. Did she, too, know about the chief's discovery that wasn't to be mentioned? "Now that it's safe to proceed, do you think your committee will be able to have at least a draft plan finished this week?"

Jana's alarm must have shown on her face. *This week?*

"It doesn't have to be detailed," Deeann continued. "I just need a general sense of what areas, like picnic grounds, and possible facilities you'd like to see at the park. We need to show by the end of the year how the grant money will be spent. That means I'm going to have to get buy-in from our facilities department, and then we'll need to hire an architect and work out costs before we present it to the city council."

The mayor sat across from her. "I know you've barely had time to settle in, and what's happened at Willow Lake hasn't been your fault or anything we could have anticipated, but it's almost September and our end-of-the-year deadline is quickly approaching. Can you do it?"

The committee had barely started conceptualizing features the park would have, but what other choice did she have? To be fair, Deeann had laid out the schedule when she'd first started.

"I can give you a very rough plan by the end of the week." Their regular weekly meeting was already scheduled for tomorrow. She bit her lip. She'd need to start putting their ideas on paper before then to push this project along. Even so, they might need to call a second special meeting if they didn't agree tomorrow on a broad-strokes sketch for the new park.

Deeann rose. "I know you're working hard, and there have certainly been some unexpected challenges. Let me know what I can do to help and feel free to call on Alyssa."

"What had you been thinking about doing with the grant money before Merritt Quinn's donation?" Jana blurted out. It was a fair question. There had been no Willow Lake park possibility until June, when Merritt Quinn had donated the land. That was half a year after the grant had been awarded. Her own position as tourism director was new, so had someone else been given this task before she'd arrived or had it been left for a last-minute push to meet the deadline?

Deeann crossed her arms but didn't say anything for a moment. "We originally planned to make improvements on the city park and zoo and use some of the money for advertising to promote the area. I can send you a copy of the application."

"But you didn't fill my position until the end of July."

The shadow of a frown crossed Deeann's face. Jana hadn't meant to sound so accusatory. She wished she could pull back her question.

"Jana, before we placed the ad you answered, I tried to appoint a tourism director, but the three people I asked turned me down. Then we advertised, actually twice before we hired you."

So she hadn't been the mayor's first choice or even her second. In fact, Deeann had been desperate—desperate enough to hire her high school nemesis.

"None of that matters now," Deeann said. "And by the way, when Merritt's gift came through, I called the grant office. They understood we hadn't anticipated that happening and are fine with the change in direction. They're happy as long as we can show we're using the money to create something new to promote tourism. Do you have any other questions?"

"No, I'll, uh, get right on that plan."

"Good. I'll look forward to seeing what you and the committee come up with."

But an hour later, Deeann returned. She closed the door to Jana's office. "Richard Hardy's attorney filed for a cease and desist order this morning. Connor wanted you to know."

"What does that mean?"

"If the judge grants it, the order would prevent you or the city from being on or flying above his property."

"I don't have any plans to do that." One drone shooting was enough.

"Then that will be the end of that, and we can all move forward. By the way, did you apologize to Aaron Reese?"

She wet her lips. "Not yet. I've called him several times, but—"

"Jana! You were supposed to do that last week. And leaving a voice message apology isn't going to satisfy him, I'm sure. You need to talk to him in person."

"I know. I've been trying, but he hasn't answered my calls. I don't want to drive to Hamblin if he's not there." Her excuse sounded pathetic, even to her. The truth was, she'd forgotten about it since her last attempt to reach him Friday morning.

Deeann's lips were tight. "I'd suggest you try harder. We

can't afford a lawsuit. The man may have been incompetent, but you're the one who publicly accused him of it. Take care of it—today."

Her *or else* was clear without being spoken, clear enough that Jana bit back her argument that she hadn't actually said Reese was incompetent.

"Yes, ma'am," she managed.

"VIRGINIA MATTHEWS?" TIM asked. The young woman who answered the apartment door didn't look more than sixteen, even with a generous application of eye makeup. She'd cracked open the door only to the extent of the security chain.

He held up his badge. "I'm Tim Birch, police chief in Crossroads and this is Sergeant Francine Compton. We'd like to ask you a few questions about Eli Carson. We understand you were friends."

She frantically glanced behind her. Tim considered wedging his foot in the opening, but he sensed the girl needed reassurance more than a demonstration of the strong arm—or foot—of the law. At least that was the impression Jana Nance had given him when she'd called an hour ago.

"I'm sorry for your loss. This won't take long. I'm sure you want to help us find whoever killed Eli."

She blinked. Closing the door, she released the chain and let them in. Sunlight from a sliding glass door in the rear of the apartment lit the entry hallway. A worn suitcase sat near the front door. It appeared they'd arrived just in time.

"This is a nice place," Francine said. "I love that you've added color in those pillows and your tablecloth. I'm guessing your landlord won't let you hang artwork. I know mine won't."

Tim resisted the urge to glance at her. He had no idea where Francine lived or whether she lived with anyone. She might just be trying to establish rapport with Ginny. If so, it was working.

"That's because my roommate loves to sew," Ginny said.

She gestured to the sofa, and they sat side by side. Tim would have preferred to remain standing, but he didn't want to appear intimidating by towering over the women. The girl folded one leg beneath her and sat in a broad faded green armchair across from them.

"Is your roommate here?" Francine asked. The apartment had only two bedrooms. That didn't mean only two individuals lived here.

"No, she works during the day."

"I understand you work at The Last Rodeo," Tim said. "Is that where you met Eli?"

"Yes." She shrugged. "He came in and we talked. We became friends."

"When did you first meet him?" Tim asked.

"It was almost Valentine's Day." Her smile was sad. "He came in two nights later and brought me one of those chocolate hearts." Her hands spanned about five inches to show the size. "It was sweet of him."

"I'm guessing he kept coming back after that," Francine said.

The girl nodded.

"Did you visit him in Crossroads?" Tim asked.

"A few times, but not at his house. He was living with his mother and sister." She paused. "He took me to the zoo, and we walked around on a path by a pond. Then he took me to Dairy Queen. We liked to do that on his day off."

"Did Eli talk about the places where he worked?" Tim asked. "We know he was a mechanic working days at the Doncaster car dealership. Did he tell you about the other jobs he was doing?"

Her face scrunched in thought. "He was working for a man at a motel. Eli didn't like him much. He stopped working there a few months ago. Said it wasn't worth the money he was being paid."

"Was that at Friendly's Motel?"

"Yeah, that's it."

"And did he say what kind of work he was doing and why it wasn't worth it?"

"He just said he was *cleaning shit* around the place. He was proud about being a mechanic. I think he thought the other work was beneath him and that the owner was too lazy to do it himself. He said the man should *get off his fat ass* and make something of the place. That's what he said."

"What about driving trucks for someone? Or helping to haul some barrels?" Tim asked. "Did he ever mention anything like that?"

"No, but a few months ago, he took me to a fancy restaurant, the Pine Lodge. He said he'd made some extra money. I asked if he'd received a bonus at work. He said, *Something like that.*"

"Do you remember when that was?" Tim asked.

Her face softened. "It was near Memorial Day, maybe the weekend before. We talked—he talked—about saving his money from then on. He wanted to have a place for both of us and maybe a June wedding in a year." She sniffed. "That was Eli. He was a sweet guy. Even then, I knew it was too good to be true."

Not for Eli. His friends had all said he had plans and was working to have his own place as soon as possible.

"Ginny, when did you last see Eli?" he asked.

"I-I hadn't seen him since the Sunday before. He called me late on Thursday night"—she hesitated. "He said he couldn't see me that weekend. He had to go away for a while and he didn't know for how long. He sounded angry but frightened too. But he wouldn't tell me what it was about. Just that it was too dangerous for us to be together for now." She picked at a thread in one of the large gashes across each knee of her jeans. "He said he'd text on Friday, but he never did. I was mad, you know? I thought he was breaking up. But then I remembered how scared he'd sounded. I tried to call him and left messages on Friday and Saturday, but he never answered."

They'd seen calls from The Last Rodeo bar on Eli's phone record. "Did you call him from work?"

"Yeah. We're not allowed to use our cell phones while we're working. I pretended to be answering the phone."

Eli had died Friday, according to the coroner.

"Ginny, is there anything else Eli said about who he was worried about or anyone he'd been arguing with?" The argument Jana had witnessed had occurred Thursday after dark. Friday Eli had called in sick and apparently holed up in the deer stand, where his killer had found him.

She gazed up at him. "Only his father. He wanted money, and Eli said he wasn't going to help him get it. Not anymore. He said his dad was going to get him in trouble, and he didn't want to be part of it. I know his parents are divorced. Mine are, too, and I thought he meant his dad was going to get him in trouble with his mom."

Tim nodded, but he doubted Eli had gone into hiding to avoid his father. The man had seemed to be all bluster—an alcoholic and possible bully who was barely holding his life together, but not a threat to his son's life.

"One more question for you," he said, "and this one's important. Was Eli selling drugs or involved with people who were?"

Her jaw dropped. "No! He used to smoke weed, but he'd given that up. He promised me."

"But did he tell you about using drugs other than weed? Pills, for example?"

"No! Eli detested that stuff. I know I probably sound like a kid who believes in fairies and Santa Claus, but I've seen plenty of people on drugs. I know who's lying to me too. I told him I didn't want that shit in my life. He didn't like how some of his friends smoked all the time. He wanted to be more than a stoner. He said he'd tried E once and didn't like it. Eli wouldn't use the hard stuff."

But would he sell it to make money to achieve what he wanted? He wouldn't be the first *good* person who let the ends justify the means.

"Did he ever mention knowing anyone making or dealing drugs?"

Her head shake was slower as she considered the question. "No."

When she didn't add anything, Tim pulled a business card from his billfold and handed it to her. "Thanks for your time, Ginny. If you think of anything else about what was going on in Eli's life that might help us, please give me a call."

"What do you think?" he asked Francine as they were buckling into their car seats for the return trip to Crossroads.

She cocked her head. "She's more street smart than she looks. She works in a bar that serves a rougher crowd than most around here. But I think she's scared too."

"The suitcase."

"Yes, and her hesitation in answering your last question about him knowing dealers or manufacturers."

"You're right about her being tougher than she looks, at least mentally tougher. It sounds as if Eli was protective of her. He may not have shared everything he was doing, like turning down work from whoever was in that truck Thursday night in front of his house."

"He confided about his father pressuring him for money."

"His father claims he was home Thursday night, so I don't think it was him arguing about a job. And he was texting Eli, according to his mother, although he could have done that from anywhere." Then again, maybe he'd misjudged Derek's criminal capability. "He lied to us about Eli wanting money from him. I think we should pay him another visit."

Chapter Twenty-Five

DEREK CARSON'S RESIDENCE in Lake Village was several blocks back from Lake Chicot, the C-shaped body of water that had probably once been part of the nearby Mississippi River. Unlike the lake, the shotgun house was neither grand or scenic: gray paint curled from the wood planks, and the small yard featured mostly dead grass and shrubs. A tricycle and a small bike had been left outside. Fortunately, they were plastic and not in danger of rusting in the August sun and rain.

The woman who answered the door had aggressively dyed red hair and carried a toddler on her hip.

"Hello again," Francine said with a smile. "This is Chief Birch. Is Derek in?"

Without answering, the woman turned around and yelled for her husband. The child, a girl, didn't even flinch at her loud call. She reached out toward Francine, who touched one of her hands and said, "Hello, honey." Her mother held the door open and invited them to come in, causing them to break contact.

Tim's guess about the house had been correct. The odor was a toxic combination of dirty diaper and urine stench, burned toast, and mildew. The loose and missing shingles on the roof no doubt explained the cause of the latter. No wonder the child had reached out to his sergeant.

Derek didn't rise from his recliner to great them. Beer in hand, he pointed to the sofa where a preschooler sat staring at the television. Her father snapped it off and told her to go see her mother. The girl's eyes widened at the sight of visitors, and then she scampered away.

"How are you today, Mr. Carson?" Tim asked, settling next to Francine on the sofa.

"How do you think? I just buried my only son." He gave a slight burp. "What's this about, you coming all the way here? Do you know who killed my boy?"

"Not yet," Tim replied calmly, "but we have some more questions for you. The first one is, why did you lie about Eli asking you for money when it was you asking him?"

He snorted. "He did ask me for money, a while back."

"But not the night before he died. You were texting him that night about it." Let him think they had the content of Eli's messages.

"So I asked him for a loan. I've got a family to support, and he owed me."

"What do you mean he owed you?"

"I'm his father. Worked all of his life to provide for him. Then when he finished school, I got him a job, didn't I?"

"At Doncaster Motors?"

"That's right. I put in a good word for him with Newt. Steered him to Friendly's, too, when he asked for money to get an apartment. I looked after my boy."

"Sounds like you have some good connections in Crossroads. Is Larry Mason a friend of yours?"

"How do you think I got Eli that job? I've known Larry

and Newt since we were in school. Played football together. The team went to state our senior year."

Tim nodded. Maybe he would have recognized Derek in the team picture on the wall in the lobby of Friendly's Motel if he'd looked closer and allowed for nearly thirty years of unhealthy eating and drinking.

"Where were you the Thursday evening before Eli died?"

His head jerked up. "What's this about?"

"Mr. Carson, just answer the question. I don't want to hear any more lies, either."

The recliner folded up, depositing Derek's feet on the faded carpet. "I told you—I was here, at home. You just talked about how I was texting Eli. Did Charly say I was there? Is that where this is coming from?"

"No, sir, but you could have been texting from outside her house Thursday night after you and Eli argued by your truck. From what you've admitted, you asked him for money. You said he owed you."

His face flushed an ugly red but then he laughed. "You think I drove to Crossroads in my truck? At night? Well, good luck proving that. My truck's sitting out in the back like the worthless piece of junk it is. Why do you think I asked my boy for money? That heap quit running three weeks ago. You can check with Rusty down at Anders Petroleum at the 82 intersection. He told me the engine was shot. I might as well shoot the truck and be done with it for the price he wanted to fix it. We had to borrow Rayellen's daddy's car to go to the funeral on Saturday."

Odd that he hadn't asked Eli to fix it, but if the truck's condition was as bad as it sounded, maybe his son had refused. "Mind if we have a look at it?"

"Can't stop you, can I? Let me know if you want to buy it."

As they saw themselves out the front door, Derek yelled, "Hey, Ray—bring me another beer!"

"Charming," Francine muttered as he closed the door behind them.

"Have a little sympathy. He's a man on *benevolence leave*." Or that's what the hardware store owner had told them when they'd looked for him at work.

"Yeah, right," Francine said.

The rusting tan Chevy pickup with bald tires looked right at home on the neglected property. The dust and pine needles covering the hood and roof suggested it hadn't been driven recently. Even so, they stopped to see Rusty on their way out of town.

"He still owes me for the tow," the grizzled mechanic said after confirming the date of his examination of the vehicle. "Hell will probably freeze over before I see a dime."

THE HARDY FARM didn't have an address that Jack's phone's GPS recognized, so he had to go old school and use a map. He knew where it was in relation to Willow Lake, but to actually drive up to the farmhouse, he had to go farther east on the highway past Jones Camp Road to the paved lane called Whistler's Way. Probably an interesting story in that name, but it would have to wait for another day. The street the Hardys lived on, Bluegill Road, wasn't paved and there was no sign. No wonder his GPS hadn't found it.

Today he was following up on Marjorie Wilkie's story of Richard Hardy shooting down the surveyor's drone when it had intruded onto his property. Man versus machine? More specifically, man protecting privacy in the age of aerial and other camera intrusion. Heck, it had been an issue decades ago when long-range camera lenses became popular with the paparazzi chasing celebrities. Now everyone carried a camera and for less than a hundred dollars could purchase small flying machines with cameras to do their own aerial shots. It was surprising there weren't more reports of drones hovering outside bedroom windows or being used to spy on neighbors or competitors.

He'd posted a small story about the drone shooting online after verifying it through a copy of the police report. He'd added a quote from the drone owner, Aaron Reese, who'd called the loss of his equipment *an expensive stunt.* Reese had also threatened to sue everyone involved, but Jack had left that tirade out of his article. At that point, it was just a threat. Still was, as far as he knew.

The self-confessed shooter, Richard Hardy, hadn't responded to his calls. Readers, however, had mostly sympathized with the farmer and his right to privacy. A few realized the drone may have accidentally ventured across the property line. The usual wits cracked jokes about enforcing a hunting season for drones or declaring them a protected species. *It's the military drones carrying bombs that are the real threat,* one apparent survivalist wrote.

Richard Hardy may not want to talk, in which case this trip out to the country might be for nothing. Usually, though, folks wanted to tell their side of the story. From what Hardy had told the police officer who'd investigated, he'd just been defending his property.

There weren't many driveways on the dead-end road branching off Whistler's Way to the Hardy place. Even if there had been, the large black mailbox had the house number painted in a bright white that would make it easy to find even for the visually impaired. Jack turned into the driveway and parked to the side. Behind the house, a barn with open doors was the backdrop to two men unloading hay bales. They looked up as he approached.

"Hey, Tuck. So this is how you stay in shape these days."

He smirked. "Why do I think you're not here to talk rodeo?"

"Because it's the off season and you're no longer competing?"

Tucker Hardy pointed his finger. "Got it in one."

"Actually, I'm here to speak to your father. Is he around?"

"He's busy," the other man said. He resembled Tuck enough to be his brother, although his features were pinched and lacked the spark of energy that made Tuck attractive.

They unloaded another bale onto a low trailer. Dust exploded when they dropped it.

"It's about the drone he shot down," Jack said, sneezing as he stepped back from the cloud of hay particles. "My readers have been really supportive of what he did."

They glanced over at him and paused a moment before tackling the next bale.

"They should be." The older man who emerged from the

barn carried two pitchforks. Jack feared for a moment that he was going to be warned off with at least one of them, but instead, the man laid them on the trailer.

"That's why I'm writing a follow-up piece. Drones are everywhere now taking pictures. We need to consider whether we need more rules or not. Are you Richard Hardy?"

"I am, but I don't want to be in another newspaper story. Folks have been calling here since that article you printed. It's a damned nuisance. Now you're here bothering me and my boys. I got nothing more to say about it."

"Can I just confirm what you told the police officer, that you shot it down because it was flying over your farm and you were defending your property?"

He glared at Jack. "That's exactly why I did it. This is private property. I didn't give anyone permission to take pictures of it. Serves him right getting a bullet through his damned camera. If they want to build a park next door, they need to keep on their side of the property line." He turned away.

"Did you have any trouble with the park folks on Saturday?"

Hardy stopped and then slowly turned around. He frowned at his sons, who looked at Jack.

"Saturday morning. The police, some volunteers from the fire department, and some folks from the tourism committee came out to search the property on foot."

"Search for what?" Tuck asked with a sneer.

Jack shrugged. "More deer stands, camps, vagrants…"

"Didn't see 'em," Richard Hardy said. "Like I said,

they're fine if they're not on my property."

"Is it true that you're planning on suing—"

"Got nothing more to say." And with that, Hardy turned around and headed back into the barn.

"How about you two? Do you think drones should be regulated more?"

"Hell, no," Tuck said. "Don't need more big government. But a man's got a right to defend his property. Don't he, RJ?"

"Sure do," his brother agreed. "We gotta get back to work."

"Yeah, have a nice day." Tuck grinned. He picked up the pitchforks and tossed one tines-up to his brother, who caught it easily with one hand. "Don't work too hard, Jack."

"Sure. Thanks."

Jack backed up a few steps before turning his back on them and walking to his car. At the end of their drive, he looked both ways, although the paved part of the road ended just beyond the Hardys' driveway. The dirt track that continued where the pavement left off led into the forest that he'd bet was on the park's land. Like so many in town, the Hardys and probably their few neighbors on this side had made use of the long-neglected property Merritt had inherited. Glancing back up toward the barn, Jack noticed Tuck watching him. He turned away from the temptation to follow that dirt road into the dark woods and pointed his car back toward Whistler's Way.

OFFICER HAL OVERMAN frowned at the report Tim had just handed him.

"Sure, it's just like I said here. I responded to the noise complaint at 12:07 Saturday night. Well, Sunday morning. Guess I should have put A.M. instead of P.M., huh, Chief? Is that what this is about?"

He wasn't that stupid or that innocent. "You said you spoke to the homeowner, Jerry Kindle. Was that inside the house?"

"Jer was outside. The party was around the pool in the back." He chuckled. "Well, most of it. Spotted a few couples in dark corners as I made my way around the yard."

"You said he agreed to turn the music down and you left. That's it?"

He spread his beefy hands. "He turned down the music. Problem solved."

"Yet less than an hour later, paramedics were called out to that address and hauled three teens to the hospital. One of them had to be flown to Little Rock and is barely hanging on. Did you see any drugs at this party? You did have a look around, didn't you?"

He squirmed and sat up a little straighter. "Well, sure, but it was a bunch of kids, maybe three dozen, on private property and the parents were there supervising."

And he obviously knew *Jer*, so why look for trouble? "You didn't see any pills or signs of drugs? Did you talk to the homeowner about that?"

"No. Jer likes a beer now and then, but I didn't see any booze."

Probably didn't look for it, either. Tim held out his hand for the report, which was returned to him. "Here's the problem. We know there are pills with fentanyl being sold to teens in the community. You had the perfect opportunity to educate the homeowner or even to spot a problem before it became a threat to life."

"Chief, if there were any drugs when I walked into the party, you know they were quickly hidden. Everyone knows I'm a cop."

Unfortunately. "Why didn't you respond when the 911 call came in about the overdoses?"

"I was on the other side of town. Raimey caught the call."

"Why'd you go to Willow Lake?" The call log had shown Hal heading to the park on the other side of town minutes after leaving the party.

"Following up on that shooter report you weren't happy with. Thought I might catch someone when they had their guard down. Didn't see anyone out there."

They stared at each other, Hal looking more bemused than defiant.

"Is that it, Chief? I should probably hit the road if we're finished here."

"Maintenance wants to check out your unit tonight. You can pick up another one at the garage."

Hal seemed genuinely surprised. "Again? They just serviced it a few weeks ago."

"Something about a part recall, I think," Tim said.

As soon as his officer left, he called the mechanic on duty to let him know Hal would soon be there and what he wanted done with the patrolman's unit that supposedly was having a recalled part replaced.

The mechanic chuckled. "You mean that engine intake valve recall? I'll take care of it, Chief. A little vacuuming wouldn't hurt that unit while I make sure we've already replaced that faulty valve a few months ago."

Chapter Twenty-Six

JANA WAS COMPILING a list of possible park features for her committee meeting Tuesday morning when Alyssa appeared at her office door. Glancing up, she smiled, expecting Deeann's assistant to offer help setting up the room.

"The mayor and the city attorney would like to meet with you in the mayor's office," Alyssa said.

"Now? Oh, uh, sure." She opened her desk drawer, intending to grab a notepad.

"You don't need to bring anything."

Alyssa's unsmiling face was beginning to alarm her.

After Jana stepped inside the mayor's office, Alyssa closed the door behind her, leaving her to face her boss and the attorney. Their somber expressions told her all she needed to know. She was about to be fired.

"Jana, please have a seat." Deeann nodded to the chair next to the attorney. "Connor here has been telling me that we may have more trouble than we thought with Mr. Hardy and Mr. Reese. Go ahead, Connor."

"In addition to a cease and desist order, Mr. Hardy has filed for damages against the city, and Mr. Reese has filed a suit against the city and Mr. Hardy. The attorneys they've hired...well, let's just say they know their business. They specialize in these kinds of actions. That doesn't mean they'll succeed, but we've got a fight on our hands."

"The amounts they're asking for are outrageous," Deeann said.

"That's normal in these kinds of filings," Connor said. "Start high and settle lower. That doesn't mean they'll win a dime, especially against the city. Unfortunately," he turned to Jana, "they've both also named you and the mayor as defendants."

Jana's throat was dry. "I-I have to hire an attorney?"

"No, Connor will represent us since we were performing our jobs," Deeann said.

"You have the right to hire your own attorney if you wish," Connor clarified.

Her gaze flew to Deeann. "But I haven't done anything!"

The silence that followed her protest offered no sympathy. Maybe if she had been able to apologize to the surveyor… But she'd stopped to check in on Nana Sue before heading to Hamblin after work yesterday, and her visit had been a disaster. Her grandmother had accused her of stealing her house and forcing her to move out. Jana's attempts to explain to her that none of that was true had resulted in a meltdown and sedation when Nana had tried to fight her and the nurse's aide who'd responded. Jana had stayed with her until she was convinced Nana was sleeping peacefully. When she'd finally left Golden Pines, she'd been too upset to drive to Hamblin.

"First, Connor is going to see if they'll dismiss the charges," Deeann said. "Local governments are immune from suits like these, aren't they?"

"That's correct, and from wrongdoing or negligence by

their employees."

"But all we did was hire a surveyor," Jana said.

"Exactly," the attorney said. "You didn't direct Mr. Reese to fly over the Hardys' property, did you?"

"No, never. You saw my email. I sent him a map of the area to be surveyed."

"Yes, and the emails you sent me should help."

"So, the case against us will be dismissed, right?"

"That's what I'm hoping, but I have to make both of you aware that lawsuits can play out in ways we don't anticipate. I don't intend to admit to any liability, but we may have to settle with either or both men to avoid the expense of a trial. As for the emotional damage Mr. Hardy is claiming, he's going to have to prove how he's suffered as a result of the shooting."

"I can give him a bullet," Jana muttered. "Seems like that's all he lost."

Deeann's lips seemed to twitch, but then she quickly looked down at the papers on her desk.

"Don't get involved," Connor said. "What should be happening is that the two men settle this matter between them and leave the city out of it." He turned to Deeann. "Hardy's attorney has indicated that he'd accept an apology from the mayor."

"What?" Deeann exclaimed. "That's ridiculous. Surveying that property was a reasonable step in planning a park. That's why I signed off on it! There was no intent to bother Mr. Hardy or anyone else nearby. This is the biggest crock of—"

"I know. Too many folks suing these days," Connor said.

"Reese is also demanding that Jana here be fired." He turned to her. "He claims you accused him of incompetence in front of witnesses, thereby damaging his reputation. The fact that there were witnesses to what you said… It's going to depend on whether the court believes he was incompetent, if it comes to a trial."

And there it was. She'd done it again—sabotaged herself by saying more than she should have, even if every word had been true. It wasn't fair, but when had life been fair? She'd always had to fight to make her way in this world, first without a mother, later without a husband. She caught Deeann watching her and raised her head defiantly.

"Thanks, Connor," Deeann said, rising. "I know you'll make this go away for us."

Her expression gave nothing away, but she had to be gloating. Only desperation had driven her to hire an old classmate she'd always disliked. Deeann would love to see her fall on her face in disgrace. Well, it wasn't going to happen. Not if Jana could help it. She wasn't going to beg for her job, either.

"There's one more thing," Connor said. "Mr. Reese says he's invoiced the city and expects full payment. He's arguing it wasn't his fault that he didn't complete the full aerial survey. He emailed the video to you, Jana. Did you receive it?"

"Yes, it arrived this morning, but I haven't had time to look at it." She'd been reluctant to open the email, wanting nothing more to do with the man. Communicating with him would mean she'd have to deliver that apology he didn't deserve.

"That's okay. Forward it to me so I have it for my records." He turned to the mayor. "I think we should go ahead and pay him. It shows good faith."

"Fine. If that's what you recommend, Connor, I'll tell accounting to make it a priority."

Jana left with the attorney, relieved that Deeann didn't ask her to stay for a private word. A summons later wouldn't surprise her, nor would a call from Golden Pines telling her they could no longer care for her grandmother. The only good news this morning had been a text from Clay Bailey telling her that he'd be able to make this morning's meeting.

"*Missed you this morning*," he'd added.

She wished she hadn't skipped her walk to arrive early at work.

Jana sighed as she checked the time. Her committee would be here in less than an hour. She wasn't going to give up on the park until they kicked her out the door. It wasn't just about doing her job or refusing to be beaten by that whiny surveyor or Deeann. She wanted to help build something that people would enjoy, maybe for generations. But it had become more than just a public park they were creating. Lawton Park, as it was to be named, would also have a memorial to Eli, who'd loved to go there and had died there. She wanted the park to be a special place for Charly and Maddy.

Alyssa soon returned to offer help on setting up the meeting room. Not that there was much to do, but the assistant produced glasses, a pitcher full of ice water, and notepads and pens. She also set up the computer and projector *just in case* it was needed.

"Does the mayor have a busy day today?" Jana asked.

"The usual—back-to-back meetings and a luncheon with business leaders. I don't think she's planning on sitting in on your committee meeting this morning."

"She's a busy woman," Jana said, relieved.

"Her campaign for reelection is keeping us all busy. Her opponent this time is really giving us a run for the money."

She'd forgotten about the upcoming election. It was another reason Deeann wouldn't want any publicity about lawsuits or a tourism director who couldn't be trusted to keep her opinions to herself. But, if Deeann was occupied all day, maybe there was time for Jana to think of a way to convince her that she deserved to keep her job.

Like apologizing to Reese? You told Deeann you'd do that.

Developing a fantastic plan for the park was more what she'd had in mind. Still, the lawsuits and the negative publicity they'd bring were more urgent than even the grant deadline.

You need to make it right.

She could almost see Nana Sue standing in front of the kitchen sink with her hand on her aproned hip. What had she done in high school to need to make right? Had it been an argument with Charly or another friend? Or the time she'd told Deeann her nose was permanently turned up so high because of the horse shit on her shoes? Not that the future mayor hadn't deserved it after saying the homecoming decorations looked cheap. Jana's wildly popular yet unconventional homecoming dance theme had beat out Deeann's more traditional one. It had been the only time Deeann had failed to come in first on anything, as far as Jana knew. She could turn up her nose all she wanted, but she'd lost, at least that time.

She hadn't apologized then, but she wasn't a stubborn, self-righteous kid any longer—or was she? She'd apologized right away to Charly and was trying her best to make that right. As for Reese, if she'd been in his shoes, she would have been angry and upset, too, especially if she knew the drone had been steered over private property where it shouldn't have been. He'd probably been upset at himself most of all. She'd have to convince him that she'd just been as shocked as he had at the shooting of his drone and like him, had perhaps overreacted. After all, the man was just trying to earn a living, just as she was.

But would that be enough?

She'd have to try. At least she'd had the satisfaction of seeing Deeann's indignant reaction when Conner had told her Hardy wanted an apology from her. Not that the mayor owed an apology any more than she did for the drone incident. Okay, even less than she did. Deeann hadn't even been there when it happened.

She finished arranging chairs. She'd dragged Deeann into this mess. The mayor had hired her and signed off on the drone survey. Her own passion for the park had been evident that first day. If the lawsuits and negative publicity hurt Deeann's chance for reelection, what would happen to the park? To this committee? To the townspeople who were looking forward to enjoying Lawton Park?

Make it right.

She had to. There was more at stake here than her job.

By ten o'clock, the full committee had arrived. Clay Bailey greeted her with a warm smile. Marjorie brought cinnamon muffins and lemon squares with paper plates and yellow napkins. Grace and Walt arrived together talking companionably. Cal was the last to arrive, striding in with his cell phone in hand. He nodded to her and clapped Walt on the back before taking the seat next to the older man.

Today they also had more members of the public in attendance. Several senior citizens—three women and a man—sat near the front in a group. She recognized the woman from the local chamber of commerce, who sat by herself. A few other people spread around the room. Surprisingly, Larry Mason didn't come this time.

Aware of her audience, Jana formally called the meeting to order. She gained confidence as they followed the agenda by approving the minutes of the last meeting. She recapped the property search on Saturday morning and thanked Walt and Clay for participating, as well as the police and fire department volunteers.

"There were no additional structures found," she said, "and we all had a nice walk through the woods. We're safe to proceed with finalizing our plans."

Before she could begin talking about the preliminary rough sketch she'd made incorporating their ideas, Grace asked, "What about the drone? Is the city going to pay that surveyor for his destroyed property?"

"I don't have an answer for you, Grace. The city attorney is handling Mr. Reese's complaint for damages."

Marjorie gasped. "He's suing the city? It wasn't our fault his drone was shot down."

Oh no. She shouldn't have mentioned the lawsuit. Trying to appear unconcerned, she glanced at their audience. They weren't exactly sitting on the edges of their seats, but it was a close call.

"Seems like he should sue Rich Hardy," Walt said. "He's the one who shot it down."

"I, uh, believe he is." Jana began to hand out copies of her sketches. "As I said, Mr. Douglas is handling the matter. Mayor Donahue wants us to proceed in developing a rough plan for the park as soon as possible, so that's what we're going to work on today."

There were mumblings from the audience. She hadn't included any time for the members of the public to speak. She'd have to ask Deeann what the protocol was. For now, she was just going to pretend they weren't here.

Jana began explaining the features she'd drawn on the map based on input from the committee members and the public response to their social media outreach. She could have emailed a copy to Alyssa to project on the screen, but she was glad she hadn't. With any luck, their visitors would soon become bored and leave. With any luck, the whole drone mess would go away too. Unfortunately, life had taught her that things usually got worse before they got better.

Chapter Twenty-Seven

"I JUST CHECKED and the boy who ODed in Little Rock is still hanging in there, Chief," Clint said, following him into his office after the morning briefing. "Maybe he'll talk about where and when they got those pills when he's awake. Haven't had a chance to ask, but how did it go yesterday with Hal?"

"He claimed he didn't see any drugs or even alcohol at the party. He knew the homeowner, who turned down the music. I verified that with the neighbor who called it in. He said it was quieter until the paramedics arrived."

"And Hal wasn't the closest unit to respond then."

"Convenient, huh? Anyhow, I reminded him about educating the public about the dangers of fentanyl every chance he has." The search of Overman's vehicle hadn't turned up anything suspicious, although it could have used more regular cleaning. A CSI tech had vacuumed the carpet and seats, but it didn't look promising. He didn't want to believe Hal had delivered the drugs to those teens, but someone had. So far, no one at the party claimed to know anything, including the two in the hospital in El Dorado.

"We need a lead from somewhere," Tim said. The CSI analysis of the drugs found in the Bissett raid he'd received yesterday had shown no trace of fentanyl. They were back to square one in locating the source of the deadly chemical additive.

"Eamon and Andrea are questioning all of the partygoers. Do you want Francine on that as well?"

"No, I need her on the murder. We haven't completely eliminated the father, although I can't see him doing it, but I want to talk to Larry Mason again. He employed Eli for odd jobs, and whoever our victim was talking to that night outside his house knew Eli had done a similar job before, a job he didn't want to do again. Derek Carson mentioned knowing Mason and going to school with him. I checked, and they're the same age. I don't think Mr. Mason told us the truth about Eli's work. Also, Francine's background check on him has turned up some bank deposits that interest me."

"And Hal?"

"I guess I'm giving him a long enough rope for now. We'll see what he does with it."

THE LOBBY OF Friendly's Motel was empty. The small television mounted on the wall was dark. The phone they heard ringing as they opened the glass door stopped abruptly when they entered.

"Hello? Mr. Mason?" Tim called. He looked for a bell on the narrow countertop but didn't see one.

"Doesn't he live here, Chief?" Francine asked.

"Yeah." There were two doors from the lobby to the interior of the motel. Guessing the one on the back wall might go to an office, he knocked on that one first. "Mr. Mason? It's Tim Birch." When there was no reply, he tried the handle, which turned and opened to a dark storeroom. Tim felt along the wall and flipped a light switch.

Small and filled with shelves and boxes, the closet wasn't a space where anyone would want to spend time. Most of the items stored looked old or seldom used, not the office or perhaps cleaning supplies he would have expected. Instead, there was a chipped ceramic Santa and boxes with other holidays written on the sides. A square computer circa 1990 and a collection of coffee machines that appeared equally old and ready for the dumpster suggested this was more of a final resting place. Dust tickled Tim's nose. He turned off the light and closed the door.

His gaze fell on the two football photos on the back wall just beyond the closet. "Have a look at this picture. Recognize anyone?"

Francine leaned over the countertop. She pointed to the first photo. "Is that Larry Mason?"

Tim tapped the second of five suited football players in the second group photo. "That's him." He tapped the man on the end next to Mason. "That's Derek Carson."

"Wow, I can see the resemblance to his son. The man in the middle looks a little familiar."

"Newt Doncaster. Owns Doncaster Motors, but he's also on the board of Southern Pines."

She nodded. "I've seen his picture in the paper."

Tim tapped the man on the far end.

"No," Francine said, shocked. "That's not Sarge, is it?"

"Looks like him. A younger version anyhow." It was

more the serious, half cynical expression Ed Rollins wore that helped Tim make the connection. He couldn't remember Sarge ever talking about his high school football *glory days*, as Larry Mason had described them.

"What about the man next to Doncaster?" Francine asked.

"I don't recognize him," Tim said. "Interesting group, though, isn't it? Take a photo of this one. I'll try door number two."

Tim again knocked and called. He thought he heard a noise on the other side, but then it was quiet. "Mr. Mason? Tim Birch, police. Please come out. We need to talk."

Again, no response. He tried the door knob, but it was locked. Francine moved to the side, her hand on the butt of her gun.

Tim tried again. "Mr. Mason, I just need to ask you another question. If you won't come out—"

"Okay, I'm coming," a female voice called.

The lock turned and the door was jerked open, revealing an angry woman with dark Asian eyes glaring at him. She had dyed red hair that hung like a tangled horse mane over her shoulders. Clutching the sides of her silky lime-green robe together, she glared up at him. "Larry's not here."

Beyond her was an empty, unmade king-sized bed. He couldn't see the bathroom that also had to be part of the space. He didn't know the layout of the motel, but it seemed odd to have what looked like a standard guest room opening to the lobby.

"Are you Mrs. Mason?"

"Fuck no." She clutched her robe closed with her right

hand and waved her left one toward his face. "Do you see a ring on this finger? Huh? Do you think I want a ring on this finger from Larry Mason or any other worthless male? Ha! Larry had better be bringing me coffee or he won't be seeing me again. That's for sure. What you want with him, anyway?"

"Ma'am, you've got me at a disadvantage here," Tim said. "Who are you?"

She put her hands on her hips. "Who are you, besides police who woke me up? Who's she? Is she your missus?"

Shaking her head, Francine held up her left hand, bare of rings and waggled her fingers.

"I'm Chief Tim Birch, Crossroads Police, and this is Sergeant Francine Compton. We need to talk to Mr. Mason about Eli Carson's murder. You were saying he might have gone out for coffee?"

"Fuck no. Not unless he grew a brain. I've been telling him for days to fix the coffeemaker or buy a new one. He doesn't do anything for me unless I tell him and then only half the time."

"Ma'am, what's your name?" Francine asked.

"Vivian Amber. I know nothing about this Eli Carson's murder. He was a nice boy. Used to work around here sometimes, but that's all I know."

Francine glanced at him, and he nodded for her to continue questioning the woman. "When did you last see Eli?"

"Eli? Not for months. Larry couldn't pay him." She sniffed. "Larry's a cheapskate. That boy was too smart to work for nothing."

"Have you seen Larry this morning?" Tim asked.

"No, I sleep late. He gets up earlier. He knows not to make noise." Something flickered in her face, and her gaze slid from his.

"Did you see Larry last night before you went to bed?"

"I come in late from work. He's sometimes...out."

"Where do you—"

Tim interrupted his officer. "Out where?"

She shrugged. "Out with friends? He do his thing, I do mine."

"When did you come back to the motel last night?"

"About midnight." She glanced at Francine. "I work at The Last Rodeo in Bastrop. It closes at eleven, but we have to clean up, sometimes have a nightcap." She scowled. "I don't drive drunk, if that's what you're thinking."

"What does Mason drive?" Tim asked Francine.

"He drives a piece of shit—" Vivian stopped and pointed at the front door and the older Charger parked just outside. "That's his car." She sounded surprised. Barefoot, she brushed by Francine and pushed open the front door. "He has a truck, too, that belonged to his daddy. It's usually parked—" She froze.

Tim reached around her and pushed the door open farther. "Is that his truck?" The faded blue pickup was parked in the first space in front of the wing of rooms extending out beyond the lobby. There were only three other vehicles parked in the lot.

Vivian recovered. "He's around here somewhere," she mumbled. Turning around, she stalked back toward the bedroom. Francine blocked her way.

"Ma'am, we need your help in finding him. Is there another room he uses or someplace he might be working on the grounds?"

Vivian scoffed. "Work? He doesn't work." Despite her harsh words, her eyes showed fear.

"Where should we start looking for him?" Tim asked.

She hesitated. "Room six. He use that for business sometimes."

He wasn't going to question her now on what business Larry was into beyond being an innkeeper. "Do you have a key, ma'am?"

Friendly's hadn't updated to computerized card swipes to open doors. Instead, Tim used the key after there was no response to his knock. Larry Mason lay spreadeagle on his back on top of the second queen-sized bed. His eyes were open and his jaw was slack. He was fully dressed, including black athletic shoes. A lime-green silky tie belt was wrapped around his neck.

Vivian pushed past Tim and screamed.

Chapter Twenty-Eight

JACK SWALLOWED THE bile that threatened to bring up the toast he'd had for breakfast as he followed Eulie Daniels through the trees encircling Crawfish Pond. His feet were heavy weights as he trudged over the pine needles, and sweat drenched his shirt. The stench alone was enough to make him sick. The bandanna his host had thoughtfully provided to wear over his mouth and nose was doing little to mitigate the smell. Worse, it brought back a sense of confinement.

The steady crunching of Eulie's feet on twigs and pine needles stopped. They had reached the clearing, the same spot where two men—one of them Eli Carson—had emptied barrels of liquid into the chemical stew. The same spot where days later he'd nearly lost his life. He pulled up his mask and vomited into the underbrush.

"Sorry," he said to his guide when he'd finished. He spit to try to clear his mouth and then wiped his lips with the back of his hand.

Eulie waited silently. He'd called this morning with the tip that had led them here.

Determined to see this through, Jack straightened and stepped into the clearing to look at the site of his nightmares.

"There it is," Eulie said.

No additional explanation was needed. Someone had

driven a white box truck into the oily water. More than likely, someone had *caused* the vehicle to go into the pond, probably hoping it would disappear beneath the surface. Unfortunately for them, only the front part of the cab was submerged. Or had they meant to leave it visible—pointing up like a middle finger to announce that they weren't going to stop using what had once been a fishing pond as their own personal junkyard?

"Well, hell," Jack said surveying it.

"Is that the truck you and Albert saw?"

"See that dent along the side? I think it's the same one." It had been dark on that visit, but moonlight had provided enough of a glow to notice the defect. He pulled out his cell and snapped a couple of pictures. "Maybe the police can pull it out and look for prints."

Eulie made a noise that sounded like a snort. "Hope they get hazard pay."

Jack's skin crawled as if he could feel the chemicals in the water burning through it. "You think there's anything in it?" Or anyone. With the front end tilted down into the pond, the cab was inaccessible, although the visible part appeared unoccupied. However, the rear wheels rested higher, barely touching the edge of the water. The door latch was within reach.

"Don't know until you look."

He didn't want to look, didn't want to spend another second by this cesspool. And there was the risk to consider, like the truck sliding farther into the pond dragging him in with it. Could even be the same yahoo who'd thrown a Molotov cocktail into the newspaper office and burned it down had planned another surprise for him, like a booby-trapped door. No, he was probably being paranoid. It was unlikely the same person had dumped this truck here, but his mind was warning him with worst-case scenarios. But what if someone were inside unable to get out? Would he ever be able to sleep again if he didn't find out?

As Eulie had said, *don't know until you look.*

The tailgate latch was stubborn, or maybe it was the awkward angle of his access to it as he reached up. He tried not to put much weight against the back of the truck in fear of it rolling forward, but it seemed stuck in place. Jack shifted his stance and gave it his best effort, but nothing happened. To his relief, Eulie's large hands joined his, and his superior strength did the trick. With a screech, the latch released and they were able to roll the door up just enough to see inside.

The cargo hold was empty. The relief of not finding anyone inside was soon replaced by frustration as he noticed the spotless state of the floor and walls.

"What do you want to bet someone's wiped down this truck? Not much chance for fingerprints, I'm guessing." Not that he'd held out much hope. The men dumping that night had worn gloves. Probably whoever had done this had, too, and they'd also apparently taken more precautions by sanitizing the truck.

"Police use DNA more than fingerprints these days," Eulie said, surprising him. "You ready to go back?"

"Yeah, let's close this up and get out of here." But as they pulled the heavy door closed, the truck began to roll. Jack let go more slowly than Eulie. With his weight still moving forward, he stumbled. To his horror, he began falling face first toward the toxic water.

"No!" he cried just as strong hands grabbed him around the waist, tugging him to safety.

"DESPITE THE TIE around his neck, it doesn't look like strangulation," Dr. Bailey told Tim. The county medical examiner, Dr. Nagashi, had taken his wife to the hospital in El Dorado for an emergency appendectomy. He would perform the autopsy, but Doc Bailey was on call tonight to certify any deaths in Crossroads in his absence.

Doc lifted Larry Mason's eyelid with his gloved fingers. "There's no petechiae, er, red spots in the eyes or on the face, and no swelling. The mark on the neck seems to have been caused after death."

"Can you tell when he died?"

"Rigor mortis has passed, so more than eight hours, I'd say, if he's been here all that time. Probably less than twenty-four."

Tim nodded. Vivian Amber—and he didn't believe that was her legal name—claimed she'd last seen Larry yesterday afternoon around three thirty when she'd left for work. Francine was checking with her employer. Doc had just eliminated Tim's first theory involving kinky sex resulting in accidental death. That didn't eliminate Vivian: The tie around the victim's neck matched her robe. Her surprise when she'd recognized it could have been an act, but why would she leave it with the dead man and go back to the other room allegedly to sleep?

"So he could have died of natural causes, like a heart attack?"

Doc cocked an eyebrow. "You'll have to wait for an autopsy for cause of death. Given his age and general physical condition, I can't rule out a heart attack."

"But?"

Doc again gently pulled an eyelid open. "See his pupils?" He then lifted the dead man's hand. "His lips and nails are blue. Could be evidence of opioid poisoning." He dropped the hand and straightened. "That's not to say he didn't have a heart attack as well."

Tim glanced at the nightstand next to the bed that contained an empty glass. He hadn't seen any drugs.

"I didn't find any evidence of recent injections," Doc said. "That glass might be important."

"CSI is on their way. I'll tell them what you said about the possible overdose." A woman had ODed here last week on fentanyl. Tim looked again in the bathroom, where two other matching glasses were still wrapped in paper. He made a quick check of the visible surfaces in the main room. No sign of drugs and no other glasses. If Vivian had been with their victim, why weren't there two glasses by the bed?

He had a new list of questions to ask Miss Vivian Amber—or whatever her real name was.

Just then his phone rang.

"Chief, Jack Hutchinson just called," Marva said as if the man were a sewer rat she had to deal with. "He found that truck used for dumping into Crawfish Pond. Says it's mostly in the water, like someone tried to dump it. I told him it didn't sound like an emergency to me, but he wanted you to know."

Tim swallowed his frustration at the reporter. An abandoned truck wasn't his priority at the moment but this one was connected to Eli Carson.

"Is he still out there?"

"Yes. Says he'll wait at Eulie Daniel's place out there if you're coming."

"I can't come now. See if Clint's available to check it out. CSI's on their way here. I'll see what I can do to have them look at it. And Marva, please call him back and tell him to wait there."

"Probably has Jack Huddleston's fingerprints all over it," Marla mumbled before she hung up without acknowledging his request.

He texted Clint to make sure the truck was processed for fingerprints and DNA. They still needed to identify the driver and whoever had hired Eli. Unfortunately, if it were Larry Mason, they'd reached another dead end.

THE COMMITTEE MEETING was productive, although the features they'd agreed on after the first hour was what anyone would expect to find at a park. If she was going to have a chance at keeping her job, she needed to come up with something new, impressive. Also, they needed a special attraction to lure tourists to Crossroads and encourage them to spend time there. Maybe the beauty of Willow Lake would be enough, but she wanted to push their vision further.

So far, everyone had agreed on a playground, several covered picnic areas, walking paths that wouldn't involve much tree removal, and restrooms with a couple of outdoor showers. Disagreement arose in their second hour on the use of the lake. The women had imagined it being used for swimming only. Walt and Cal wanted a boat launch.

"Folks around here love to fish. More will come use the park if we encourage fishing," Walt said.

"There are plenty of places around here to fish," Grace argued. "Nothing against it, but who wants noisy motorboats on that beautiful lake? No one will want to swim, especially if the lake becomes polluted by boat fuel and oil."

Jana winced. Walt was right but so was Grace. Could they have fishing without risking contaminating the lake?

"What about a fishing pier?" she suggested. "Bring a chair, cast a line, but no noisy motors?"

"The best fishing is out more in the middle," Walt said. When everyone turned to look at him, he mumbled, "That's true of most lakes."

Cal snapped his fingers. "What we need is to make this park unique. Our job is to attract more tourists to the area, correct? What if we made Willow Lake a waterskiing venue? We could attract ski competitions and have our own teams. Folks would come to see the skiers practice. We could build a small bleacher stand on the shore farther down from the swimming area."

A moment of surprised silence followed his suggestion. Jana sat up straighter.

"It would be a unique feature," Marjorie said slowly.

"My grandchildren love to water ski. My son has a house on the river. I don't know how they ski with the cottonmouths and who knows what else is in that muddy water. Lake skiing would be much nicer."

"You'd still have outboard motors on the lake," Grace pointed out.

"But only during the summer for skiing." Cal grinned sheepishly. "I know, that's also when the swimming would take place."

Walt chuckled. "Maybe we need a winter sport for the park."

"Deer hunting?" Grace said drily.

"Okay," Jana said. Their time was almost up, but she was reluctant to stop. "We've accomplished a lot today. I'd like to suggest we consider Cal's idea and the use of the lake for boats and fishing."

"And hunting," Walt suggested. "Might as well consider using it year-round."

"Hunting, too, then is on the table. I'll update Clay so he can give us his thoughts." The doctor had been called out soon after the discussion of the plan had begun. "Thank you for coming," she said to her committee and then nodded to the audience. "Please let me know if you can meet again Thursday morning so we can finalize the first draft of our plan."

"Jana, one more question, if you don't mind," Marjorie said. "I thought we were going to consider a second entrance to the park from the other side, where Bluegill dead ends."

"We were considering that," Grace said peering at Marjorie over the top of her reading glasses, "*before*."

Jana glanced nervously at the audience. Jack Huddleston hadn't shown up today, although she didn't know if any of the others were stringers for his paper or bloggers who might post something online.

"You could show it as a future possibility by drawing it with a dotted line and indicating what it is in a key," Cal suggested. The others nodded their approval.

"It makes sense to consider access on that side for folks coming from the north or east," Walt added. "Far as I know, it's not a private road."

"I'll check that out, Walt. Good suggestion, Cal, as long as it is a public road."

When there were no more questions, she ended the meeting. Gathering up her notes, she approached Cal, who was snagging an extra muffin to take with him. "Hey, Cal, didn't you say you're a friend of Merritt Quinn? I was wondering what her ideas were for the park."

He took a napkin and opened it to bundle his muffin. "Er, that's a good question. She'd heard locals used the lake over the years for swimming and picnics. It was a well-kept secret they didn't share with outsiders. I never heard her mention anything else she'd like to see, other than a place for families to enjoy. If you want, I could ask her." He grinned. "Maybe I should see what she thinks about waterskiing on the lake."

"Would you be willing to give me her number? I'd like to talk to her. I know she's donated the land to the city, but I'd still like to know if we're on the right track in creating the kind of park she envisioned being named after her great-aunt." Maybe Merritt's support if she liked what the committee was planning could help Jana keep her job. Besides, she was genuinely curious to know what the young woman's vision had been when she'd given the land to the community for a park.

Now Cal laughed. "Merritt probably won't like the idea of hunting. Maybe no boats, either. She's a professor of environmental science. I think she might side with Grace on the potential pollution of gas engines."

"But you don't agree?" Cal had been adamant about preserving as many of the trees as possible. She'd assumed he was in favor of protecting the environment.

"I'm more pragmatic, and besides, the boat engine manufacturers are catching up to the auto industry in cutting down on air pollution. Electric boats are becoming more popular, and there are hybrid models. Eventually, they'll become cheaper."

"Maybe we only allow watercraft that doesn't pollute," Jana said, excited about the idea. Did any other park in the country have that restriction? They could be the first to take the next step in being environmentally sensitive. Theirs could be the park of the future.

Cal wasn't convinced. "I doubt that there are many electric models sold around here. Not yet, anyway."

"Maybe not, but there are rowboats, canoes, sailboats, or even those paddleboats you can rent at some lakes. Not that they'd be good for fishing. And if we only allow electric motorboats, we'd be sending a message that we want to keep Willow Lake pristine for future generations to enjoy."

His smile widened. "I'll send you Merritt's number. I think you're going to hit it off."

When she returned to her office, Jana checked her phone, which she'd silenced for the meeting. She winced when she saw the voicemail waiting from the director of Golden Pines. The message was brief: "Jana, could you please call me? Your grandmother has had a stroke."

Chapter Twenty-Nine

NANA SUE HAD been taken to a hospital in El Dorado, about an hour's drive from Crossroads. She was still in the emergency room. The young doctor with dark circles under his eyes led her to a small waiting room that was probably used for meetings with family members about their critically ill relatives.

"Your grandmother is resting comfortably," he assured her in a low voice that sounded too calm to be reassuring. "She's breathing on her own, but given her age and the likelihood of another stroke, I'd encourage you to consider whether you want us to take any extraordinary measures to keep her alive should her condition worsen."

Jana's brain felt numb. The walls of the small room closed in on her, although she'd never been claustrophobic. "Can I see her?"

"Of course, but I wanted to talk to you first. Your grandmother is ninety-four, I believe?"

"Yes, but she's always been healthy."

"I understand she has Alzheimer's."

Of course. The doctor was right: Nana hadn't been healthy. She'd been slipping toward this moment for the last few years, if not longer.

Jana nodded. "That's why she was in the nursing home. I

know, I mean I've been expecting something more might happen. I guess I'm not as ready as I thought to lose her."

He looked sympathetic, but surely he was too young to have personally suffered the loss of someone close to him?

You lost your mother when you were fifteen.

Jana blinked back tears. "You're talking about a DNR, aren't you? Wh-what kind of care will you give her if I agree?"

"We'll give her fluids and medicine to help ease pain or relieve symptoms—*comfort care*, we call it. We won't resuscitate her if she goes into cardiac arrest or put her on a ventilator or take other measures to prolong her life. Given her age and general frailty, chest compressions or electric shocks to resuscitate her could cause more problems and leave her in a worse condition, even if she survived."

"Is she conscious?"

"No, but she's stable, although she shows indications of partial paralysis on her left side. If she does regain consciousness, she might not be able to speak. We're waiting for a room to be prepared for her. That's why she's in the ER for now."

Ninety-four. What would Nana Sue want? She thought of calling her father or Uncle Jasper, who had set her up to be his mother's medical surrogate when he no longer could travel due to his wife's illness and his own debilitating kidney disease now requiring dialysis. She was the one who was here now and had been trusted to make the right decision.

"I'll sign it."

Nana looked even older and more frail in the hospital bed than she had at the nursing home when Jana had first visited her at Golden Pines. As the doctor had warned her, the left side of Nana's face sagged, pulling down her eye and half of her mouth. Jana kissed her soft cheek.

"I'm here, Nana. You're not alone."

There was no response other than the beat of the heart monitor. Outside the curtained cubicle, life in the emergency room went on but seemed part of another world. All that mattered was Nana Sue's battle to live or die.

Jana pulled up a chair and enfolded her grandmother's hand in both of hers.

TIM YAWNED. HE should go home, have dinner with Adam and Audra. Or was it Becky's day to watch the boy? Come to think of it, Aunt Skeet had fussed about needing to spend time with his six-year-old. She'd moved to Wilmot when she'd remarried just before Adam was born, so it wasn't as convenient for her to take a shift. Her arthritis also bothered her at times. Audra, a nurse who still helped out at the clinic even though she'd supposedly retired, claimed that her middle sister would ache less if she was more active. Skeet had just winked and said her husband was making sure she had plenty of exercise.

"You'd think they were still newlyweds," Aunt Becky, the youngest sister, had commented with an eye roll when she'd told him about the conversation.

More power to them, if that was the case. His own marriage, much less the honeymoon glow, hadn't lasted six years before his wife had given him divorce papers.

His next yawn was interrupted by a knock on his door.

"The team's in the roll call room, Chief," Clint told him.

Eamon didn't look up from his laptop when Tim entered. Francine broke off her conversation with Andrea. Sarge was seated off to the side with his arms crossed on his chest. Tim rested his hip on the table in the front.

"Thanks for staying a little later. As you've heard, we've had another death. Larry Mason was found dead this morning at Friendly's Motel. Preliminary indications are that drugs may have played a role in his death. The coroner is out of town, so the autopsy won't be until next week."

"Eli Carson worked for Mason," he continued. "We also had a fentanyl OD at the motel last week. Given those *coincidences*"—he stressed the word as he didn't believe that's what they were—"I think we should consider this death possibly related to Carson's and to our drug investigation."

"Could be a coincidence," Sarge said, "if he was a user, like the hooker who ODed there."

"I understand you went to high school with him and played football. Were you two close?"

Sarge shrugged. "Not so close I'd know if he was using these days."

Tim nodded. He had no reason not to trust him. "In any case, we'll have to wait for the autopsy to confirm COD and whether fentanyl was involved. Meanwhile, we're holding the woman apparently living with him, Vivian Amber." He explained about the robe tie connection. "Francine?"

"Chief, her boss at The Last Rodeo confirmed she worked last night from four until they closed at eleven. He also confirmed she stayed later to clean, and they all left just after midnight."

"That's what she told us." For the benefit of the others, he added, "She claimed she returned to the motel and went to bed in the room she shared with Mason, which wasn't where he was found. She said she hadn't seen him since that afternoon when she'd left for work."

"Did they have sex, Chief, before she left?" Andrea asked, her hand half raised like a schoolgirl in class.

The others turned to look at her. Her face colored. "I was just thinking it might have been an accidental death and his girlfriend had thought he was asleep…" Her voice trailed off as lips twitched. If she'd been less new and male, they wouldn't have been so restrained about teasing her.

Tim kept a straight face. "It looked like a sexual encounter gone wrong, but she denies they had sex that afternoon." He didn't share Vivian's comments about Larry's ability to perform. "Doc Bailey didn't see the usual signs of strangulation but his pupils were pinpoints and his lips and nails were blue, which is common with opioid poisoning, as you know from our training."

He glanced at Sarge. "No evidence of injecting drugs or any sign of pills or powders in the room. Also, there was only one glass on the nightstand. Two others were wrapped for guests on a tray in the bathroom. According to the motel cleaner, there should have been four glasses and a water pitcher. It was missing. Francine, what about the other guests?"

"There was a family of four in town to visit relatives, a couple on their way to New Orleans, and a salesman. They didn't hear or see anything unusual, although both the couple and the salesman mentioned hearing a motorcycle. The couple couldn't tell if it was on the highway or not. They were saying good night to their granddaughter on the phone, and she asked what the noise was. The salesman assumed it was on the highway, although he heard it around ten thirty, after he'd turned off the television and gone to bed. That was it, other than they all complained that the rooms weren't very clean. I'm still waiting for a call back from the salesman's supervisor, Chief, but they all seem to be legit."

"And the cleaner?" Tim asked.

"She works independently, and the motel is her main gig. She worked for the original owners too. She had lots of complaints about Mason and her bad knees and back, but she denied knowing anything about him taking drugs. Said she wouldn't be surprised if Vivian Amber was bringing them in. She considers her a bad influence and called her a *ho*."

"Thanks, Francine. Eamon?"

"Larry Mason inherited the motel from his grandparents, Chester and Annmarie Friendly, who were the original owners. That was about ten years ago. Financially, the place doesn't seem to be making it. He hasn't paid his property taxes this year and only renewed his business license after several notices threatening to shut him down."

"No surprise there," Francine said. "The place is a dump."

"Yeah, but he seems to have another source of income, judging by some cash deposits into his checking account at irregular intervals." He shifted his gaze to Clint. "There was a deposit of two thousand in cash the day after the dumping Jack Huddleston witnessed at Crawfish Pond. There was another last week for two hundred."

"Could they be from motel business? Maybe he only takes cash."

"No, sir. He had a separate account for that and does take credit cards. The balance was nearly zero. Looks like he's averaged only a few customers per night this summer. More in June around rodeo time. There were transfers from his personal checking to the motel account after several of the bigger deposits in the past."

"Chief, CSI isn't very hopeful about prints on the box truck dumped at Crawfish Pond," Clint said, understating the disastrous loss of evidence Jack Huddleston had caused, "but what if Mason was the driver? That could explain the deposit in his account in May. Eli was working for him then and looking for extra cash. Makes sense that they might have done the job together."

"And now they're both dead," Francine said. "Someone is trying to silence them?"

"Why not kill Mason first?" Tim asked. "That would have scared Eli to keep silent. Besides, if Mason was the driver, he probably knew who they were working for."

"And who killed Eli," Eamon said. "Maybe he tried to blackmail the killer for money."

"Or maybe he killed Eli and was a loose end?" Francine guessed.

"Or it has something to do with the drugs," Clint said. "Any link between Mason and the Bissett brothers?"

Tim answered. "That's more bad news. There was no

trace of fentanyl on the Bissetts' property and no evidence they were making the blue pills. None in the Mexicans' truck, either. Turns out they're weed growers from over by Texarkana who've been selling their product to the brothers for years. If they're connected to a cartel in Mexico, the feds aren't aware of it."

He rubbed his neck. "It's getting late. Let's go home and regroup tomorrow. Good discussion. All of your theories are still on the table, but we're missing something here. Someone out there is still making those fentanyl pills, and I want to find 'em. Have a good night."

"Chief," Eamon said closing his laptop as the others filed out the door. "There's something I need to talk to you about."

Tim's fear that he was about to be told he was losing another officer must have shown on his face.

"It's not about me, Chief," Eamon said. "Didn't mean to give you a heart attack."

Clint hesitated at the door, but Tim shook his head at his inquiring look. "We're covered for the night shift?" he asked his deputy chief.

"All set." He named the patrol and duty officers—all three of them.

"Fine. Go home, Clint," Tim said.

After the door closed, Eamon dropped his bombshell. "That research I've been doing today on Larry Mason?"

"Yeah?"

"Well, I was curious why his mother or a sibling didn't inherit the motel, so I did some research on the family line. Turns out Larry's mother died in a car accident when he was young. There was another daughter, who, according to their will, had no interest in running the motel. They left her money. I thought we might want to talk to her or notify her of Larry's death, so I tracked her down. Turns out she married a man named Cole Overman. They had three children, and the oldest was a son, Harold."

"Hal," Tim said. "Well, now."

"Hal and Larry are first cousins."

"Lots of folks are related to each other in this town. It could just be a coincidence."

But Eamon's skeptical look mirrored Tim's own thoughts. Was it also a coincidence that Hal had looked the other way when called out to scenes where drugs were being consumed? He'd had Hal pegged as lazy and incompetent, but was something else going on?

"Let's talk to Ms. Vivian tomorrow after she's had her rest. I want to know just how close these cousins were. Well done on the research, Eamon."

He grinned. "I thought I was going down a rabbit hole tracking that family. Easy to happen digging on the internet."

"Yeah. Let's not mention Hal's connection to the team just yet."

Eamon nodded. "Might not mean anything."

"That's right. The man's innocent until proven guilty." But the circumstantial evidence of him at least being complicit or covering up for someone was growing.

"Also, that picture from the motel that Francine took of the football players? The man you couldn't identify is Thomas Fielding."

Tim shook his head; the name wasn't familiar. "Is he still around town?"

"He's the manager of Forest Truck Traders, out on—"

"Yeah, I know it. Go talk to him. Ask him about his recent contact with our victim and also whether he ever employed Eli Carson in any capacity." He quickly explained about Jack Huddleston's interest in tracing the white box truck possibly sold by Southern Pines to the trucking company. "Tell him we're tracing one of the trucks possibly involved in a crime and need his sales records for that model for the last year, at least to start with."

After Eamon left, Tim stayed in the conference room alone. Forest Truck and its manager probably had no direct connection to the murders of Eli Carson or Larry Mason, but he'd told Jack he'd look into their truck sales. As angry as he was at the reporter, it made sense to follow up to find the owner of the mostly submerged truck who might have hired or even killed Eli.

They also had no proof that Larry Mason had any connection to Eli Carson other than as a former employer. Vivian had confirmed that Eli hadn't worked for him for several months. Not at the motel, anyhow. Possibly the autopsy would show that Mason had been killed by the same fentanyl that had been found in the pills in the deer stand, but Eli had been shot by his own rifle. Jack had identified Eli as one of the men dumping in Crawfish Pond, but they had no ID on the driver or any information on what had been dumped. Now they had the truck, or, more accurately, knew where it was, for all the good that would do them. Bottom line, they were no further along in connecting the dumping to Eli's or Mason's deaths. There was also no proof that the two killings were related, much less committed by the same person or persons.

At this point, he wasn't even sure Mason's death was murder. Most overdoses were accidental.

He interlaced his fingers behind his neck and arched his back. For now, Eli Carson's murder was his number one priority, at least until he had a new lead on the fentanyl. The young man had been scared of someone or something and gone to his deer stand to hide out. The day before he called in sick and left, he'd been pressured by his father for money and he'd had an argument that night about a job he was turning down with a man in a pickup outside his mother's house.

Tim jerked his hands free as he sat up. Larry Mason had an old truck. Jana Nance had said the engine made a peculiar noise. It would be easy enough to check. He gathered up the photos and files spread out on the table and headed out the door. Dinner would have to wait.

THE FRIENDLY INN'S VACANCY sign flickered in the dimming daylight as the sun made its way toward the horizon. Tim pulled up in front of the entrance. Inside the glass door, a woman untangled herself from a man behind the desk and hurried into the attached bedroom, a pink robe billowing behind her. Her long hair was dark brown or black. Apparently, the vacuum Vivian's absence had caused had quickly been filled by whoever was now minding the store.

"Chief," Hal Overman said rising behind the reception counter. His beefy face flushed. "Are you looking for me?"

"No, but I'm surprised to see you here. Aren't you working tonight?"

"Sarge gave me the night off. Had to take care of family business." He jerked his thumb toward the football photo behind him. "Larry was my cousin."

Hal didn't seem to need any commiseration, so Tim didn't offer any. "I'm surprised the motel is open."

"The family's keeping it running for now. Might as well have it pay for itself."

Good luck with that. "You have any customers tonight?"

"A couple of linemen from Entergy in Louisiana returning from Florida."

"Ah." Tim glanced at the photos on the wall. "Were you and Larry close?"

Hal turned around awkwardly in the narrow space to look at the pictures. "Larry was about ten years older, but yeah, we saw each other now and then."

"Did you play football too?"

"Nah. Didn't have enough speed. So, what can I help you with, Chief? I don't suppose you want a room?" His attempt at humor fell flat.

"No, there's something I want to check in Larry's truck. Do you have the keys?"

Hal knew he had a right to search the vehicle since it was part of a homicide. Standing to one side, he opened a drawer and rummaged around. "Haven't seen any vehicle keys. I can look for 'em for you."

"Appreciate that. By the way, if this gig is going to be

ongoing, you'll need to report it to HR."

He chuckled. "Give up writing reports? I'll have to think about it, Chief."

Outside, Tim walked to the vintage truck with plates registered to Larry Mason. He wasn't surprised that he was able to open the door. The keys were in the ignition.

Idiot. No matter how often he and his officers warned the public, too many folks still kept their vehicles unlocked. As for the keys dangling in the ignition like an invitation, maybe Mason was hoping someone would steal the heap and save him the cost of having it towed away.

The interior of the cab smelled like old cigarettes and fast food. The engine started right away.

Tim leaned back in the seat and listened. The sound reminded him of hiccups. The mechanical gasps happened every ten seconds or so.

The front door of the motel opened, and Hal's bulky form filled the entrance. Tim shut off the motor and climbed out.

"Found the keys," he said, holding them up. "Gonna need to tow this truck. I'll give you a receipt."

Hal didn't object.

Chapter Thirty

NANA SUE HADN'T moved or shown any signs of regaining consciousness. Not long after Jana had begun her vigil, orderlies had come to move her grandmother to a room on the third floor. They'd tucked her in, and a nurse had then checked her vitals. Hooked up to machines, Nana continued to be oblivious to her surroundings.

A meal had been delivered around five.

"You might as well eat it, honey," the kind woman told her after glancing at the unconscious woman on the bed.

Jana hadn't touched the food. Her irrational thought was that if she left it for her grandmother, Nana would awaken.

Time passed, and the meal grew cold. When her stomach growled, she took a packet of crackers from the tray and nibbled on them. Nana wouldn't mind if she ate the saltines. She and Grandpa had always been amused at how excited Jana had been as a child to receive crackers wrapped in pairs in clear plastic with tomato soup when they'd eaten out. She'd loved the oyster crackers best. What a surprise it had been to discover a different shape and to receive so many in one packet! Grandpa had handed over his crackers with a chuckle, but Nana Sue had dropped hers into the vegetable soup she'd ordered telling Jana she wasn't the only one who enjoyed them. Afterward, Nana had begun stocking them for her visits to Crossroads.

A gentle knock at the door dispelled the memory.

"How's she doing?" Charly whispered. She carried a vase of flowers that she set on the shelf beneath the wall-mounted television.

"She hasn't awakened," Jana said, unable to stop her voice from hitching.

Charly wrapped her arms around her and gave her a quick hug, which almost undid Jana.

"I'm sorry, hon. What do the doctors say?"

"That it's probably just a matter of time. She's partially paralyzed. She may not be able to talk if she does wake up. They don't know how severe it is."

"I'm guessing she knows you're here, and that's all you can do for her right now. Have you had anything to eat? If you want to grab a bite, I can stay with her."

Jana shook her head. "I'm fine. I don't want to leave her. Thanks for coming." She glanced around. "Did Maddy come with you?"

"No, she's with my sister. And of course I had to come. I love Nana Sue. I'm glad you texted me." She moved the other visitor chair next to Jana's and reached out to stroke Nana's arm.

"I'm glad you came. I thought I was ready for this but I don't think I am."

"Of course not. No one is."

The grief for Eli joined them in the room. Jana reached for Charly's hand and squeezed it. After a moment, her friend squeezed back.

"Do you remember the time Nana Sue took a broom to

those beetles attacking her pecan tree?" Charly said.

"She didn't usually swear, but she was sure mad that day. I'd forgotten about that." The pecan tree still stood in the front yard, although it didn't produce many nuts anymore.

They talked of old times and childhood memories involving Nana Sue, who'd always loved Charly. *That girl has a heart as big as Texas*, she'd say.

"I'd better head back to Crossroads," Charly said just before eight. "Maddy will be worrying. Let me know how she is tomorrow."

"I will."

She hesitated a moment, looking at Jana, and then left without another hug.

Jana reached for Nana's hand. It felt cool, not surprising in the air-conditioned room. The light blanket covered her, except for the hand she clasped. Was she warm enough? Nana hated to be cold.

The hospital was quiet, too quiet. It was just the two of them alone in the room as the second bed was empty. She thought of calling her daughters, but she didn't have the emotional stamina. Terrible to think that way. They would be concerned, more for her. Nana had always been old to them, and they didn't have the same bond with their great-grandmother as she had. Although they'd experienced loss and grief as teenagers when their father had died, this would be different. Nana was in her nineties; it was expected. *So sorry, Mom.*

Her father would be more sympathetic, but he, too, would regard Nana's death from a distance of time and space. He hadn't seen Nana Sue in decades, although he always told her to say hello for him. He had a new wife, a new family. Hadn't her oldest half brother and his wife just had a new baby? There had been talk about going to Wisconsin to spend time with the new grandchild. Why spoil that joy?

The one person she needed to call was Uncle Jasper. He couldn't travel, but he needed to know what was going on.

"Uncle Jasp? Nana's had a stroke," she said without preliminaries when he answered.

"Oh, darlin'," he replied with a sigh.

JANA WAS ASLEEP in her chair beside Nana's bed the next morning when a man called her name and touched her arm. She blinked, struggling to awaken from a troubled dream involving trying to escape from something or someone pursuing her through a forest of pine trees.

"Jana?" Clay Bailey's eyes were the gray of a cloudy sky.

She blinked and sat up. "What time is it?"

"Almost seven." He released her arm. "Sorry to wake you."

Nana. She straightened to look at her grandmother, but Clay's body blocked her view. A nurse and an orderly stood just outside the open door to the room watching her.

"Jana, your grandmother has passed," Clay said softly. "I'm sorry."

She gazed up at him and then at the still form under the white blanket. Clay stepped aside.

Nana still looked like she was asleep, but her skin color

grayed. All of her smile and worry lines had smoothed out. No more laughter, no more tears. She was gone.

Her grandmother's hand was cool to the touch. "Oh, Nana," she said, and then her tears started to fall.

JACK HUDDLESTON DIDN'T exactly ambush him, but the reporter was waiting in the lobby at the station the next morning when he arrived.

"I've got nothing for you, Jack," Tim said as he crossed the lobby and swiped his card.

Jack caught the door before it closed. "Look, I know I shouldn't have touched the truck. I was just—"

Tim turned to face him. "I don't care what reason you thought you had for tampering with evidence. I should arrest you right now. That truck's almost completely submerged. What do you expect we can do—send in divers? It's going to take a crane to bring it out, but I'm not risking anyone's life. They'll have to drain the pond first."

"Tim—"

"It's Chief Birch to you, and I have nothing more to say except that you need to leave or I will arrest you." He raised his hand to push the door closed.

"I was worried someone was inside."

That was enough to stop him.

"I had to know if someone was being…disposed of along with the truck." Jack's eyes were haunted behind his glasses.

"You told Clint it was empty."

"It was. I don't know about the cab, but there was nothing in the back. It looked like it had been scrubbed really well. I don't think there was any evidence left to discover." When Tim glowered at him, he quickly added, "Not that I don't regret causing it to go deeper into the water."

Tim shook his head. "You don't know what DNA traces may have been found. Also, a serial number would have helped us trace the truck. Thanks to you, we're not any closer to finding who's responsible for the dumping you're so concerned about or possibly Eli Carson's murder. Just go, Jack."

This time the reporter released his hand from the door. Closing it firmly behind him, Tim went to his office.

At his morning team meeting, he asked Clint to report on the truck at Crawfish Pond and what had happened to make it inaccessible, at least for now. In the interest of keeping last night's meeting short, he'd saved the sorry saga for today. There were a few head shakes and looks of disbelief from his officers as Clint provided a summary of events.

"Eulie Daniels observed dents on the back fender indicating another vehicle may had been used to push it into the water. Also, both men said the license plate had been removed."

"Did they take any pictures of the truck before it rolled into the pond?" Francine asked.

Clint shook his head. "Nope. Also, none of the other neighbors saw or heard anyone the night it was abandoned."

Tim told them what Jack had said about the cargo area possibly being cleaned. "I don't know if CSI would have gotten any evidence, but we're not going to get any now. Even if we could safely remove the truck from that chemical death pit, there probably isn't anything left to analyze. It would have been nice to have a serial number, though. Eamon, what did you find out from Forest Truck Traders?"

The detective didn't have to look at his notes. "The manager, Tom Fielding, confirmed that they'd been buying used box trucks from Southern Pines. Eli Carson never worked for them. He's pulling their customer list for the box trucks and should have it to me today."

"Good. It's a long shot, but maybe we can find a purchaser who might have hazardous materials stored in barrels."

"Yes, Chief."

"None of the locals closest to the pond have security cameras," Clint said, "not that they'd show anything through the trees anyway. I was thinking SP might have them, maybe one focused on that back road that goes in to the dump site. Thought I'd check that out this morning."

"Good idea, although I'd be surprised. It's worth checking out, though."

Things could be worse, Tim figured. At least the hospitalized fentanyl kids were still alive and there had been no overdoses overnight. But damn it, Jack Huddleston had really screwed up and cost them a possible lead on at least one of the murders. It was going to be a long time before he did the reporter any more favors.

NANA'S HOUSE SEEMED quieter and sadder than normal as if it, too, were mourning. Jana sat in the living room for a few minutes and then made herself shower and change clothes. She called Deeann's office and explained to Alyssa what had happened.

"I'll tell the mayor right away, and I'm so sorry for your loss. I'm sure she'll want you to take all the time you need."

Jana doubted it. Deeann would still want that plan by the end of the week, come hell or high water. Nana's death wasn't going to stop the clock counting down to their December deadline. "Just today for now, but thank you."

She toasted a slice of bread, deciding to layer it with peanut butter and strawberry jelly. She'd bought peanut butter, but couldn't find any jam or jelly in the refrigerator. She checked the cabinet Nana called her pantry. On the top shelf was a box of oyster crackers. Jana pulled it out. The expiration date was four years ago.

"Oh, Nana," she said aloud, blinking back the tears that stung her eyes. She threw the crackers into the trash and then checked the other boxes on the top shelf, most of which were also too old to keep.

Preparing to tackle the next shelf, she remembered her toast. The bread had popped up but was now cold. She set it to toast a little longer and managed to heat it without burning it. Sitting down to eat, she realized she was hungry. But the simple meal was satisfying enough; she didn't want any more.

She tried to focus on making a list of what needed to be done. She'd have to make arrangements with a funeral home, but it was too early to call anyone. At some point, she'd have to clean out Nana's house, but that seemed too final and too emotionally treacherous right now. Did she need to notify

Golden Pines? They'd probably already heard from the hospital or would soon if they checked on Nana's status. At some point, she'd have to settle with them and collect Nana's personal items, but that, too, could wait.

Jana clicked her pen closed. What was she going to do now? Staying in Crossroads without Nana seemed unthinkable, but where else would she go? She'd cut most of her ties with Indianapolis. She was still young enough to move and start over again, although it was unlikely Deeann would give her a good reference for quitting. Of course, if the mayor fired her, she wouldn't really have any choice but to move on.

Make it right.

But was it already too late?

She jumped up and went to the bathroom to comb her hair and add some makeup. She couldn't sit around the house all day. Maybe she could catch Aaron Reese before he left for whatever jobs he had today. She had to try, to show Deeann she'd kept her word. Not that Deeann would ever trust her.

You get what you give.

Her hand stopped, the comb halfway through a stroke. She didn't trust Deeann. How could she ever expect the mayor—her boss—to trust her if she wasn't reflecting back trust?

But why should I trust her? She—

Oddly, she couldn't think of one thing Deeann had done since she'd started this job that had given her a reason not to trust or respect her. Fear her maybe or her authority to fire her. True, Deeann hadn't been forthcoming at first about advertising the tourism director job several times or offering it to others first, but she hadn't rubbed that in. She also hadn't made any promises of support in the face of the lawsuits and the demands to fire Jana. Now that she thought about it, Deeann could have quietly dismissed her and perhaps settled the lawsuits more quickly by tossing the petitioners that bone. If she was worried about reelection, wouldn't that have been the obvious step to take?

It was all too much for Jana's tired brain to deal with. For now, she needed to keep her options open. More than that, she needed to keep her word that she'd apologize to Reese. She was tired of her conscience—and Nana Sue's voice in her head—nagging her.

JANA NANCE SOUNDED as if she were coming down with a cold when Tim called her after he'd returned to his office with a cup of coffee.

"I'm sorry to bother you. Is this a bad time?" Traffic sounds were in the background.

"I'm driving, but I can talk." She sniffed. "How can I help you, Tim?"

"I think we might have found the pickup truck you heard that night at your neighbor's."

"Oh?"

"I was wondering if you could come to the garage where we towed it and see if you recognize it."

There was a pause. "I-I'm not sure when I could come. My grandmother passed away last night."

Tim silently swore. “I’m sorry. And your grandmother was—”

“Sue—Susan Ffyfe.”

The name didn’t ring a bell, but his father, the town’s barber, probably knew who she was. “Again, I’m sorry. The truck can wait until you’re ready.”

“No,” she said sounding stronger. “I want to help you find Eli’s killer. I have some business to take care of in Hamblin, but I could probably come by later this morning.”

Relieved, he gave her directions to the garage they used to store larger items and vehicles related to crimes. “Tell Xavier to start the engine and let me know if it’s the one you heard. And thank you.”

Chapter Thirty-One

THE SURVEYOR'S BUSINESS address on Oak Street in Hamblin wasn't hard to find. The city seemed smaller than Crossroads but also had a Main Street and a downtown area of about two blocks. Oak was only one street over. The red brick office in a row of businesses had a sign out front and a truck she recognized parked nose into the curb.

The door was locked. Jana knocked, but there was no answer. She checked for any posting of hours, but there was none. Reese probably worked by appointment. She tried calling the phone number on the door, which was the same one she had. There was no answer.

Well, she'd tried. The drive had at least been a distraction.

She placed her hands on the glass and peered inside. A light glowed from what appeared to be a back room. Maybe he just hadn't heard her. Jana knocked again. "Mr. Reese? Are you there?"

There was only silence.

She could try the back. There must be another door—

"Ma'am, are you the one who called the police?"

Jana jumped. The Black officer studying her was bald with a thin mustache above a generous mouth.

"Didn't mean to scare you. We had a report of a possible

break-in here. The caller didn't leave a name. Said she didn't want to be involved."

"It wasn't me. I just arrived. I was hoping to catch Mr. Reese at his office, but he doesn't seem to be here. He didn't answer his phone, either."

He peered in the glass door. "Appears to be a light on in the back. I'll check the rear."

He walked to the end of the row of shops and disappeared around the corner.

A break-in?

Jana headed in the direction the officer had taken. The shop next to the surveyor's was also dark. The one at the end appeared to be vacant, like the lot at the end of the block. She found the officer talking on his radio by what appeared to be Reese's rear office door. She kept her distance as he finished reporting his location and donned his gloves. Then he reached for the handle.

The door opened easily, too easily. He disappeared inside.

What did a surveyor have that would be worth stealing? It seemed unlikely he'd have cash in his office. Did Reese have other drones? Her impression was that he only had the one *bird* that had been shot down. Maybe the thief didn't know about that.

The officer emerged from the building, talking on his radio.

"...deceased, appears to have been—" He noticed her and stopped. "Ma'am, I need to you wait over there." He pointed toward the end of the row of offices. "I'll be with you in a minute."

Another death? "Is it Aaron Reese?"

"I'll be with you in a minute." He waited until she'd moved farther away before resuming his call. A siren sounded not far away and came closer.

Jana rubbed her arms. Her timing absolutely sucked.

HAMBLIN'S CHIEF, JOHN Newbauer, called Tim just after he read the coroner's report on Larry Mason.

"Hey, John. You have a lead for us on the fentanyl business?"

"Wish I did." He had a voice like James Earl Jones. "What I have is a murder, and one of your citizens was on the scene. The deceased is Aaron Reese, a surveyor. He was killed at his office in town sometime after five last night."

"I know him. Reese did a job for the city. His drone was shot down by a farmer who didn't like being spied on."

"I read about that. From what I can gather, he did decent work."

"You thinking revenge was a motive?" Rich Hardy had been angry enough to shoot down the drone, but he had no record and was respected in the community.

"Too early to tell. Looks like the perpetrator was searching for something and intent on finding it."

"Any idea what it was?"

"No, but he or they made a mess. Smashed the guy's fancy computer and other equipment. That's how we pinpointed the time: The owner of a neighboring business heard noise like someone hammering. He assumed Reese was putting up shelves, which he'd mentioned wanting to do soon."

Probably good that the neighbor hadn't checked further. "Cause of death?" Tim asked.

John chuckled. "You know how that works. Can't say for sure until the coroner's worked on him. In this case, there are several possibilities. He was beaten and possibly tortured."

"Geez. Tortured?"

"Yeah, but we're keeping that quiet. I can send you the coroner's report when I have it."

"Appreciate that."

"Thought you would, especially if Reese's death turns out to be related to that drone shooting. By the way, the woman found on the scene mentioned that. Her name's Jana Nance. Says she's your tourism director." He sounded as if he didn't believe they had one. "She claims she came to talk to our victim. It appears another woman called in the suspected break-in. When my officer arrived, he found her at the front door, not the back where the break-in had occurred. Is there anything we should know about her or her relationship to the deceased?"

"As far as I know, her only involvement with your victim was hiring him to do that drone survey of our new park." He told John about his earlier call to her. "I could hear traffic noise and she said she had business in Hamblin this morning. Sounds like she might have just been at the wrong place at the wrong time." She seemed to have a knack for that. "Is she all right?"

"Shaken, but she says she's okay to drive. Just wanted to give you a heads-up on this."

"Thanks, John."

"Send me what you have on that drone shooting, Tim. We need to catch whoever did this."

"Will do."

He emailed the report filed on the drone incident. Another death connected to the park. Coincidence? The method of killing was different. There had been no sign of torture with Eli Carson, and he'd been shot with his own rifle, not beaten. Reese had filed a lawsuit against the city and Richard Hardy, whose son Tucker said *they* kept an eye on the property next door where Eli had been killed. But for now, the surveyor's murder was Hamblin's case, which was frankly a relief. He didn't have the manpower to handle another major case.

He glanced at the coroner's report on Larry Mason. Picking up the phone, he called Clint. "I need to meet with whoever's available from our task force—ASAP."

JANA LEFT HAMBLIN as soon as she'd given her contact information to an officer and been allowed to leave. She'd begun to worry that the police were going to arrest her.

If she were superstitious, she'd suspect Death was following her or, more accurately, leaving his victims for her to find. She hadn't warmed up to Aaron Reese prior to the drone shooting. Not that he was repulsive—just smug. He obviously related better to men and tended to mansplain to women like her. Maybe he'd rubbed someone else the wrong way, or maybe he was into spying with his *bird* and someone else hadn't appreciated it. It seemed unlikely that Richard Hardy would have killed him. Why go to the trouble of suing the surveyor if he'd wanted to do him physical harm? At least the police officer had arrived before she'd checked the rear of the office. If she'd tried the door and it had opened… She shuddered. How did Clay, police, and other first responders live with the horrors they'd seen?

Heading back to Crossroads, she turned on the radio, now set to a local station. Reluctant to return to Nana's house and the sad chores that awaited her there, she decided to stop by the police garage. If she could identify the truck of the man who'd argued with Eli, maybe that would help solve one of these murders.

She was nearing Crossroads when the local news came on.

"Police have not yet announced the cause of death of local motel owner Larry Mason. Mason, who was found at the Friendly Inn on—"

Jana gasped. What on earth was going on in Crossroads?

The garage where Tim had directed her appeared surprisingly clean and well ordered. Several cars, including a police cruiser, were parked in the lot, and at least two mechanics were working on vehicles on the two lifts. The owner, Xavier, smiled and told her she'd been expected.

"The truck's in the back, ma'am. I'll just get the keys. Tim, er, the chief, wants you to listen to the engine."

Jana followed him through the large bay to a back door. The yard outside had been fenced in. The pickup was the only truck; two other vehicles with serious crash damage were nearby. Xavier opened the door and started the motor.

At first the engine sounded like any other. Jana closed her eyes and imagined herself standing at Nana's carport door, watching and listening that night. Eli's voice arguing with the unseen driver. Words from the man inside the cab she couldn't make out. And in the background—

Her eyes popped open. She listened another minute to make sure she wasn't just remembering the sound.

"That's it!" The hiccuping or *revving* as she'd described it came as regular as a heartbeat.

"Noticed it myself," Xavier said. "Engine needs tuning and probably some other work. This truck's been around a long time."

And wasn't well maintained is what he didn't have to add.

"That's the sound I remember. It was dark, so I couldn't tell the color." She backed up and tried to find the angle she'd viewed the truck from that night. There wasn't room for her to recreate the distance. She squinted, trying to picture the pickup at dusk. The shape was right, if her memory could be trusted.

"That blue color has faded over the years," Roscoe said. "Probably looks gray or even a dirty white at night."

Jana blinked and rejoined him. There was no doubt that this was the engine she'd heard. "Whose truck is it?"

He raised his ball cap and scratched his head. "I don't know that I'm supposed to say, but it's no secret around town. This old truck belonged to Larry Mason."

TIM HELD UP Dr. Nagashi's report. "According to the

coroner, Larry Mason was murdered by a fatal fentanyl injection," he told Clint, Eamon, and Francine, the only members of his task force available for this meeting. "Doc Bailey was right—he wasn't strangled."

"So, he was a drug user," Francine said.

"Maybe, but there were no signs of regular injections. This one was in the neck."

Eamon swore. "That's cold."

"That's murder," Tim said. "Dr. Nagashi is ruling it homicide."

"We don't have much from the people at the motel that night," Clint said. "Just a possible motorcycle."

"If it was on the motel property," Francine said. "The couple weren't sure if the sound came from highway or the parking lot."

Tim pulled the witness statements again. "It was there all right. The salesman heard it at eight and the couple heard it about an hour later. The salesman heard it again then too. He's sure it was the same one."

Eamon said, "Could have been someone visiting—"

"They all said they didn't have any visitors," Francine interrupted.

"So, someone had come to see Mason," Eamon said. "If his girlfriend is telling the truth, he would have been the only other person on site, at least that we know of."

"Timing is right," Tim said. "We have that glass and water pitcher missing. There was alcohol in his system but below the legal limit. It looks like someone came to see Mason, visited a while, had a drink with him, gave him the fatal shot, and cleaned up the scene."

"What about the kinky sex thing with the robe belt?" Eamon asked.

"Maybe our killer has a warped sense of humor," Clint said.

"Or wanted to frame Vivian Amber." Francine clearly wasn't a fan.

"Could be any of the above. CSI did get some hairs from the victim they're trying to match. Meanwhile, have we confirmed Vivian's alibi with someone other than her boss?"

"Her coworkers that shift confirmed it, Chief," Francine said. "I stopped by The Last Rodeo last night around eight." When the men all raised their eyebrows, she added, "Jay was with me. I hadn't been able to reach one of the servers, so I was hoping to talk to her and get a feel for the place."

"Francine—" Even if her weightlifting, six-four boyfriend had escorted her, Francine had no business scouting out a bar in the next county at night.

"Chief, there was a guy delivering beer, so I asked him quietly outside if he'd been there the night of the murder. Turns out he was and he remembered talking to Vivian. Flirting was probably more like it."

"Good work." In other words, they had a witness whose employment or loyalty to Vivian might not have influenced his statement.

Eamon grinned. "Tried it on you, did he?"

"Okay," Tim said before Francine could answer with more than a look. "I guess Vivian's in the clear. Talk to those guests again. They might have remembered hearing something else or seeing someone else."

He put the coroner's report on the table. "There's one

more thing that may or may not be related. Aaron Reese, the owner of the drone shot down over Hardy's farm was murdered last night in his office in Hamblin. He'd been beaten to death." He described the condition of the office but omitted John Newbauer's news that he'd apparently been tortured.

"Can't imagine a surveyor keeping much money around his office," Clint said.

"Sounds like the computers and equipment were being targeted," Eamon said. "Maybe the owner was collateral damage."

The torture indicated otherwise. Reese may have been the target. The perpetrator needed something from him, perhaps something to do with his equipment.

"Is our farmer a suspect?" Francine asked.

"It's HPD's case, but Hardy certainly had a motive. I told Chief Newbauer about the drone and the lawsuit."

"The camera was on the drone, but the video was downloading to his phone," Francine said. "If a video was what his killer was after—"

"He'd want to destroy his computers too," Eamon finished for her. "He'd probably downloaded the video to his computer. It might also be saved in the cloud."

Tim wasn't sure how all of the technology worked, but what Eamon was describing made sense. The city had hired Reese to do the aerial survey, so presumably they'd receive a copy of the video, which John might need if he started checking into the surveyor's recent jobs. He'd check with the mayor. He didn't want to bother Jana again today, if he didn't have to.

"I'll check on whether the city received a copy of his video. He may not have shared it since the job was incomplete and he's suing. In any case, the crime could have to do with another customer or someone who wanted to destroy him and his business. At this point we have enough to deal with."

A sharp knock on the door was followed by Marva bursting in. "Chief, I've got a man from Pine Bluff calling about Eli Carson's Mustang. He found it abandoned in his lot. Figured you'd want to talk to him."

IT WAS ONCE again Jack's favorite time of the week—crunch time. Which story would be his headline and which other stories would appear on the front page? Sometimes, like today, he didn't have enough facts yet to move a developing story to headline status. Aaron Reese's murder had been brutal, according to two of his sources, including the Hamblin PD officer who'd called him this morning. Normally, he put news from neighboring towns inside, but the article about the murdered surveyor's drone being shot down by a local farmer had sparked a lot of discussion online. However, there was no indication that Reese's death was related to the drone shooting. More likely, he'd surprised his killer or killers burglarizing his office.

And then there was Larry Mason's death at Friendly's. Unlike Reese, he was a local, a former Crossroads High School football player who'd managed the motel for more than a decade. The coroner's report had just been released, calling the death a homicide due to injection of fentanyl.

That was explosive news, given the recent accidental death of Officer Rollins and the outbreak of overdoses in the community. Also, the maid at the Friendly Inn had told him her boss had been found with a silky belt around his neck and had probably been drinking and doing drugs. Quite an ignoble end for a one-time local sports hero, even if he had been an unwitting victim of a crime.

Two Cokes later, Jack made his decision. Larry Mason's death—LOCAL HOTEL OWNER FOUND DEAD—would have to be his headline. Lower on the front page, the story he'd written about the tourism committee and plans for the new park would be a more positive note to counterbalance yet another murder. There would also be a photo and a tease to a story inside with his interviews of the two mayoral candidates.

Even though it was big news today, the surveyor's murder would be on page three. After all, the man wasn't from Crossroads. But Reese had customers here, and folks would be talking about his death. Under the headline HAMBLIN SURVEYOR MURDERED, he'd written several paragraphs with the details he knew of the crime, followed by information on the victim from the police report. He'd concluded with a mention that Mr. Reese had recently been hired by the City of Crossroads to survey the property at Willow Lake. There was no point in mentioning the lawsuit the dead man had filed as it would now probably be dismissed.

Jack sat back and looked at his mock-up. The news this week wasn't good, not at all. Two dead men and a park. A park property surveyed by one of the dead men whose drone had been shot down. A park searched by local first responders on a sunny Saturday after another dead man had been found there—a young man who'd been seen dumping barrels illegally one night from a box truck later abandoned at Crawfish Pond (story on page five). A third dead man who'd employed the first victim briefly.

It was like looking at a jigsaw puzzle with half the pieces missing. He sighed. And now he'd upset Tim Birch. That would be the headline today if his life were a paper: NEWSPAPER EDITOR DESTROYS EVIDENCE—POLICE CHIEF THREATENS ARREST. Thanks to his reckless action, he'd now be the last to hear about any breaks in the murders. Worse, he'd probably lost his chance to catch the driver and find out who was behind the dumping at Crawfish Pond.

Sorry, Albert. I'm an idiot. The dead man would probably chuckle at that and forgive him, but the police chief was a source he couldn't afford to lose. Somehow he was going to have to convince Tim that he deserved a second chance.

Chapter Thirty-Two

"THE TRUCK BELONGS to Larry Mason? Why do the police have it?"

Charly had come over with the obligatory casserole minutes after Jana had arrived home. After she'd again expressed her condolences and asked how she was doing, Jana had told her about visiting the police garage. After all, her grief over Nana's expected death meant little in comparison to Charly's grief over losing her son and not knowing who had killed him or why.

"I guess they're looking into his death. At least they know now who Eli argued with that night." She'd left a message for Tim Birch after she'd finished at the garage but hadn't talked to him.

"I heard that Larry died." Standing in front of the open refrigerator, Charly handed her a plastic container with a single piece of fried chicken. "We can put this in something smaller, if you still want it."

"I do. It's delicious—even cold." She'd planned to eat it last night, but she'd stayed at the hospital instead.

Her neighbor slid the new casserole into the space she'd created. "I guess Larry wanted Eli to come back to work for him. I wonder why Eli didn't want to?"

Jana had no idea, but Eli had been a grown man, even if

he had still been living with his mother. He'd sounded adamant about not wanting to do whatever job was being offered.

Charly closed the refrigerator. Apparently, the question had been rhetorical. "I'm glad you saw them that night and told the police. Maybe they're getting closer to finding his killer. It's just so frustrating thinking someone's getting away with murder."

"I'm sure they are." It was hard to picture the motel owner who'd talked about his *glory days* as someone who would track Eli to his deer stand and shoot him in the face. But if Larry Mason had been the killer, it was too late to bring him to justice.

Charly didn't have to ask where the foil was and quickly wrapped the lone chicken breast. Washing her hands, she gestured to the refrigerator. "You're going to need more room, although there's space in the freezer. Word's traveling fast about Nana Sue's passing. Get some rest while you can." On her way out, she touched Jana's shoulder as she passed her. Another positive sign?

After Charly left, Jana sensed an even deeper emptiness than she had when she'd first arrived in Crossroads. Or maybe it was just her dark mood. She rolled her head to ease the crick in her neck from sleeping in the chair at the hospital. There were calls to make, people to notify, arrangements to organize. Her trip to Hamblin this morning now seemed more like a desperate attempt to flee the reality of Nana's death than a mission to live up to her values. Why hadn't she taken care of that apology sooner or not criticized the man in the first place? She was a screwup. And now the person who'd loved her despite her many character flaws was gone. She filled a glass with water from the tap and drank it, ignoring the tremor in her hand. Staring out the window at Charly's driveway didn't ease the sadness or the heaviness in her heart.

Wiping a tear from her eye, she cleared her throat and called Uncle Jasper.

"I had a dream about Mama last night," he said. "Is that when she crossed over?"

"Yes."

"We can't come, and I'm truly sorry. You know she has a plot at Crossroads Cemetery next to Papa. It's already paid for. She made all the arrangements with Jackson Funeral Home for a casket and a service. She said she put the paperwork in an envelope addressed to you in the china cabinet."

Tears burned her eyes. Trust Nana to have planned ahead, and thank god she had before Alzheimer's stole her mind.

"That's a relief, Uncle Jasp. I'll see if I can have someone video the service so you won't miss out."

"That would surely be nice. You call me if you need me, you hear?" His voice was deep with emotion.

"I will."

"That house is yours now. She left it to you. I told her I wanted you to have it."

"Uncle Jasp—"

"I got no need for it and no one to leave it to except you. I just wish I could be there to help you. I love you, girl."

She found the envelope addressed to her in Nana's writing in the china cabinet and left it out on the kitchen table to read later.

Her daughters must have also sensed a shift in the universe. They answered her calls, despite being at work.

"Do you want me to come?" they each asked. It was a silly question. Of course she wanted them here. What they were really asking was if a trip to Arkansas was necessary, given they had work, relationships, plans, and not a lot of extra money to spend on a flight bound to be expensive on such short notice. There would be a car rental involved too.

"I know you're busy and haven't seen Nana in a long time," she'd replied. "I'll leave it up to you, but I'll be fine if you don't come." They were adults now, as she frequently reminded herself. Their consciences would guide them, and she was being truthful about understanding if they couldn't make it. She promised to let them know when the funeral would be.

Her father sounded jovial hearing from her but soon turned sympathetic after she told him. "Sue lived a long life," he commented and then asked about Jasper. There was a pause when she explained the physical problems that prevented her uncle and aunt from making the trip.

"Let me know when the funeral is, honey. I'll try to make it."

"Thanks, Dad, but if you can't, that's all right." She didn't want to get her hopes up.

Next, she contacted Jackson Funeral Home, who promised to pick up Nana Sue from the hospital in El Dorado and assured her they had her grandmother's arrangements on file. All she had to do was come in and sign papers at her convenience. It was surprisingly easy and a relief to not have to choose a casket or a gravestone. Maybe she should make her own arrangements to save her daughters from being burdened. But surely it was too soon—she had years ahead of her.

Yet that was what Marcus had thought. He hadn't lived to see forty.

Her stomach growled, and Jana realized she hadn't eaten more than a packet of saltine crackers since yesterday at noon. Clay Bailey had encouraged her to have breakfast at the hospital before driving back to Crossroads, but she hadn't been hungry then. She made herself a pimento cheese sandwich and choked it down as memories of sitting at this same table eating with her grandmother made her tear up. Nana Sue had loved pimento cheese.

Not long after she'd finished eating, another neighbor, Mrs. Perkins, arrived. She'd lived behind Nana for as long as Jana could remember. The back alley separated their backyards. Although different personalities and members of different churches, they'd shared a love of gardening and a mutual dislike of a yappy dog that had aggravated them until it had run out in front of the garbage truck in the alley.

"I've been watering your grandmother's black-eyed Susans along the back property line," Mrs. Perkins told her after handing her a plate of oatmeal cookies—plain, no raisins. "I always thought she had too many, but she told me they were like having an audience of smiling faces in her garden." She sniffed. "Used to think of them as weeds, but I guess they've grown on me."

"You could plant some yourself," Jana suggested.

"I prefer my petunias and camellias. Besides, I don't have

room for any more perennials."

She could make room, but to each her own. Jana thanked her for the cookies, promising she'd enjoy them later.

"I suppose you're going to sell the house," Mrs. Perkins said, looking around the living room where she was seated. Her nose seemed to be turned up, but Jana didn't take it personally. There was no denying the sofa was faded, the furniture dated.

"I haven't thought that far ahead yet." She'd only just learned it was now hers.

"Let me know if you decide to sell or if you decide to dispose of your grandmother's gardening tools. I might be interested."

Two other neighbors stopped by that afternoon with chicken casseroles, making a nap impossible. Jana didn't remember them, but they had kind things to say about Nana Sue and told her how much her grandmother had talked about her. Neither commented about how long it had been since her last visit.

Giving up on the idea of a nap, she wandered into Nana's bedroom. The funeral director had been kind on the phone as he'd confirmed that he would arrange for the service and burial Nana had planned and thankfully paid for. He'd requested that she provide the clothing Nana would wear in her casket. Taking a deep breath, Jana opened the closet.

Empty hangers must have contained the clothes Nana had worn at Golden Pines. The clothing was organized by type, a practice she'd adapted in her own closet. The dresses were together at one side. Jana sorted through them, pushing each hanger aside to see the next one as many memories flashed through her mind. There was the lilac dress with long sleeves she'd worn to the girls' high school graduations in Indianapolis. The black dress, decades old, she'd called her funeral dress. The summery floral print and the pink suit she liked to wear to church this time of year. Jana pulled those two out and laid them on the bed. They'd been Nana's favorites and reflected her love of spring and summer. And gardening.

She held up the pink suit. Nana would want this one, she sensed. She sniffed it, but the fabric smelled more of dry cleaning than her grandmother. She located the blue and pink blouse that went with it. How long had it been since this outfit had been worn? Would it fit Nana? It wouldn't be too tight, she realized. Nana had shrunk in the last five years.

She set the outfit aside and chose a pair of shoes. Yes, Nana would approve of her burial outfit; the suit was dignified and cheerful. Strange that her detailed instructions hadn't mentioned what clothes she wanted to be buried in. As it had turned out, she seemed to have the same wardrobe today as she'd owned when she made her funeral arrangements a decade ago.

Determined to keep busy and not feel sorry for herself, Jana started filling a trash bag with Nana's underwear and then the clothes that were too worn or dated to be donated. Before she knew it, the daylight had dimmed and she was hungry again. She was surprised to see it was after eight.

She didn't bother to turn on the hall light. When she entered the dark kitchen, a shadow shifted just as she felt for the light switch. Suddenly, strong arms grabbed her, jerking her away from the wall. She struggled in her captor's grasp as her feet searched for solid ground.

"Let me go!" She screamed then as loud as she could.

His grip loosened as a gloved hand covered her mouth and nose. She twisted her head from side to side, desperate to breathe. Then she kicked him, hard.

"Son of a bitch!" he growled. He threw her to the ground.

Jana rolled instinctively. *Away from him, get away!* The cabinets stopped her and she scrambled to her hands and knees, not daring to look back to see where he was.

Hands grabbed her ankles, yanking her legs out from under her. He flipped her, dropping onto her chest with enough force to leave her breathless. She struck out at him, but he seized her wrists. Jana screamed again, squirming and bucking to try to throw him off.

She was no match for him. He wasn't a big man, but his arms were like iron. His face was hidden under a black ski mask. All she could see were dark eyes narrowed with intent. He shifted his weight as he pinned her wrists with one hand. She screamed again and he backhanded her.

The surprise and the pain paralyzed her. She'd never been struck by a man before. Her jaw and cheek felt numb.

He chuckled. "Should have brought a rope. Didn't expect an old heifer to put up a fight."

Anger burned through her shock. She wasn't sure she could speak, but the words came out clearly. "What do you want?"

"Who did you send the video to?"

"What?"

"The video from the drone. Who else has it?"

Tempted to deny she had the video, she guessed he already knew she had a copy. "No one." She wasn't going to put anyone else in danger.

He seized her neck below her jaw in his gloved hand, forcing her head back.

"I-I haven't had time to even look at it! I swear!"

His hand encircled her throat. "Where's your computer?"

Oh god, he was going to kill her. Was this the man who'd murdered Aaron Reese? "My...my laptop's in the living room on the coffee table."

"Is that the only one?"

Fear was paralyzing her. The video was on her work computer. Was he too stupid to realize that? "My-my grandmother has...had one. It's in the bedroom." Her bruised jaw ached, but she ignored it. "I can show you."

"Yeah, I bet. I have other plans for you." Releasing her neck, he shifted on top of her, placing her wrists under his knees. She grunted as the air again left her chest. He reached into a pocket of the zippered vest he wore over his dark, long-sleeved top and pulled out what looked like a leather case for glasses. He used his teeth to unsnap it.

"Can't breathe," Jana said, exaggerating the difficulty she was having but not by much.

He didn't answer, but shifted off of her, pinning her legs with his folded right one and again capturing her wrists with one hand. He pulled up her shirt with his thumb and tipped out a syringe from the case onto her bare abdomen.

Before he could reach for it, Jana screamed and bucked

for all she was worth, twisting her torso and trying to pull her wrists free. The syringe rolled off, and he swore. When he reached for it, she turned beneath him as he lifted up from her torso, thrusting her hip bone into his crotch. He yelped and raised his hand to strike her. She screamed for all she was worth.

The kitchen door burst open. “Jana!” Charly’s shout was followed by the *rachet* of a rifle being cocked.

Her assailant froze and then lowered his hand.

“Let her go,” Charly said. “Hands up, now!”

“Hey, now, we were just having a little fun. You want to join our party?”

“Hands up!” Charly stepped closer and sighted him along the rifle’s barrel.

“Easy,” he said, sounding less sure of himself. He released her and raised his hands.

“Stand up, slowly.”

He used one hand to push himself up from the floor to his feet. Charly never took her eyes off him. Freed, Jana drew her legs in and scooted backward away from him before she sat up. She pushed the syringe under the cabinet with her foot.

He didn’t notice. His eyes were locked on the rifle and the woman holding it. “You look kinda familiar,” he said. “What’s your name, darlin’?”

Charly ignored him. “Take off your mask. I want to see your face before I shoot you.”

She was serious. Anger and grief burned in her eyes, a desire to kill someone, anyone, even though it wouldn’t bring Eli back.

Her assailant must have understood that too. He reached for the ski mask.

Jana grabbed the countertop and pulled herself up. They needed help. Her phone was in Nana's bedroom. She edged away from him.

"Now!" Charly demanded.

Jerking his mask off, he threw it at Charly, ducking sideways and then running toward her. The rifle fired, the sound blasting Jana's ears. She ducked, covering her ears as her assailant shoved Charly out of his way and ran for the open door, escaping into the night.

"Charly!"

Her friend had fallen but still held the rifle. "I'm okay." She pushed herself to her feet as Jana reached her. Outside, an engine started.

They raced down the steps into the carport. There wasn't a vehicle in the driveway or the street, but they could hear an engine rev.

"He's in the alley!" Jana cried. Charly hurried around her into the side yard, again cocking her rifle. Jana followed more cautiously into the backyard. There was no one in sight. Hearing another revving noise farther away, they stepped into the alley.

A single red reflector bounced down the narrow unpaved lane and then disappeared.

"Well, shit," Charly said. "Too bad that bullet didn't hit him." She lowered her rifle and began to shake. "I really did want to shoot him."

Careful of the gun, Jana gathered her brave friend into her arms. "I know. You're something else, you know that?"

Chapter Thirty-Three

JANA SOON DISCOVERED just how fast the small town of Crossroads could react. A patrol car arrived minutes after she called 911. Charly made her an ice pack for her sore face and insisted she sit on the sofa. Neither of them wanted to be in the kitchen.

The young officer who interviewed her—could he possibly be out of his teens?—had only just settled in a chair and written down their names when Tim Birch arrived. He'd taken one look at her and called the paramedics.

"It's just sore," she said, lifting the ice pack so he could see. "I really don't need any attention."

"Let's make sure you're all right."

Charly nodded at her, siding with him. Jana sighed. Her face must look as bad as it felt. She moved her jaw. It throbbed, but it didn't seem to be broken. If he'd hit her again or injected her with whatever had been in that syringe… She shivered, which prompted Charly to fetch her a sweater. It was one of Nana Sue's and felt like a hug from her grandmother.

Tim requested another police unit and CSI on his radio before coming to sit with her. He was dressed in jeans and a T-shirt with the image of Tim McGraw on it. His usual ball cap was missing, revealing his short brown hair. "Tell me what happened, Jana."

She described the attack as he watched her intently.

"Did you see what he was driving?"

"It was a motorcycle," Charly said, "in the back alley. We didn't see it up close."

"What makes you sure it was a motorcycle?"

Charly scoffed. "I know the sound of a motorcycle engine—I used to have one. And there was only one taillight."

Jana looked at her in surprise. Charly had a motorcycle?

Tim turned back to her. "What did he look like?"

Jana hugged her elbows. "I couldn't tell much about him. He wore a black ski mask." She described his other clothing and the gloves he'd worn. "He had brown eyes. He was maybe five ten? And strong. I'm sorry—I wish I could tell you more."

"White, Black, Hispanic? Young, old?"

"He was white," they answered together.

"Jana's right about the height," Charly said. "He sounded local. Thought he was a real charmer. Tried to convince me that they were just having fun."

"He called me *an old heifer*," Jana said. "I wouldn't call that charming. He said he should have brought a rope to lasso me. Instead he brought that hypodermic."

Tim's eyes blazed. "Did he inject you or even scratch you with the needle?"

"No, I fought him, and it rolled away before he could grab it. That's when Charly came in with her gun. The syringe is under the counter by the sink. I kicked it there."

He glanced at the kitchen and then back to her. "Did he say why he wanted to hurt you, Jana?"

"He asked about the video—I assumed it was the one Aaron Reese took with the drone—and whether I'd sent it to anyone. I told him no, but I sent it to Connor Douglas two days ago. He wanted a copy for the lawsuits Aaron Reese and Mr. Hardy had filed."

"That might be why Aaron Reese is dead. Whoever killed him smashed his computer and some other equipment."

"He asked where my computer was. I told him my laptop was here, but that wouldn't have done him any good. The video is on my work computer."

"I need to see it," Tim said, rising and pulling out his cell. To her surprise, he called Deeann Donahue. He briefly told the mayor what had happened.

"Yes, a little bruised," he said, glancing at her, "but I'm having the paramedics check her out. I'm going to need to go into city hall tonight." He explained about the video. "Jana didn't tell her attacker that Connor had a copy, but I'll send an officer around to his place to warn him just in case."

Two male paramedics arrived then. While they were checking her out, two more police in uniform entered the house. When Tim finished giving them directions, he looked around the kitchen, squatting down where she'd pushed the hypodermic under the counter.

"Your blood pressure is a little high," the paramedic told her. He'd been one of the searchers at the park on Saturday. The name above his uniform pocket said Alan Curtis.

"I'd be surprised if it wasn't," Charly said. "She was nearly killed tonight!"

He smiled patiently. "In that case, your blood pressure is a little low." The twinkle in his eye lowered her stress level and made her smile. "I don't see any signs of concussion, or fractures, although you're going to have a nasty bruise." He asked her a few more questions about how she felt. "We can take you to the clinic and have the doctor check you over."

"No, I don't need to do that." The ice pack was helping. Besides, she didn't want Clay called. He'd driven to El Dorado early to check on her and two other patients. He didn't need to be called out this evening, at least not by her. Besides, the temptation to beg him to hold her would be too great. She wasn't sure either of them were ready for what that kind of closeness might lead to.

Tim rejoined them as the paramedics packed up. Alan advised her to keep her jaw iced and take ibuprofen for pain, and told the chief that she seemed well enough not to need further treatment. She thanked them and they left.

"Is there somewhere you can stay tonight, Jana? CSI will be working here. I don't know when they're going to arrive." Tim didn't need to mention that her attacker was still out there.

"I can show you that video if I can get into my office. I don't know if the building is open at night."

He studied her. "Are you sure you're up to it?"

There was no question in her mind. And from what she'd learned watching television, the first twenty-four hours were critical in an investigation. "You have to catch him, especially if he killed Aaron Reese. If the video will help..."

"Okay. We'll wait for CSI. They should be here soon. They'll want to take the clothes you're wearing to examine for evidence."

"They might be interested in his mask too," Charly said

with a satisfied grin. She pointed to it.

TIM WASN'T SURPRISED to see Deeann Donahue's car parked by the well-lit employee entrance at city hall when they arrived. The mayor turned off her engine and emerged. She was dressed casually in jeans, short boots, and a plaid shirt with the sleeves rolled up.

"Jana! Are you sure you're feeling up to this?"

"Yes. My face probably looks worse than it is."

Tim had to give her credit. The woman had nearly been murdered tonight but was still determined to help him find the SOB who'd attacked her.

"I'm so sorry about your grandmother." Deeann raised her arms as if she wanted to hug Jana but then lowered them. "You've been through hell today. Come on, let's see this video."

Inside, they flipped on lights as they made their way to Jana's office. Logging into her computer, she soon had the video pulled up on her screen. Tim pulled up a chair for Deeann beside Jana and stood behind her to look over her shoulder.

The drone camera showed the liftoff, and soon the machine was flying over the trees to Willow Lake. It turned and began to cruise above the shoreline.

"How long was it flying before it was shot down?" he asked.

"About forty minutes." She moved her mouse and a bar tracking the length of the chip showed at the bottom of the screen. "Forty-three minutes, to be precise."

"Let's fast-forward to when it leaves the lake."

The drone appeared to fly faster and soon there were trees again below it. Jana clicked on pause, rewound a little, and then moved it forward.

The forested area didn't last long, and soon the drone was circling over farmland. A road came into view intersected by a shorter stretch. Bluegill, he guessed, and if the drone was approaching from the north, the Hardy farm would be on the south side. As it drew closer, a man emerged from the main house, holding a phone at his left ear. His right hand was at his side, but Tim could only guess what was in it. Still apparently talking on his cell, he gazed upward at the sky, looking toward the end of Bluegill or beyond where the park boundary began.

Don't cross that road, he urged the drone as if it could hear him and time would bend for it to react.

"What's that?" Deeann asked, leaning forward.

Jana rewound a few frames and then resumed playing it.

"There!" Deeann said pointing at the screen.

Jana froze the picture.

He didn't see anything except a small house set back by a stand of trees just east of the Hardy's main house and barn.

"I thought I saw something."

"Let's look again." Jana rewound the video and then played it forward.

"There!" both women said as Jana again hit Pause.

This time he'd seen a flash of blue in the trees behind the smaller house before Jana again had paused it. The detached garage set back from the house on the left would hide whatever it was from the main road, Whistler's Way, but not from a drone flying overhead toward it.

The video timer showed two minutes and thirty-seven seconds remaining.

"Let's see if it goes any closer," he said.

Jana clicked Play.

The drone continued its circle, sweeping over Bluegill and closer to the Hardy homestead. A man wearing a cowboy hat emerged from the smaller house and strode toward the garage. Tucker? He halted and turned around, apparently reacting to another man by the barn facing him and pointing at the drone. Shading his eyes, he gazed upward.

Less than a minute remaining.

Oblivious to the attention it was receiving, the drone swooped closer to the smaller house, and the blue object came into view. This time Jana hit Pause at exactly the right moment.

They stared silently at the screen. She zoomed in.

The still photo was blurrier, but they were looking at the back of a blue Mustang. Twin white stripes ran over the roof and across the trunk. The license plate was too blurry to read, but someone on his team or at CSI might be able to clean up the image.

"That's Eli's car!" Jana said. "Do you think that's what they didn't want us to see?"

"I'm guessing it is." He noted the time on the video. "Let's watch the rest."

The man standing in front of the main house raised a rifle and aimed it upward toward the drone. His body recoiled as he fired. As he lowered his rifle, the screen went dark.

He wanted to watch it again, but Jana's shoulders were drooping, and she had to be hurting. For now, he'd seen enough—maybe enough for a warrant.

Chapter Thirty-Four

TIM HAD JANA email him the video and then drove her home with Deeann following in her car. Charly Carson, waiting on the carport steps, seemed surprised to see the mayor.

"Deeann," she said in greeting before asking Jana, "Are you okay?"

"Yes, I just need to pack an overnight bag. They probably have a room at the Redbud Inn." She looked at him, as if for confirmation.

"Forget that," the mayor said. "You're coming out to the ranch. We have plenty of room."

"Perfect," Charly said, smiling. "If my sister weren't still here, I'd have you stay with me. You'll be safe out at the ranch."

They ignored her protests about not wanting to impose and escorted her inside before disappearing into her bedroom to help her pack. Tim checked in with the CSI supervisor in the kitchen.

"You're keeping us busy these days," Etta Wainwright said. The hood of her white overalls covered her salt-and-pepper hair. "Is this related to the motel owner?"

"I think so. Looks like the same MO. That's why I need this one prioritized, Etta. At least let me know if there's fentanyl in that syringe."

"I can tell you that right now. The answer's yes. But if you want to know if it's identical to the drugs in the other two cases, I'll need to analyze it in the lab. By the way, we found a motorcycle track in the alley, a good fresh shoe print too. The owners of the house behind this one must have watered their garden not long before your suspect arrived. I can get some information to you on that tomorrow morning."

"The sooner, the better," Tim said. "Thanks, Etta."

"My pleasure. As a woman living alone, I'm as anxious to catch this creep as you are. Oh, by the way, if you do find the boot that matches our print, there could be some black-eyed Susan petals caught in the tread, unless he cleans it in the meantime. The dirt alone can be matched if you can bring the boots to me."

"I'll do my best."

After the women had left, Tim walked to the street to his SUV. The night was clear with a waning gibbous moon. As he opened his door, the sound of a motorcycle disturbed the quiet evening. It passed by on the cross street, the driver keeping a steady speed within the posted limit. Tim slid into his seat. Making a U-turn, he headed in the direction the cycle had taken.

The red of the reflector glowed ahead of him, and he began to close the distance. He flashed his brights, curious to see what the driver would do.

A turn signal winked a moment before the driver took a right into Cedar Street. Tim reached the corner in time to see the cycle pull into the driveway of a white house with a neatly maintained yard.

He slowed, but the house was the third from the corner, not leaving him enough distance to pull over and avoid being noticed. The driver parked and dismounted. The lantern-style lights on either side of the double garage door confirmed the subject was wearing clothes matching the description the two women had provided: dark jeans, a black jacket, and boots. The height looked right too. Making up his mind, he pulled into the driveway behind the cycle.

The man turned around and removed his helmet. Ed Rollins frowned at him.

Tim rolled down his window. "Evening, Sarge."

"Chief." Rollins walked over to him.

"I just left Jana Nance's home two blocks over on Beech. She was attacked tonight. Thought you might want to know the assailant could still be in your neighborhood."

Rollins stared at him, his expression giving nothing away.

"Her neighbor scared the intruder off before he could hurt her. He was trying to inject her with a syringe."

"Sounds like Larry Mason's killer."

"Yeah, exactly." Wherever Rollins had been recently, his tires appeared relatively clean. In fact, the bike shone like it had just been washed.

"Anyhow, if you hear anything from neighbors, let me know. Have a good evening."

His lips twisted. "This is my sister's house…Chief."

Of course. He remembered then. Sarge lived in North Crossroads.

"Tell her to keep her doors locked, just in case." He put his car in Reverse and backed out. He could have made a bigger fool of himself, but at the moment he didn't see how. Rollins knew from the briefings the suspect in the Mason killing had probably been riding a motorcycle.

He reached the end of the driveway and looked up. Rollins was still watching him.

TRUE TO HER word, Etta confirmed the next morning that the tire track lifted in the alley was from a motorcycle. More importantly, it matched a print found near the deer stand in the area where they believed Eli's Mustang had been parked. Even better, they had a DNA match from the ski mask. The judge agreed an arrest was warranted.

The SWAT team met them where Whistler's Way intersected the highway. Tim and Cliff followed them to the Hardy farm, and Francine and Eamon trailed in a second vehicle. At the house, the SWAT team quickly split up to check the two houses and the barn. Soon Richard Hardy and his wife were escorted outside. The two CSI staff who were waiting for the site to be secured were waved in. Eamon and Francine suited up to join them.

Hardy blustered about his rights and claimed retaliation for the lawsuit he'd filed against the city. Oddly, his protests quickly died. His wife, wide-eyed and frightened, didn't say anything.

"Where's Tucker?" Tim asked.

"I don't keep track of his business," Hardy said in a toneless voice.

It was an odd comment from a man who seemed to

dominate his sons. He almost sounded as if he regretted not knowing what Tuck was up to.

"And your other son?"

"RJ lives in town," Corine Hardy answered when her husband remained silent. She twisted her wedding ring. "He's going with his wife to see the doctor this morning in El Dorado. She's—they're trying to have a baby."

Richard Hardy didn't react.

Leaving the couple with Eamon, Tim walked to the smaller house where two SWAT officers were banging on the door and yelling "Police! Come out now!" They then used a ram to breach the door.

The house was empty. SWAT soon cleared the simple two bedroom, one bath structure. The bed was made, but that didn't prove it hadn't been slept in last night. Farmers rose early. Tim put on gloves and had a quick look in the bedroom closet. There were plenty of boots, both tall cowboy style and work boots, but none had mud on them. He checked the other rooms, which had only a few personal items. Maybe Tuck didn't regard the place as his home—just a temporary residence where he could store his clothes and boots.

The SWAT team had opened the attached garage's broad door as they cleared the buildings. Tim walked into the dark space, large enough to hold three pickups. The only vehicle was a motorcycle, the one Tucker had been on the day they'd responded to Eli Carson's body in the deer stand when he'd claimed his family *kept an eye on the place.* Tim squatted and looked closer. The tires had fresh mud with speckles of yellow flower petals.

He rose.

"Chief?" Francine called. "You need to see this."

He followed her toward the barn where a kneeling CSI tech was gathering samples of a darkened patch of grass.

"I saw it from the upstairs window in the house," Francine said.

Something had bled substantially on the spot, but the farm had chickens and horses—maybe other animals he hadn't seen. Could have been a wild creature wanting a chicken dinner that had to be shot, maybe a fox or raccoon. But there was more blood here than one of those animals would have bled. It also looked fresh.

"From the window it looked like something had been dragged around the barn."

Tim could see it then, the flattened grass with smears of blood. Careful to walk wide of the trail, he followed it. When they reached the back of the barn, there was less of a blood trail but thicker grass. The trail ended at the tree line where the forest began.

They found Tucker Hardy not far inside the wooded area sprawled face down between two pines as if he'd been tossed there. The bloody hole in his back appeared to be an exit wound. His clothes—the black T-shirt beneath a nylon black vest, black jeans, and work boots—matched Jana's description of her assailant. He was dead.

Back at the main house, Tim made sure the guns in Rich Hardy's safe were taken by CSI. He then returned to the front porch where Hardy and his wife sat with Eamon.

"Mr. Hardy has something to say to you, Chief. He wanted to talk only to you."

The farmer met Tim's gaze. "I've known your daddy a long time," he said slowly, his voice as rough as gravel. "He did a good job raising you on his own. Comes a time when you have to let your boys make their own decisions, though, and that's when they either take the right path or they don't."

"Mr. Hardy—"

"I believe in taking responsibility for my mistakes." He held his hands out to be cuffed.

"Richard?" His wife said alarmed.

He turned to her, still not showing any emotion. "Tucker is dead. I shot him." He turned back to Tim. "I found those pills he was selling in the hayloft where he hid them. I knew he had something going on over there on that property with men I'd never seen around these parts coming and going. I went to destroy it, but I didn't find anything except a place in a clearing where there had been a pole tent. It's up in the loft too."

"Did you know about the blue Mustang?"

Something flickered in his eyes. "He said a mechanic friend had fixed it up and sold it to him. I had no reason not to believe him until I read about that boy you found in the deer stand. I told him he needed to call the police and let them know he had it. That night he drove off in it. He told me he'd turned it in."

Tim shook his head. "We found the car in a lot in Pine Bluff, abandoned."

Rich Hardy didn't look surprised. "Just so you know, RJ wasn't part of any of this. I guess I raised one of them right."

Corine Hardy's quiet sobs turned into heartbreaking

wails.

Tim nodded to Eamon, who cuffed the farmer and read him his Miranda rights before turning him over to the pair of patrol officers who had been summoned in anticipation of the arrest of Tucker Hardy. Then Tim called the coroner.

TIM HAD ALMOST become comfortable holding press conferences when there were only a few reporters in the audience, but two days after Richard Hardy's arrest, a larger group, including television teams from the Monroe stations viewed by the southeast Arkansas area, were waiting for him to speak at the podium set up outside the station. Next to him stood John Newbauer. Hamblin's police chief cleared his throat several times, reassuring Tim that he wasn't alone in his dislike of these events. The mayor and Jana Nance stood off to the side in the audience. They already knew what he was about to say, and both nodded encouragement as he waited for the audience to become silent. Jack Huddleston, as promised, had a front row seat, but that wasn't Tim's doing.

"Today I'd like to share with you more information we've received about the deaths of Eli Carson, Aaron Reese of Hamblin, and Larry Mason, owner of Friendly's Inn here in Crossroads. Forensic evidence, including DNA, has linked all three deaths to one man, Tucker Hardy, now deceased. Mr. Hardy's father, Richard Hardy, is now in police custody after confessing to shooting and killing his son. In addition, we've learned that Tucker Hardy was operating a business selling illegal substances, including fentanyl-laced opioid pills. His business has been shut down. The pills located on the Hardy property are identical to those involved in recent overdoses of young people in this town and the death of Officer Josephine Rollins. The Crossroads and Hamblin police departments will continue to do everything we can to keep Chester County free of dangerous and illegal drugs. Any questions?"

Several reporters shouted at once. After answering most of their questions, mainly about Tucker's activities and death, Tim reluctantly called on Jack.

"Was Eli Carson involved in manufacturing or selling the drugs, and why was he killed by Tucker Hardy?"

"We have no proof that Carson was involved with Hardy's drug business. As for Hardy's motive, the deer stand built by Eli Carson and his father was located in what will be our new park near Willow Lake. From what we've uncovered, Hardy was also using that property for his operation. It could have been a case of Carson being in the wrong place at the wrong time."

They might never know if that was what happened. Perhaps Eli had been involved as a lookout. He could have been the person who shot at Cal and Merritt in June to warn them away. Or, he might not have been aware that Tucker was using the park for his pill mill. Tuck might have even taken advantage of the usually vacant deer stand to meet his suppliers and make deals. It could have been as he'd said, that Eli had just been in the wrong place at the wrong time, prompting Tuck to kill him and plant the pills in the deer stand and possibly even the marijuana in his work locker.

But until they had proof one way or another, he was considering Eli innocent of illegal activities, other than the dumping at Crawfish Pond. That was still an open investigation.

Another reporter asked about Mason's cause of death and connection to Tucker Hardy.

"The coroner determined that Mr. Mason was injected with an opioid containing fentanyl and died of a heart attack as a result. As evidence has been found that Tucker Hardy was at the motel that night, we believe he supplied the fatal injection. Next question."

The reporter frowned, apparently dissatisfied with his answer. Tim didn't blame him. The truth was that they simply didn't know why the men had met that night. Given the age difference and lack of witnesses, including Vivian Amber, who was only able to confirm that the men knew each other and had enjoyed beers together once or twice at The Last Rodeo, a close friendship seemed unlikely. Nonetheless, it appeared Mason had invited Tucker into the room where he'd died. They'd spent almost an hour together, according to the motel guests who'd heard the motorcycle arrive and leave. Tucker would have brought the hypodermic and fatal dose to the meeting, which suggested premeditation. Whatever business arrangement they might have had remained unclear. As in the case of Eli Carson, there was no proof that Larry Mason had been involved in the drug business.

The next question concerned Aaron Reese's death, and he stepped back from the microphone so John could answer it. After that, they alternated answering or declining to answer several more questions before Tim thanked everyone for coming.

"Sounds like you have some holes to fill in there about that motel owner's death," John said to him after they'd returned to his office. "Are you sure those two weren't just partying with drugs and got carried away?"

"That's still a possibility, but the attempted murder of Jana Nance by hypodermic injection that we linked to Tucker was exactly the same method. Larry Mason had a high alcohol reading but no evidence of previous drug use. Even if he willingly took that shot, why would he inject himself in the neck?"

"Folks do strange things—not that I don't agree with your logic."

Tucker Hardy as a drug kingpin wannabe was still hard to buy. "There's something more going on here, John. Someone else is still out there pulling the strings." And it bothered the hell out of him. They still hadn't caught whoever had supplied the fentanyl, and there were pushers out there who wouldn't need to wait long to find another supplier.

"Any leads on that?"

He sighed. "We're following up on some phone numbers in Tucker's recent contacts. One shows up several times, but it appears to be a burner. I'm also questioning his parents and brother. I think they know more than they've said, especially his brother."

"Hard to trace those burners, unless you find the phone in the owner's possession. Could be whoever was supplying him with the drugs or the dealers who bought from him."

"The calls came in right before each of the attacks. Also, Tuck liked money. He liked flashing it around and being the local hero. I can see him getting into something illegal and highly profitable like the drug trade, but I can't see him running that kind of operation alone. He stayed under the radar for months. By the way, the anonymous tip for the raid on the Bissett brothers? It was from another burner. I asked CSI to see if they could match the voice to Tucker. He might have phoned it in to steer us in a different direction."

"And eliminate some competition." John crumpled up his paper coffee cup and tossed it into the trash can. "I'd better head back up the road. Thanks for solving our murder, but next time, keep your crime local, you hear?" He chuckled and stuck out his hand. "I hope you find whoever set that boy to killing. It's a damn shame he couldn't stay on the rodeo circuit longer and stay out of trouble."

Tim shook his hand. "As you said, people do strange things." Whatever had caused Tuck Hardy to go bad had been there all along. It was like his father had said—you raised 'em and hoped they chose the right path when they were grown. Tuck had made a series of poor choices and now he was dead.

Chapter Thirty-Five

THE OCTOBER AIR had a nip to it that foreshadowed winter. Cars, SUVs, and pickups continued to arrive at Willow Lake, causing Jana to revise her estimate of how many parking spaces they would need at the new park. A bigger lot would mean cutting down more trees, and she could already hear Cal objecting to that. There was room for some parking on the Bluegill Road side of the park, which would be close to the playground area for families. Maybe they could add some picnic tables nearby and—

"I know that look," Deeann said. "She's visualizing what else she can add to the park."

"What you've planned is already amazing," Merritt Quinn said. They'd met yesterday when the young professor had arrived in Crossroads for a long weekend visit, but they'd been emailing for weeks. Merritt's suggestions for an eco-friendlier park had been widely accepted by the committee, although Walt had been disappointed to be outvoted on allowing hunting in season on the property. There really wasn't a need, with all the other state and federal parks in the area that allowed it. Cal's idea of a waterskiing venue might happen one day, but they'd decided to wait until electric boats became more popular. For now, only vessels without gas engines would be allowed, to protect the environment and preserve the tranquility of the park. Fishing would be permitted from a pier they'd included in the plan now being formally drafted by an architectural firm.

Jack Huddleston joined them. "Looks like half the town is here for the park dedication."

"If you feed them, they will come. Don't you know that, Jack?" Deeann said. "Besides, Jana's set this up as a family festival with face painting and games for the kids. It was a smart idea."

"Thanks, boss." She wasn't sure she considered Deeann a friend yet, but after staying two days at the ranch, she had a better idea of who the mayor was. The former Deeann Ferris had taken over her parents' horse ranch, but she'd also worked hard juggling marriage, motherhood, and her career. At home, she was more relaxed, casual, and down-to-earth than Jana would have ever guessed. They'd gone riding and talked, more about families and raising children than about their competitive high school days. She'd also enjoyed talking to Logan, a veterinarian, and their youngest son, Kyle. Their older two boys, like her girls, were no longer living at home.

"Well, you obviously drew in a crowd," Deeann said, "proving it was a great idea. Did you tell Merritt about our latest grant application and the community center you're planning?"

The grant proposal had taken a lot of their time this past week, but Jana knew they were right to ask for more money this year, a sum that had taken Deeann's breath away. She'd helped with even larger grant proposals when she'd worked tourism in Indianapolis and was confident they'd at least receive some of the amount requested. It usually paid off to go after what you really wanted, even if it involved taking risks.

Jack's eyes widened. "Community center?"

"Now, Jack," Deeann said. "One step at a time. At this point it's only a proposal to convert that old general store building on south Main into a multipurpose center. That's not ready for publication yet. Today we're focusing on dedicating this park."

"Aren't you rushing it?" he asked, looking around. "Nothing's built yet."

Deeann waved her hand. "The city council has already approved what Jana's committee suggested. They'll have to sign off on the final plan and funding, but we won't have any problem with that. They love it!"

She wouldn't have any problem. Deeann was passionate about the park, and she'd already won over the council members. Even so, Jana would feel much better when the final approvals were in and actual building was underway. One of these days she'd learn to have confidence in everything working out for the best without having to bare knuckle through ten rounds with only one hand. After all, her committee and Merritt Quinn had confidence in her. Even Deeann had confessed she'd admired Jana's determination and vision all those years ago for the homecoming dance their senior year in high school.

They'd cleared a lot of air that morning riding horses at Deeann's ranch. She'd also apologized to Charly for suggesting Eli might have been involved in drugs. Their relationship hadn't quite returned to what it had been, but her friend was still grieving her son's death. There were still so many unanswered questions surrounding it. They were talking, and that was enough for now. She'd always be grateful that Charly had saved her life, despite not being ready to forgive her.

Jack was grinning at Deeann. "Chalk up this park as another achievement for our mayor, who looks to be winning reelection."

"Don't be so cynical, Jack," Merritt said, amused.

"Just an observation. Facts are facts."

"Still a month to go before the election," Deeann said. "Speaking of which, I need to shake some hands and kiss some babies before the dedication. Y'all have a good time."

"If you'll excuse me, I'm going to catch up with some friends before we start," Merritt said.

"That just leaves us," Jack said, "and a few questions I have before you have to give your speech. Tell me about this community center idea."

"You heard the mayor. Are you trying to get me fired?" Jana said before steering him back to today's events and providing him with a couple of quotes about what great work her committee had done and her hopes that they'd be breaking ground in the spring, if not sooner. Clay Bailey then wandered over, rescuing her from more questions. Apparently he'd managed to escape from a recent epidemic of seasonal allergies and flu that had kept him busy.

"I'm glad you're here," she said after Jack left them. She smiled at the man who had become her friend. Recently, he'd shared with her his struggles dealing with PTSD from his military service in Afghanistan and his childhood trauma of losing his parents in a small plane crash that he'd miraculously survived. She understood the loss of a parent and also the importance of having fulfilling work and strong relationships with people who cared about you. Her daughters and father, for example, who had come to be with her for Nana Sue's funeral and burial.

"Have you decided to go back to Indianapolis?" he asked her, his gray eyes troubled. He'd just accepted a permanent position at the Crossroads Clinic. Clearly, he'd found his home here. And while he hadn't said he wanted her to make this town her home and stay, he'd shown her in other ways that their relationship—and what it might soon become—was special to him.

"Yes, I bought my ticket last night. I'm leaving next week." She considered drawing out the suspense, but she decided not to tease him—much. "My house sold and I need to be there for the closing. I'll only be there a week, but I need to sort through the things I put in storage—"

He didn't wait to hear any more. His strong arms drew her in for a hug and a promise that she'd made the right decision to stay in Crossroads.

The End

Author's Note

Thank you for reading *Death Watch*, the second of my Southern Secrets mystery series for Tule Publishing. If you read the first book, *Deadly Inheritance*, you probably understand why I chose the name Crossroads for the fictional setting of the series. Jana Nance, like Merritt Quinn, has reached a turning point in her life and makes a move from the Midwest to the South, taking a risk to finally have her dream job. When she discovers who her new boss will be, she fears she's made a terrible mistake.

The town, too, is ready to try something new but afraid to leave the past behind. Like many places in this country, Crossroads is threatened with the loss of their biggest employer, Southern Pines, due in part to competition from overseas. Too many young people leave for the cities and better jobs. Years of passive neglect have taken a toll on the town's infrastructure and pride. There is hope: Newcomers like Jana, Merritt, and Cal and residents with vision and love for their hometown, like Mayor Deeann Donahue, Tim Birch, Jack Huddleston, and Curt McMillan, are working hard to revitalize Crossroads. The future is looking brighter, despite the occasional villain surfacing now and then. This is a mystery series, after all.

In case you're wondering what's next for Crossroads, I'm

pleased to announce that the third book in this series will be released in early 2026. I hope y'all will come back for another visit!

While you're waiting for your next Arkansas trip, spend some time in Chicago with Crystal Ward, the amateur sleuth and professional organizer of my Cluttered Crimes mystery series. The titles are listed below and are available in paperback, e-book, and audiobook formats at your favorite online book retailers.

I would love to hear from you! You can contact me at info@carollightauthor.com or visit my website at www.carollightauthor.com. For news and peeks behind the curtain of my writing life, please sign up for my free monthly newsletter at www.carollightauthor.com.

And finally, please consider writing a review—even a sentence or two—about this book on your retailer's site, Amazon, Goodreads, and/or BookBub. Reviews help readers connect to authors and find their next book to read. I'd appreciate it!

All the best,
Carol

Acknowledgments

I'd like to thank the Tule editorial board for encouraging me to create the community of Crossroads, Arkansas, and plot crimes for Tim Birch and my cast of characters to solve. My mother's family is from southern Arkansas, where I spent many happy hours of my childhood with my cousins and extended family. Research is helpful but doesn't always provide all the details needed for authenticity. Any errors in portraying this region or police procedures are strictly mine.

I'm proud to be part of the supportive team at Tule Publishing. Jane Porter, Meghan Farrell, and Cyndi Parent are always willing to answer my questions and provide assistance. Mia Gleason and Jaiden Colling do wonderful work coordinating book releases, designing promotional graphics, and running the Tule Book Club. A special thanks to Lee Hyat for an incredible book cover design and to Hossley Kallassy of HPK Creative Arts for the author photograph.

A huge thanks as always to my editor, Julie Sturgeon, who knows just how to tweak the manuscript to make it better than I'd dreamed possible. Nan Reinhardt, my copy editor, and Marlene Roberts, my proofreader, also have my gratitude for finding my mistakes and missteps and for giving this story its final polish.

And finally, thanks to my readers, including family,

friends, neighbors, and fellow authors. Your support and encouragement boost my spirits and creativity every day. Thank you for coming on this journey with me.

If you enjoyed *Death Watch*,
you'll love the other books in the…

Southern Secrets Mysteries

Book 1: *Deadly Inheritance*

Book 2: *Death Watch*

Available now at your favorite online retailer!

More Books by Carol Light

Cluttered Crime Mysteries Series

Book 1: *Room for Suspicion*
Book 2: *Deadlier Than Fiction*
Book 3: *Killer Close to Home*
Book 4: *No Room to Hide*

Available now at your favorite online retailer!

About the Author

Carol Light is an avid reader and writer of mysteries. She loves creating amateur sleuths and complicating their normal lives with a crime that they must use their talents and wits to solve. She's traveled worldwide and lived in Australia for eight years, teaching high school English and learning to speak "Strine." Florida is now her home. If she's not at the beach or writing, you can find her tackling quilting in much the same way that she figures out her mysteries—piece by piece, clue by clue. You can also follow me on BlueSky.

Thank you for reading

Death Watch

If you enjoyed this book, you can find more from all our great authors at TulePublishing.com, or from your favorite online retailer.

Made in the USA
Columbia, SC
26 June 2025

59670258R00202